THE
PRESIDENT'S
LAWYER

THE
PRESIDENT'S
LAWYER

— A Novel —

Lawrence Robbins

ATRIA BOOKS
New York London Toronto Sydney New Delhi

ATRIA
BOOKS

An Imprint of Simon & Schuster, LLC
1230 Avenue of the Americas
New York, NY 10020

First Atria Books hardcover edition October 2024

ATRIA B O O K S and colophon are trademarks of Simon & Schuster, LLC

Simon & Schuster: Celebrating 100 Years of Publishing in 2024

For information about special discounts for bulk purchases, please contact Simon & Schuster Special Sales at 1-866-506-1949 or business@simonandschuster.com.

The Simon & Schuster Speakers Bureau can bring authors to your live event. For more information or to book an event, contact the Simon & Schuster Speakers Bureau at 1-866-248-3049 or visit our website at www.simonspeakers.com.

Interior design by Jill Putorti

Manufactured in the United States of America

1 3 5 7 9 10 8 6 4 2

Library of Congress Cataloging-in-Publication Data has been applied for.

ISBN 978-1-6680-4719-4
ISBN 978-1-6680-4721-7 (ebook)

To my greatest loves:
Leslie, Jeremy, Ethan, Noah, Sasha, and Casey

Part I

DEFENSES

I

The news broke in June, while I was trying the Karinsky case in D.C. Superior Court. It arrived like a summer hailstorm, just after Judge Sam Edgerton announced the jury's verdict.

Abel Karinsky, a distant cousin of one of my partners, had gotten the best (in truth, the only) criminal lawyer at Lockyear & Harbison. He'd gotten me. Abel was not, to be sure, my usual sort of client. Yes, "Mr. Green" hadn't shown up, but I was used to doing my fair share of unpaid cases, either voluntarily or involuntarily. Nor was Abel unusual just because he was nasty, brutish, and short. Very few of my clients were likely to replace Andrew Jackson on the $20 bill.

No, Abel Karinsky, alleged check forger, was unusual because he might well have been innocent. Not suppress-the-evidence innocent; not throw-out-the-confession innocent; not guilty-but-entrapped innocent. Abel seemed to be actually-didn't-do-the-crime innocent. An albino moose. A triple-yolk egg.

I don't see many of those.

Abel had supposedly stolen three pension checks from a retired Metro engineer, then forged the victim's signature, Arthur F. Hodges, before cashing the checks at a downtown pawnshop. The surveillance footage was grainy, but I could see why the cops had focused on my client. Abel had done two bids for previous forgeries. He'd been seen cruising this particular pawnshop. He had no visible means of lawful support.

And Abel's handwriting seemed a dead-on match for the endorsements on the back of the checks.

The FBI's handwriting protocol was simple enough. The Feds started with the three stolen checks, then directed Abel to make seventy-five exemplars—to write the name Arthur F. Hodges on seventy-five little slips of paper. When a suspect has to write the same thing seventy-five times, he usually betrays some handwriting idiosyncrasies that an expert can compare to the signatures on the checks. In this case, it was the distinctive loops in the capital letters and the upward thrust in the script that supposedly fingered my client as the forger.

Even so, by the time the prosecutor, a blond fellow from Harvard, called the pawnshop manager as his final witness, I figured we were about even. I'd done a decent enough cross on the FBI handwriting expert, pointing out two defendants he'd helped convict who were later exonerated. If the government's chief witness had screwed up twice before, maybe the jury would take his testimony with a grain of salt.

The prosecutor must have been thinking along the same lines. So after establishing that the pawnshop manager had seen Abel in the vicinity a day before the incident, Harvard Man tried to turn the witness into a second handwriting expert. Someone to corroborate the Fed, whose credibility I'd tarnished on cross.

"Have you seen other writings by Mr. Karinsky?" the prosecutor asked.

"Yes," said the manager, "I saw his phony ID when he cashed the checks."

"Do you think you'd recognize his handwriting if you saw it again?"

"Oh, sure. I'd know it anywhere."

"I show you these three pension checks, Mr. Cooperstein. You see the signature on the back, Arthur F. Hodges? Whose handwriting do you recognize that to be?"

"The defendant's," Cooperstein confidently declared.

Abel slumped in his seat, defeated. "Buck up," I whispered. "It's our turn."

I started my cross by planting a few seeds—a few preliminary questions to establish that Harry Cooperstein, though doubtless a competent pawnshop manager, knew nothing about handwriting analysis. Then came the punch line. Picking up the seventy-five exemplars, I approached the witness.

"Do you recognize this stack of papers?" I began. Before venturing further, I needed to know whether the prosecutor had acquainted the pawnshop operator with the actual evidence. He hadn't. Cooperstein had no idea what the exemplars were.

"Well, Mr. Cooperstein, take a look at the signatures on these seventy-five slips of paper. Do you see that each one is signed Arthur F. Hodges?"

"Yes," Cooperstein acknowledged.

"Well, here's a pencil, Mr. Cooperstein. On these seventy-five slips of paper, I want you to put a check mark next to each Arthur F. Hodges signature that you believe Mr. Karinsky made. If you think Mr. Karinsky is *not* the person who signed Mr. Hodges's name on a particular page, just leave that page blank and go on to the next one. Fair enough?"

Cooperstein got to work. After a minute or two, he'd put check marks on only three or four of the first ten pages. By then, some of the jurors, in on the joke, were eyeing me with amusement. By page thirty or so, with just half of Cooperstein's pages bearing check marks, the jurors were openly snickering. Even His Honor, usually no fan of criminal defendants, had to suppress a smile.

Cooperstein knew he'd stepped in it, but he couldn't tell which way to pivot. Should he:

A. check off every signature?
B. check off none of them? or
C. keep splitting the difference as he'd been doing?

Finally, Cooperstein made his choice: B. "This is a trick," he announced. "These signatures were crafted to *look like* they were made by Mr. Karinsky, but they actually weren't. They are elegant forgeries by a master deceiver."

"So there shouldn't be a check mark on *any* of them—is that your testimony, Mr. Cooperstein?"

"Yes," said the witness, with some well-deserved hesitation.

"Okay, then. Please erase the check marks you've made so far, since your testimony is that *none* of the signatures were made by my client."

Cooperstein complied.

At this point, Harvard Man was turtling for safety beneath the prosecution table.

"Shall I let you in on the joke, Mr. Cooperstein?" I asked. "These seventy-five slips of paper are what the FBI calls handwriting exemplars. That means *all* the signatures were made by Mr. Karinsky."

"Oh," said the witness. Glumly.

"Does that cause you to doubt your prowess as a handwriting expert?"

"Yes, it does," Cooperstein admitted.

"Would you like to withdraw the testimony you gave the prosecutor on direct?"

"I would," said Cooperstein.

The jury stayed through free lunch on the government and acquitted Abel at about half past two.

Which is when the courtroom imploded. The crime-beat reporters bolted from the pews, barking into their iPhones, accompanied by shouting from folks in the cheap seats. Couldn't be on our account, I thought—acquittals are rare, sure, but Abel's case was small potatoes. While Judge Edgerton gaveled for quiet, I grabbed one of the press stragglers, who fed me that evening's headline:

Five months after leaving office, John Sherman Cutler, former president of the United States, had just been charged with the murder of Amanda Harper, a junior lawyer in his White House Counsel's Office.

Jesus, they charged the president.

I'd been wondering about Amanda's killer since last February, when the D.C. police had recovered her body in Rock Creek Park. According to the cops, Amanda, thirty-two years old, had been strangled and bore what seemed to be rope burns on her wrists and ankles. Not far from the victim, police recovered a small, locked briefcase with a silver, dull-edged knife wedged into its lining.

Couldn't be the president, was my first thought when the news flashed through the courtroom. No fucking way it's him. I'd cycled through a passel of theories since the news first broke of Amanda's death. This one had never crossed my mind.

Impossible, I thought again. *Cannot* be the president.

As I was leaving the courtroom, I noticed, sitting conspicuously in the last row, a vaguely familiar-looking man in his early thirties. He was decades too young and much too smartly dressed to be one of the courtroom buffs who regularly attended my Superior Court trials. I was about to exit through the double doors when he grabbed my elbow. "Rob Jacobson?" he asked. "Can I have a quick word?"

We stepped into the corridor and huddled a few feet from the courtroom.

"Jack needs to talk to you," he said.

II

Jack's emissary turned out to be Will, one of Jack's former Assistant Secretaries of Something. Will drove me to Jack's Georgetown townhouse and briefed me on the few case details that had been publicly released.

When we pulled up around the corner from Jack's place, news vans, camera crews, and a half block's worth of inquiring minds were already camped out. You could hear the crowd buzzing: What was going on between the former president and Amanda? Had Jack used the knife to force open the briefcase? What was inside? And what about those rope burns on the victim's wrists and ankles? Was the former POTUS really into that stuff? (Traffic on bondage websites had quadrupled. Or so I'd been told.)

My face was not yet familiar to most reporters, so I managed to elbow my way to the front door, and Jessica, Jack's wife, let me inside. She'd obviously been crying. Her eyes darted anxiously over my shoulder, as if the hordes were poised to storm the castle and all she had as protection was a balding, middle-aged Jewish lawyer.

We hugged, a beat longer than usual.

"Robbie, thanks for coming so quickly," she said. "Jack's in his study."

"Of course," I said. "Tell me how the kids are managing."

"Well enough, though I may not be the best judge. Mostly in shock, I guess. Smith Universal and Fox News are crowing, naturally."

It was hardly surprising that Jack's media enemies were having a field day. Fox News still had the largest slice of conservative viewership, but former president Smith's upstart network, Smith Universal TV (or SMUT, to its detractors), was now a close second. "Vultures," I commiserated.

"And social media's worse, of course," Jess added. "The memes with ligature marks and dominatrix outfits. Jokes about Jack and his 'sex slave.' I can't screen the kids from all that garbage."

"Jesus, Jess, I'm so sorry."

"Let me leave you with Jack."

She knocked softly on the study door, opened it a crack, and left me to enter alone.

Jack's study was a presidential library in miniature. The framed photos captured a mostly charmed life in politics. Jack, the junior senator from New York, chairing the congressional investigation into President Smith's self-pardon. Jack, as president, bestowing the Presidential Medal of Freedom on the founders of Global Forest Generation. Jack attending the unexpected inauguration of the first Israeli Labor government in decades. Jack, grayer but still dashing in his final year, thundering condemnation at the United Nations when Russia annexed Moldova. And barely two months later, Jack, the defeated candidate for reelection, thanking a ballroom of supporters for all their hard work.

I always fixed on the most obscure photo in the bunch—Jack, Jess, and me, dazzled with weed and adrenaline, the night Jack was first elected, against all odds, to the New York state assembly. Jess and I had spent late evenings crafting Jack's position papers, but Jack sealed the deal. He was an electric campaigner, a natural. He'd always had the gift. We were all so young. And, I thought, so happy. There was Jack, towering over me as always, beaming at the clubhouse crowd. Jess was by his side, all smiles, too, staring up at Jack with an air of hopefulness. I was smiling as well, I suppose, but my eyes, caught in a peripheral glance at Jess, betrayed a dash of melancholy. Did Jess feel some of that, too? What was in *her* mind that moment? A vision of the years to come? Plans for Jack's life in politics?

It's easier to predict the future, I suppose, after the future has arrived.

As I moved across the study to embrace the former president, he got up from his Dartmouth rocker to greet me. "It's been too long," he said. "I trust Will has shared the news."

"Yeah," I said. "He gave me the basics on the way over."

Jack's eyes were lined with worry and sleeplessness. He gathered himself for a moment, then spoke slowly and with emphasis.

"I had nothing to do with this," Jack said. "Nothing. I know you were . . . close . . . to Amanda during your law firm days together, and I promise you—I did not fucking do this."

I get that a lot from clients. Hard-earned experience has taught me not to take clients' denials at face value. Even Jack's.

"Jack, how long have you known these charges were coming?"

"Well, Amanda's death, of course, was all over the news in February. I'm sure you remember. But until the prosecutors called late last night, I had no reason to think that I'd be targeted as her killer."

Really? I thought. *No prior notice?*

"Okay, Jack. Here's the basic rule from this moment on: You don't speak to anyone about this case besides Jess and your lawyer. You don't talk to your kids, your buddies on the Hill, and especially not to reporters or cops. No one but Jess and your lawyer." That meant, I explained, no spur-of-the-moment pressers on the front lawn.

Jack winced. "Got it," he said finally. "But what's this 'your lawyer' horseshit? *You're* my fucking lawyer."

I paused a moment. My old friend would not like my answer. "I'm sorry, Jack, but I'm not the right guy to defend you." *Plus, case of the century or not, I don't want to.*

"How can you not be the right guy, Robbie? You're the dean of the defense bar, for chrissake. I've seen you in action. No one can dismantle a witness like you. And how long have we known each other? You're Gretchen's godparent—you were with us at Sibley when my little girl was treated for leukemia. You've been to both kids' christenings."

"But that's just the problem, Jack," I explained. "If a lawyer knows all the players, he may be too close to do the best job. And here it's even trickier because, as you were kind enough to mention, I was 'close' to Amanda once upon a time. I'll find you someone else. Someone just as good but without the baggage."

"Robbie, I know how you felt about Amanda. I know this is a big ask from an old friend. But I'm in trouble here, deep fucking trouble. You're the only guy I know who accepts me, warts and all. That's what I'm gonna need here."

"Tell me about the 'deep fucking trouble.'"

Jack's eyes moistened, I thought.

"Everything stays in this room, Robbie?"

"Every word," I assured him. "Even if you need to find another lawyer, I'm bound to keep your secrets until you tell me otherwise."

Jack lowered his voice and began.

"There's just no easy way to say this—Amanda and I, we had an affair. Started a couple of months after she joined the Counsel's Office. We were working closely on some issues, and it just happened. I didn't mean for it . . . I wish I could take it all back." Jack's voice was quivering.

I wasn't altogether surprised—some part of me had imagined as much. Still, I paused to gain composure. "How long did the affair last?"

"Until she died. I saw her in late January, at her place, for the last time."

"How long before her death, Jack?" My suspicions were piqued.

"A week, maybe ten days. Obviously I can't be positive. I *wasn't there* when she died, Robert."

"Does Jess know about the affair?"

"She may have suspected. One evening she walked into the White House dining room when Amanda and I were having dinner. But she's never said a word about it, to me anyway. And I don't want all of this to become public, Rob."

"Jack, there's no way to keep a lid on the story. It's bound to come out if you testify at trial—and you'll almost certainly have to. Any defense lawyer with an IQ north of eighty will tell you that."

"I can't admit any of this publicly. No goddamn way."

It wasn't too early to push the client a little, even if some other lawyer had to finish the job. "Why not, Jack? It's not as if you have some unblemished romantic history to preserve for posterity."

"That's a little cold, Counselor, don't you think? Let's just say that Amanda and I liked to play things a little rough, and I don't want that in my obit, thank you very much. I can see it now: 'Jack Cutler, former president of the United States, died today at age eighty-two. He was best known for tying up his thirty-two-year-old lover during an extramarital affair.' No way I'm copping to this stuff. That's why it's got to be you at my side, Rob. No one else has our history together. No one else will suspend judgment."

I explained that hiring someone else was almost certainly in Jack's best interests.

"Why the fuck is that, Robert?"

"It's pretty basic. If the government learns about my own affair with Amanda, they'll raise holy hell with the judge. They'll argue that I can't do the best possible job for you, since I'm still carrying a torch for the victim."

Which, as it happens, didn't begin to capture how I felt.

Jack raised his voice a notch. "I get it, goddamn it," he said. "But I can't be without my wingman. I'm not sure I can count on a jury of my peers. As you may have heard, I took home the silver medal in the last election. I'm gonna need your coattails, Robbie. There's no one else I can trust."

I loved hearing Jack's praise. He *needed* me. But still.

"I'll think about it, Jack. In the meantime, I can at least tell you what to expect at the arraignment. Will says that Judge Edgerton has drawn the case. I was just in front of him today in another matter. Edgerton is a formidable old bastard, but he calls balls and strikes and lets lawyers try their cases. You could have done worse."

Jack looked relieved. "So what happens next?"

"You know about arraignments from TV: The judge will ask if you've read the indictment. You'll say yes. He'll ask you how you plead to the charges—you'll say, 'Not guilty.' The judge will then set bail, but he'll almost certainly release you on your own recognizance, or perhaps with a minimal cash bond. So it's short, but it's not sweet. The press will stalk you from here to the courthouse. There'll be photographers lining the corridors, and a swarm of reporters clamoring for seats in the pews."

"I have some passing familiarity with the press and the public," Jack noted.

"Yeah, that's the whole problem, Jack. You love them. You love working the crowd. But this is not the Jefferson-Jackson Dinner. You're not running for office. So I repeat: *do not* talk to anyone. In the meantime,

I'll give some thought to whether I can represent you. But for now, let me tell you my number one condition for taking a case, Jack, yours or anyone else's."

My friend leaned forward in the rocker.

"Rule one is you tell me the truth. Every last ounce of it. Whatever the truth is, I can handle it. The same goes for whoever ends up defending you. Your lawyers cannot get blindsided by the prosecutors. The government must not know anything your lawyers don't know."

Jack nodded, said he understood.

"Before I leave, do you mind if I talk to Jess for a few minutes alone?" I asked.

Jack said he was fine with this. He then drew me closer and lowered his voice. "Please tell her I had nothing to do with Amanda's death. Jess doesn't seem to hear me when I say that. And for god's sake, Robbie, don't make me shop around for another lawyer."

I found Jess downstairs, paging listlessly through some magazine. "Jack seems shell-shocked but reasonably composed," I said. "He wanted me to tell you what I'm sure he's told you himself. He didn't do this. And, Jess, I believe him."

Jess gave me a look I'd seen a thousand times before—she wasn't convinced. "I'm so grateful we have you in our corner, Robbie."

"Listen, Jess. I wish I could tell you that the days ahead will get better. But I'll do everything possible to carry some of the burden."

"Thanks, Robbie."

"I'm sure this is all a terrible shock. Did you know Amanda Harper?"

"No," Jess said. "Until I saw the *Post* story online this evening, I couldn't have told you what she looked like." Jess paused. "She was pretty, wasn't she?"

"Yes," I acknowledged. *Very pretty*. "But I take Jack at his word on this, Jess." (That's what you're supposed to say, right?)

Jess nodded and returned to her magazine.

I saw Jack again as I readied to leave. "She's in your corner."

Jack smiled, ruefully I thought, then clasped my hand in both of his and watched from the leaded-glass window as I ducked into a back alley. Will was waiting in his car and I asked him to drop me off in Rock Creek Park.

The place where Amanda's body was found.

III

Rock Creek Park, established in 1890, was the third national park designated by the federal government. The park comprises some 1,754 acres, but I cut a narrow swath as I walked along Military Road toward the Horse Center, where the cops had located Amanda's body. I knew that riding spot—Jack and Jess were regulars during Jack's Senate years, even stabled a horse there, and my family had joined the Cutlers a few times. East on Military, south on Glover, and I was there. (You actually smell the horse barn before you see it: the park makes manure available—free of charge!—to enterprising gardeners.)

I reminded myself that Amanda was not killed on a soft summer day like today. According to media accounts, it had been late January and frigid, during a blinding snowfall that shuttered the city for a week and scattered white bluffs across Northwest D.C. As far as I knew, the police had not yet determined whether Amanda was killed in the park itself or had been moved there after her death. If she'd been moved, the killer must have driven the body into the park, leaving the car at the

Horse Center or in one of the adjoining lots, perhaps capitalizing on the midwinter camouflage.

Amanda had always hated the cold. Her apartment, a fifteen-minute walk from the park, was toasty, yet she still needed an extra blanket or two on winter nights. I could picture her in flannels, a space heater nearby, wrapped in the gray cashmere shawl I'd given her for Valentine's Day last year, with that single crimson band running lengthwise. We used to debate the meaning of that one red thread.

"Rosy-fingered dawn," she suggested.

"The river of slime from *Ghostbusters II*."

"More like a vein. Pulsing."

"Like a strand of your hair."

That hair. The smell of it. The curled red torrents I'd get lost in. Amanda's locks framed a broad, freckled face that creased into a wry smile—the kind of smile that suggested she was the only one in on the joke. Her beauty was enhanced, in my estimation, by a thumb-sized birthmark just below her neck that invited you to look more closely.

The barn at the Horse Center has an open space for riding and dressage—not, I thought, the likeliest spot to hide a body. But the adjoining horse stalls, which house upward of sixty horses at a time, had the requisite nooks and crannies, each stall separated by faded wood beams and facing a broad pathway with bits of strewn hay. Maybe Amanda had been stowed in one of those berths.

———————

"Come on, just one taste," she taunted as she handed me a pill. "It puts the *x* in *sex*."

"It's not for me, Amanda. I'm too old for this."

"Robbie, really, age is just a construct."

"Tell that to my hairline."

A trail of kisses across my forehead. Reaching up to circle my earlobes with fingers strengthened by years of Czerny piano exercises.

A girl from the only family of Democrats in Rapid City, South Dakota. Getting up at dawn for Yale crew practice on the Connecticut River. An Olympics tryout. Articles editor on the *Harvard Law Review.* Soon after, my associate at L&H.

Then: Room service at the Mayflower after a heated deposition. A chocolate sundae with two spoons.

Then: Concocting elaborate meals together in her garret or at my place. The smell of roasting garlic. Oh, God, how I loved those nights.

But later: Concert tickets I got stuck with. A last-minute nominations memo she had to get out. And somehow, a cold January dumping ground, somewhere in the Horse Center.

———

I walked south and east to the Capitol stones quarry, a set of sandstone and marble blocks taken from the Capitol when a former one-term congressman, with no architectural training, was put in charge of renovation in the 1950s. Whatever his faults, Jack had always prized genuine expertise. No more talk-show hosts running foreign policy. No more TV lawyers running the Justice Department. No more radiologists posing as infectious disease advisers.

Could Jack have done this?

I sat on a sandstone and gazed toward the Capitol as the sun dipped into twilight. Here's how I cry: First a tingling runs up and down my nostrils; then the first tears gather in my eyes. Next come the heaves, spaced apart at first, then drawn in large gulps, like a boxer taking a standing eight count. The park is deserted tonight, so I let it all out of me.

How could I even imagine taking this case? How badly did I need Jack's approval?

I looked east down Military Road to Fort Stevens, where the Union Army had repelled the Confederacy's march up Georgia Avenue. Where Lincoln was shot through his top hat—the only sitting president to have personally drawn fire during war. Who signs up to be commander in chief? What does it take?

I always knew that Jack had what it took. I could have told you that back in orchestra class. Jack's passion for control. His magnetism. His street smarts. His relentless energy.

His casual cruelty.

"I can't do this," I protested as I dropped my hands to the pillow. "I'm sorry, Amanda."

"It's fine, Robbie, we'll do it the usual way."

I grabbed a cab and headed home. Jack's arraignment was fast upon us, and I had a decision to make. Could my old friend have done this? I couldn't take the case if I thought he had. There was no way to know for sure, but at least one way to learn more.

All I had to do was get Jack to agree.

IV

Three days later, Jack and I sat in the anteroom at Chevy Chase Imaging. As it turned out, my heaviest lift was purely logistical—spiriting the former president, unobserved, out of his Georgetown townhouse after midnight and delivering him to a specially arranged session at CCI's offices on upper Wisconsin. Jack barely put up a fight.

Admittedly, I hadn't given him much choice. Before signing on for the defense, I needed to know, at least to a reasonable certainty, that he was not Amanda's killer. Of course that's not how I pitched the idea to Jack. "It will help the defense," I explained. "If you pass the lie detector swimmingly, I'll find some way to publicize the results. Even if we can't get the test admitted at trial, it will easily be worth an hour of your time."

"But what if I fail, Robbie? Innocent people flunk these things all the time, don't they? How will that look to the potential jurors?"

"They'll never know, Jack," I answered. "If the test goes south, no one but you, me, and the examiner will ever know you were here, and the examiner is an old friend of mine. Your secret will stay with us."

A little before 1 a.m., Jack and I walked into the scanning room, where Jedediah Beresin was waiting for us. "Mr. President, it's an honor," Jed said. "Has Rob explained how this imposing contraption works?" Jed was pointing to a long cylindrical machine with a raised bed for the human subject, a see-through cover, a white helmet for the subject's head, and a series of magnets at the top and sides of a tunnel.

"Only the basics," Jack said. "Maybe you can walk me through it. I take it we're not using the polygraph from the cop shows of my youth."

"No. Polygraphs are too easy to fool. The scanning machine you see in front of you is state of the art, just off the assembly line. It uses what we call functional magnetic resonance imaging, or fMRI for short. I will ask you a series of questions while your body glides into the tunnel, and you should answer each of them truthfully. The fMRI will then take images of fluctuations in the blood flowing to your brain every second or two. When an area of the brain is activated by some task, such as answering one of my questions, there's an onrush of oxygenated blood to the region, which creates a magnetic field that the fMRI can measure. When a subject is lying, roughly three times more areas of the brain get activated than when the subject is telling the truth. So basically, if your answers don't light up the whole scoreboard, you're likely telling the truth."

"How likely is *likely*?" Jack asked. A reasonable question, I thought.

"Well, nothing is foolproof, Mr. President," Jed answered. "But the early data give us about a 90 percent confidence level. If the machine says you're telling the truth, then nine chances in ten, you are."

"What about false positives?" Jack persisted. "Isn't there a chance that the results will say that I'm lying when I'm actually telling the truth? What if I simply get nervous?"

"Again, there is a slim chance of that," Jed acknowledged. "That's why judges are still unwilling to permit the results into evidence. But we've made enormous strides at filtering out the noise. While it's still possible that a truthful subject will flunk the test, those instances are pretty rare."

Personally, I wasn't nearly as worried about a false *positive* result as I was about a false *negative* result. What if the fMRI indicated that Jack was telling the *truth* when he denied being the killer, but he was actually *lying*? Sure, Jed said that the odds of an invalid result were low. Even so.

"Okay," Jack said at last. "Let's get started."

Jed handed Jack a thin robe that tied in the back and directed him to a changing room. When Jack returned, Jed fitted him with one of the helmets and a gray leaded shield. The former president, now decked out like a crash-test dummy, eased himself onto the bed.

"Not claustrophobic, are you, sir?" Jed asked.

"Not that I'm aware of," Jack answered as Jed gently glided Jack into the cylinder.

"Great. I will start with some straightforward questions so that I can chart your baseline reactions. Please answer with a simple yes or no, if possible. Is your name John Sherman Cutler?"

"Yes."

"Do you go by Jack for short?"

"Yes."

"Did you serve as the most recent president of the United States?"

"Yes."

"Are you forty years old?"

"No."

"Are you fifty-five years old?"

"Yes."

"Are your eyes brown?"

"No."

"Are your eyes blue and gray?"

"Yes."

"Did you score 590 on your math SAT when you were a senior in high school?"

"No."

"Did you score 800 on your math SAT when you were a senior in high school?"

"Yes."

"While you were president, did you negotiate a nuclear freeze agreement with North Korea?"

"Yes."

"While you were president, did you sponsor a UN resolution condemning the Russian annexation of Moldova?"

"Yes."

"While you were president, did you sign legislation permitting oil drilling in the Bering Sea?"

"No."

"Were you and Mr. Jacobson in high school together?"

"Yes."

"In high school, did you ever play embarrassing pranks on Mr. Jacobson?"

Jack shot me a quick look. I tried to keep a poker face.

"Yes, I guess I did."

"Just a simple yes or no, Mr. President," Jed interjected. "Let's continue: Have you ever broken the law?"

"Yes."

"Did you assault your father when you were in high school?"

Jack paused a bit longer this time, wondering, I suppose, how Jed learned that biographical nugget. It came from me, of course.

"Yes," Jack said finally.

"Do you know a woman named Amanda Harper, who served as an associate White House counsel in your administration?"

"I did, yes."

"Did you have an affair with Ms. Harper?"

I had told Jed as much. We needed to gauge Jack's reactions, and now was as good a time as any. Jack paused again before answering.

"Yes."

"Did your affair with Ms. Harper last more than a month?"

"Yes."

"Did it continue after you left office?"

"Yes."

"Did you eventually break it off?"

"No."

"Did you and Ms. Harper ever use physical restraints during sex play?"

A longer pause this time. "Yes," Jack said softly.

"Were you the submissive in the relationship?"

"No," Jack answered with more conviction.

"Was Amanda the submissive?"

"Yes." Jack turned his eyes to me. "Robert, must we?"

"Yes," I broke in, "we must."

Jed continued. "Was Amanda's submissiveness what attracted you to her?"

"Partly, yes," Jack whispered.

"Is Amanda Harper alive today?"

"No."

"Do you know how she died?"

Jack hesitated again. "I know only what I've seen in the media."

"Do you know whether she was killed by someone?"

"That's my understanding, yes."

"Did you kill her?"

"No." Jack answered that one emphatically.

As we had plotted the other night, Jed asked me to step into a private

room with him, leaving Jack alone in the tunnel. We closed the door behind us, waited three or four minutes in silence, then returned to the room.

Jed restated his last question. "Mr. President, did you kill Amanda
Harper?"

"No, I did not."

Jed called me over and pointed to something in the scan results—but
it was all pantomime, intended to increase the pressure on Jack and take
account of any emotional reaction. All according to plan.

"One more time, sir. Did you have anything to do with Ms. Harper's
death?"

"No," said Jack for the third time.

"Do you know who killed her?"

"No."

"That's it, Mr. President. We're all done. As far as modern science can
determine, you're an innocent man. I'll send my report, and bill, in the
next day or so."

———

Jack's car was waiting for us in the parking garage, and we headed back to
Georgetown. It was nearly three a.m.

I told Jack I was ready to go to battle with him. His eyes welled with
relief.

"Robbie, it isn't lost on me that the real reason for tonight's exercise
was to assure you that I'm not Amanda's killer."

I started to protest, but Jack cut me off. "Listen, I get it. I understand.
You loved Amanda. You told me so at the time. I'm just grateful . . ." Jack's
voice trailed off, and I put my arm around him.

V

Some kids in America, I'm told, hope to be president someday. I wanted to be a president's best friend.

Jack Cutler and I went to high school together in Brooklyn—Briar Country Day, class of 1988. Nearly forty years later, it's still hard to believe I attended a school with the words *Country Day* in its name.

The Final Jeopardy answer is "What are scholarships?" The school paid about 90 percent of my tuition for all four years.

The high school—or upper school, as such places call themselves— monopolizes twenty-five acres in a southwest Brooklyn neighborhood known as Dyker Heights. My family and I lived due north, in Borough Park. I commuted on the D train. It took about forty minutes each way, depending.

Briar has been in business almost as long as Lockyear & Harbison, dating back to 1856. It's got a roster of famous alumni, from Arthur Levitt, who once ran the SEC, to Bruce Cutler, no relation to Jack, lawyer for the eighties crime boss John Gotti, whose mug graced the tabloids during our sophomore year.

Effective Inauguration Day four years ago, Briar added a U.S. president to its Wall of Fame.

Jack Cutler was not, to put it mildly, a scholarship kid. His family owned a five-story brownstone in Park Slope, and Jack did not take the subway to school. Most days, his father's limo driver chauffeured him and, later, his younger sister, to Briar. In good weather, the car stopped around the corner so that Jack and C.C. could walk the final block or two. You know, to mingle with the peons.

Jack was the popular kid even then. He was a good student but a truly standout athlete, a starter in lacrosse in the spring, soccer in the fall, and basketball in the winter, always wearing his letter sweater in case you'd forgotten. He won the student government presidency both junior and senior years. He was the boy most parents hoped their daughters, or sons, would bring home for dinner. Strikingly handsome, but in a casual way: well over six feet but slightly slumping, an imposing Roman nose, and dark wavy hair always in search of a barber.

I didn't know Jack during freshman year. I was new to the school, having transferred from the local public school after eighth grade. By sophomore year, I had ferreted out my crowd, mostly the shorter, dorkier kids who lettered in things like chess club and did tech work for the school plays. Jack, of course, was out of our league. And yet Jack and I formed a lasting, if improbable, friendship.

It started in music class. I played the upright bass (pretty well, actually), and Jack played clarinet (badly). What we had in common, as we discovered one memorable afternoon (instead of practicing some Virgil Thomson piece for the tenth time), was a reverence for 1960s rock and roll, especially the little nuggets you'd never hear on Oldies 102.5 FM.

Jack was especially good on mid-sixties trivia. (Q: "The name of the band that recorded 'Little Girl'?"; A: "The Syndicate of Sound." Q: "The flip side of 'Satisfaction' when it was released in the United States?"; A: "'The Under-Assistant West Coast Promotion Man.'")

We started hanging out the middle of sophomore year. Sometimes we worked on class projects together, although Jack, perhaps anticipating his presidential future, delegated most of the work to me. I didn't mind—I felt lucky that Jack had redeemed me from Nerd Patrol. Not that I became one of the cool kids; my bona fides as tragically unhip were too deeply rooted. Still, being one of Jack's friends—one of his *closest* friends, to this very day—gave me a perch from which to see how the other half lives.

Jack had his flaws, don't get me wrong; I saw some of those early on, and more as we got older. He has deep pools of anger, even cruelty, that can sometimes bubble to the surface. He loves, he *needs*, to dominate— every conversation, every personal relationship, every everything.

But even now, with forty years of hindsight, I can see why I've always been drawn to him. Jack is quick-witted and sardonically funny, often at his own expense. He's generous. Bighearted. Kind to us underdogs. If you find yourself in Jack's charmed circle, he focuses on you like a tracer. You suddenly become the most important person in his life.

And when you're the most important person in Jack's life, your own life seems shinier, jazzier, sparklier. Jack was always quick to pick up the tab when we went out for lunch together, as we did on special occasions. But it wasn't just largesse that Jack doled out without breaking stride. Even though he was, by universal acclamation, Big Man On Campus, Jack always took an interest in what I was doing, and never intimated that my life was less fascinating than his. (Though it surely was.)

In the summer before our senior year, for example, I became obsessed with Steve Winwood, whose "Back in the High Life Again" had been re- leased earlier that year. I found myself humming the title track around the clock. Not long after school began in September, Jack stopped me in the hall and asked me to drop whatever I was doing that evening. It was all a big mystery until we got to Town Hall in Manhattan, where, as it turned out, Winwood was headlining. Jack's old man had evidently invested a few shekels in renovating the venue, which gave Jack enough swack to get the man himself to dedicate his performance of "High Life" to me—to me, Rob Jacobson, Jack's sidekick—in front of the whole damn crowd.

Jack also had a sensitivity about him. When one of my nervous twitches—and I have a small army of them, to this day—made me the butt of schoolyard jokes, it was Jack, more often than not, who stuck up for me. I loved him for that. I could, and did, forgive a thousand sins on account of his kindness in the face of my vulnerabilities.

Of course, I was only a visitor in Jack's world. He was born with bumpers that kept his bowling balls rolling down the middle of the lane, while the rest of us had to worry about staying out of the gutter. Jack could screw up, blow off an assignment, smoke a joint en route to class, and he would know—to a *certainty*—that he'd get by. Jack had a margin of error, a permanent hall pass, a get-out-of-jail-free card.

I was not as lucky.

My parents should not have had children. They probably should not have gotten married, at least to each other. They had only one thing in common.

They were both batshit crazy.

My mother, Evie, was bipolar but undiagnosed throughout most of my childhood, medicated only after I left for college. Evie went through long periods of depression, during which she struggled just to get out of bed. At the other extreme, she could pinwheel with energy that overwhelmed any sense she had of how a parent is supposed to raise children.

Take, for instance, this one New Year's Day, when I was about twelve. I was sitting with my brother, watching the new plasma TV we'd just gotten for Hanukkah. As Evie came downstairs from the bedroom, she announced, as if with a drum roll, that she and our dad had started out the new year "with a bang."

Who says shit like that to their kids? Our mom, for one. I now know all the clinical terms—*boundary issues, manic phases, mood disorders*—but at the time, none of us understood anything. All we knew was that when Evie finally got out of bed, she sucked every molecule of air out of the room.

My father, Nathan, dealt with his seriously depressed wife by hoisting his hand precisely to eye level and telling her to "snap out of it," a directive he accented by snapping his fingers. He managed his own spooled rage with a studded utility belt, a thick wraparound with a large American flag buckle in the front. When one of the kids got out of line—or was just too kid-like—Nathan would remove the belt, double it over buckle side out, and hunt down the prime offender. That was usually me, which meant I received the leading edge of Old Glory. Depending on whether I resisted, the imprint could last for hours, even days. And the belt buckle was only one of Nathan's resources. There were also Evie's high-heeled shoes, which Nathan would fling, end over end, like a throwing knife but less aerodynamic. There may have been other weapons of mass destruction. I forget.

My father ran the floor operations at Woodchik's, a hardware store on Flatbush Avenue, which meant that he made the spare keys, handed out paint swatches, and recommended the latest in butterfly hinges and drain snakes. I imagine that Nathan resented his days on the floor. Nathan's bosses had bosses, and in plumbing supplies, as in life, shit flows downhill.

Nathan was reliably home from work between 6:15 and 6:30, and dinner had to be on the table within fifteen minutes of his arrival. The meal lasted no longer than the time it took to eat it. My father then retired to his lounge chair with the spotted olive covering to read the *New York Post* and smoke Tiparillo cigars until bedtime.

That was life with my dad until my senior year at Briar. One evening in late November came the horror—Nathan was fatally assaulted on his way home from work. The police found my father's body, skull crushed, crumpled behind some dumpsters in an alleyway about two blocks from the D train. Nearby, the cops recovered a Louisville Slugger sprayed with what proved to be Nathan's blood.

The detectives investigated the crime for what seemed like an eternity. My family's hopes swelled with each encouraging lead—like the day a witness reported seeing a tall white male in his mid-thirties with an athletic build in the vicinity of the alley where my dad was killed. That jibed with the forensics: from the angle and force of the blow, the cops figured the killer to be taller than Nathan and powerfully built. But that single lead scarcely narrowed the possibilities. Although the authorities managed to lift a partial print from the bat handle, they were never able to find a match.

I became obsessed with my dad's case. *How can you not match a fingerprint?* I remember thinking. *Isn't there some national database you can use? Is my father's case not important enough to be taken seriously? Can we get the feds involved?*

Because I was the "smart one" of the two kids, my mother tasked me with pressing the cops about the progress of their investigation. In time, I was on a first-name basis with Captain Reagan at the 66th, spending hours in the squat faded-redbrick building and competing for the cops' attention with the neighborhood Hats (our slang for the ultra-Orthodox). With no further progress to report, Captain Reagan eventually foisted me off on underlings, and our family finally gave up the hunt. I imagine the cops did as well.

Evie weathered the loss of her husband surprisingly well. She actually seemed to blossom after Nathan's death. To be clear, Evie was always capable of a certain kind of love. But you had to earn it, and the struggle began afresh every day. My mother treated me like a competitor. She went to temple, so I went to temple. She'd been a diligent student, so I had to study hard and excel. But whatever I did, she assured me she could do better. And when you're a kid, there isn't much your parents *can't* do better than you.

My mother also convinced me that, like her, I was an "overachiever." In her vernacular, that meant that any success I garnered was the result of hard work, not natural talent, and would probably never recur. So I grew up thinking that around every corner lurked a manhole with a false cover, and that no matter how gingerly I stepped, I was bound to fall through. No amount of prior success assured against imminent failure. But at least when failure arrived, it would not be unexpected. I expected it *constantly*.

That's probably why I always prepare for the worst. As a kid, I studied for every test. I did all my homework. I was a good student, though not, to be sure, a perfect one. Teachers reported that I sometimes spaced out, and I guess that's true. My mind wanders. I'm easily distracted.

The only family member I was close to was my brother, Evan, who is a year and a half older than me but was only one grade ahead. Even as a teenager, Evan was what they call a "tough Jew." He cursed. He was confident. He had an easy smile. And he took absolutely no shit, none, from our parents or from anyone else.

For one thing, he was nearly a foot taller than the rest of the family, and much, much beefier. By fourteen, Evan was working out regularly and taking lessons (on the sly) at the local Silver Gloves club in Brooklyn.

When he turned seventeen, he entered the Golden Gloves circuit in the 175-pound weight class. Evie and Nathan couldn't be bothered to watch his fights, but I was transfixed. All I could think was that my big brother was in the ring and more than holding his own.

When he wasn't boxing, Evan dabbled in rooftop graffiti—more precisely, the artistry you see on buildings as the D train snakes across the Manhattan Bridge to DeKalb Avenue. Look for Evan's initials, *EHJ*, with the two verticals in *H* formed by a pair of obelisks, each with a single ruby-red eye staring out at the audience. How Evan got the stones to go up on those roofs, I'll never know. I inherited Nathan's fear of heights, but Evan didn't.

Evan did not attend Briar Country Day, but he kept close tabs on me in those years. You couldn't ask for a better protector (Golden Gloves!). I remember one time, in my senior year, when Jack played a practical joke on me and the girl I was seeing. I didn't clock it as any big deal, just some high jinks involving the photographer for the school newspaper, I forget the details. But when I got home that afternoon and told Evan, he was ripshit. Next thing I knew, Evan had cornered Jack, picked him up by his shirt collar (and Jack was built like the lacrosse player he was), and shoved him up against the high school facade. "One more prank like that, asswipe," Evan said, "and I will end you." Or so Evan told me when he got home later that night. (Jack, of course, gave me a different account when I saw him the next day at school.)

After Evan graduated from the local public high school, he worked in the neighborhood, mostly as an auto mechanic. But soon after I finished Briar, Evan left home for good, resolving that he would never set foot in Borough Park again. My mom barely seemed to notice once he was out the door, announcing, with her usual subtlety, that she had only one son—me.

I, on the other hand, was heartbroken. For the next thirty-plus years,

I never saw or heard from Evan once, despite my many efforts to get in touch. But for occasional googling, I could not have told you whether he was still alive. As it turns out, he is.

———

In our junior year at Briar, Jack's sister, Clara Cutler, C.C. for short, entered ninth grade. One spring day after school, when Jack and I were heading over to the Parkway Restaurant on 13th, C.C. passed by with a classmate, whom she introduced as Jessica Friedland. Jess lived in Cobble Hill and, like me, had transferred to Briar from a local public junior high. She was an inch or two shorter than me, with black curly hair that she somehow managed to fix in a ponytail, soft green eyes, and a snub nose that could pass for a shiksa's. She was gorgeous.

Grabbing Jess's arm, C.C. pointed to me and proposed "joining this stud muffin" and her brother for a late lunch at the Parkway. I suppose I had grown a few inches the previous summer and filled out some, though *stud muffin* would not be the first phrase you would have thought of if you'd met me back then. I was about five-eight, en route to five-ten, with muddy brown eyes and an unruly mop of sandy hair that has thinned (to say the least) over the years, and wore wire rims that looked better on John Lennon in the sixties. Jack, on the other hand, had already topped out at six-four, with the Mediterranean good looks he'd inherited from his mom. Jet-black curls; blue eyes flecked with gray chips; an easy, inviting smile. Jack was all stud; I was mostly muffin.

But as Jess confided to me in bed two years later, Jack was traife—unkosher food—off-limits to her in those days. I, on the other hand, was exactly the kind of boy that Jess's parents, Avram and Lenora Friedland, wanted for their daughter. A good student, but not showy. Quick to laugh at Avram's dad jokes and Lenora's puns. A mildly observant Jew, but no fanatic. (We did the High Holidays at our house, maybe a little something for Passover, but never passed up a cheeseburger or a good roast beef and swiss on rye.)

I was also a first-class debate team partner in those days. Jess and I spent countless hours after school working on our arguments, carefully cataloguing obscure facts to dazzle our opponents. There was a lot of time spent in close quarters, cribbing notes from all possible sources, marinating in a witch's brew of ambition and hormones.

Late in my junior year, when Jess and I first paired up, the citywide debate topic was "Resolved, CEO compensation should be regulated by the federal government." Jess and I competed as the negative team, so we prepped arguments against the resolution. We got plenty of help that year from Jess's dad. Avi Friedland was a "financial engineer" at a large savings and loan bank, who spent most of his time buying up smaller banks and inventing new financial "products." S&L stock prices had been skyrocketing for years, 1987 looked to finish higher than ever, and why shouldn't past be prologue?

Avi specialized in mergers and acquisitions, "M&A," as he called it. As best as I could tell, Avi scooped up S&Ls with crappy balance sheets and stuffed them into his bigger bank's portfolio. His own financial success had convinced Jess's dad that government intervention in the market was always a drag on profits. So Avi was happy to explain to his daughter and her lovestruck boyfriend why the government should keep its mitts off CEO compensation.

The debate finals were hosted that year at Bronx Science, our archrivals. Jess and I had been prepping around the clock. We also had our very own superpower. In what passed for juvenile delinquency among the smart set, Jess had created a file called "Successfully Faked Quotes," a collection of bogus quotations to support the arguments we planned to make. So if one of our opponents pointed out, for instance, the vast disparity between CEO pay and the comp of your average employee, Jess might whip out a fake quotation from the Fed chairman or the Treasury secretary about how regulating the salaries of private actors would stifle economic growth. Nonsense, of course, but calculated to impress the judges, who wouldn't know that we'd simply invented all those juicy quotes.

The judges were duly impressed that year, though only enough for a second-place finish. Still, a silver in a citywide contest in my junior year was nothing to sneeze at. Jess and I were in high spirits as we drove back to Brooklyn. Approaching Jess's block, I willed my right arm to drape across her shoulders in the front seat. No luck. My hand stayed rooted to the steering wheel.

Then, in a moment I've replayed in my head a million nights since, Jess leaned her head against me as I drove. I could feel a few tangles of her hair against my flushed cheek. I tried to freeze the moment in my mind—successfully, it would seem, since the memory still scorches nearly four decades later.

Jess wasn't the first girl I'd ever kissed, but she was the first girl I actually wanted to. She was also the first girl I slept with, prom night senior year.

"How the fuck does anyone get these studs on, Evan?"

"Don't you look lovely, Liddle Man?" My brother was trying not to bust a gut. "Smile," Evan said as he took a quick photo.

"Posterity can wait, asswipe. Help me get the clasp done on the necktie. Why do people put up with black tie events?"

"Enough already, Robbie. You look good. Got the corsage? Got the tickets?"

"Check and check."

"Okay. Mom's resting, so say your goodbyes softly. We won't wait up, in case you get lucky."

I grabbed the car keys and headed to Cobble Hill to pick up Jess.

That year's prom theme was Bread Lines—the kind of smartassery you'd expect from private-school kids whose parents were still licking their wounds from the market collapse on Black Monday, October 19, 1987. I pictured the gymnasium walls plastered with Walker Evans photos from the Great Depression. Maybe some shots of Civilian Conservation Corps workers. Some Dust Bowl pics, perhaps.

But Jess and I didn't see any of that because we were heading into Manhattan to spend the evening at the Waldorf. I'd saved up for months for this one splurge. All I had to do was get Jess back home for her two a.m. curfew.

Jess helped me undo all the finery that Evan had helped me put on. The shirt studs, one by one. The idiotic cummerbund. I slipped her gown over her shoulders, and it fell in a chiffon pile at the foot of the bed.

VI

Just after the July Fourth break, Jack was arraigned in Superior Court. Judge Edgerton set some pretrial motion dates and released Jack without bail. To my relief, Jack kept his promise not to engage the press.

Ducking the Fourth Estate was actually the toughest part of the morning. The scene in front of the Superior Court was right out of a Bruegel—you know, the paintings with plump red-faced couples drinking and making merry, cattle walking aimlessly across the square, dogs and cats living together. The crowd that day had a certain *democratic* feel to it—reporters from CBS and *The New York Times* jostling, cheek by jowl, with their counterparts from OAN and the *New York Post,* not to mention dozens of others whose journalistic cred consisted of blog posts they wrote under their bedsheets at two a.m.

Needless to say, Smith Universal was present and accounted for. Even before Jack beat him four years earlier, President Smith had launched his network as a 24/7 platform for the New Nationalism. No populist fable was too preposterous for the network's lineup of prime-time lickspittles.

America on the brink of socialist revolution? Check. Caravans of Canadian elderly poised to invade America on their walkers, all in search of better healthcare? Check. Even that soon-to-be-disbarred Texas lawyer, with her antic claims about made-in-China machines that supposedly flipped votes from Smith to Cutler, was rewarded with hours of unrebutted airtime.

Fortunately, Judge Edgerton runs his courtroom like a Rolex, but with even greater precision. Sam Edgerton has been on the bench for thirty-plus years. He still has the brush cut and military bearing of his Marine days. As I had told Jack, Judge Edgerton is tough but fair. He'll give you an evenhanded trial, but heaven forbid you ever have to stand before him for sentencing.

A Republican appointee, Judge Edgerton had been an insurance defense lawyer before taking the bench. And not one of those big-firm insurance lawyers who arbitrate billion-dollar coverage disputes in The Hague. No, Edgerton was a meat-and-potatoes insurance lawyer, a trench warrior who defended slip-and-fall cases against the kind of lawyers who advertise on highway billboards. (You know—the guys with the perky jingles and the 1-800 numbers.) Naturally, Judge Edgerton brought to the bench a hard-earned skepticism about human nature.

His Honor and I have always gotten along famously. Maybe that's because he's a Fordham evening-school grad, too, and sees me as a kindred spirit. It also helps that I come to court prepared and don't push the envelope too far. If you test the judge's patience, he lets you know. Edgerton has a set of eyebrows that come with their own gardener. If he isn't buying some argument, he gives you the Full Eyebrow, peering over the top of his half-rims, raising the shrubbery, and shooting a look that says, *Not in my courtroom.*

As usual, the judge was all business today. He took Jack's plea at the bench, to avoid any unnecessary spectacle. The whole thing took about ten minutes. Jack and I then navigated the river of photographers, and I deposited him with his driver. I was scheduled to meet Jess at my office at Lockyear & Harbison in half an hour.

———————

A few minutes past noon, Alec, my assistant, brought Jess to my office. Looking at Jess never fails to break my heart. She wears her neediness like a hairpin. You could spot it if you knew where to look—hooded eyes, some reddening, a slight bearing of fatigue. But to my eyes, the same drop-dead beauty I'd first glimpsed at Briar decades before.

As we walked to the adjoining conference room, I asked how she and Jack were doing. The news was not good.

"Jack is shutting down," Jess said. "He gets an hour, maybe two, of sleep, then lies awake scrolling through online chatter. I can't persuade him to ignore it, and the more lurid the stories, the more he seeks them out."

I wasn't surprised. Jack had lived his entire professional life by the sword of public opinion. Why would now be any different?

"How about you and the kids?" I asked.

Jess hesitated. "Worse by the day. I want to support Jack, of course, but I'm just so fucking angry. I may take the kids elsewhere for a while."

"If that time comes, let's discuss first, Jess. Jack will need his family, now more than ever." Not to mention that it would be a bad look in front of the jury.

"Of course," Jess replied.

"Let's talk about Jack and Amanda," I said.

Jess frowned. "As I told you at the house, Robbie, I don't recall meeting this woman. And I don't think Jack ever mentioned her—until the charges, of course. I really can't tell you anything about the two of them."

"The government will be poking around anyway," I said. "Is there anything the prosecutors are likely to learn about your marriage that I ought to know?"

"How is that relevant?" Jess was understandably defensive. "It was bad enough when we were in the White House. We signed up for that fishbowl when Jack entered politics. But we're out of it now. What possible business is our marriage to the people prosecuting my husband?"

"No business of theirs at all," I acknowledged. "But we've got to prepare for the worst, Jess. If witnesses were to testify that you and Jack were unhappy, the government might insinuate that Jack found companionship elsewhere. With Amanda Harper, for example."

"Well, we're not unhappy, no more so than other married couples with complicated lives. Listen, Robbie, can those bastards really make me talk about my marriage? Don't I have some kind of immunity?" Jess asked, her voice breaking just a little.

Maybe it was the wrong moment to press the point. "You're right, Jess. So long as you remain married to Jack, the prosecutors can't make you testify *against* him. But you *can* testify *for* him, so let me ask you: Can you provide Jack with an alibi for the time of the murder? Can you vouch for his whereabouts at the tail end of January?"

"Nothing special comes to mind, but I'll give it some thought. Jack and I live pretty active lives. We don't always keep each other posted on our comings and goings."

"How about violence?" I asked. "Has that ever been an issue?"

Jess hesitated—a few beats too long, I thought. "No," she said at last.

"So no fits of anger, no threats, nothing like that?"

"Well, with his dad, of course. Sherm can still touch a nerve with Jack, even after all these years, if you can believe it."

I could believe it. I'd seen Jack's violence with his dad firsthand. Twice, in fact.

I first met Sherman Cutler when I was invited to dinner junior year of high school. The Cutler home was on Carroll Street, a tree-lined block just off Prospect Park. It was one of those stately brownstones built in the late nineteenth century to house Manhattan gentry seeking a more bucolic lifestyle. When I got the full tour from Jack that evening before dinner, the house looked as I imagine it did when such mansions hosted the Rockefellers at the fin de siècle.

The double door entrance to the Cutlers' home was at the top of a flight of stone stairs rising above the garden level. Just inside, an entryway with a sweeping staircase lit by a magnificent crystal-drop chandelier opened onto an expansive living room with parquet floors and a couple of Rothkos on the walls. The room was framed on the street-facing side by windows with their original mahogany pocket shutters. At the other end was a formal dining room and a gleaming spacious kitchen that looked like the family ate out every night. On the level below were two bedrooms, a wine cellar, and a narrow but deep garden, appointed that fall with hybrid tea roses, shining sumac, and uncomfortable-looking outdoor furniture. Upstairs were three more bedrooms, a wood-paneled and gilded library, a music room with a Steinway grand, and Sherm's study, complete with leather wing chairs and a large cigar humidor.

Sherm Cutler was CEO of a hedge fund called Sovereign Capital Asset Management, a fund that invested in distressed sovereign debt, issued by countries that suffered the worst losses during the last recession. Jack's dad wasn't home much—he was usually jetting off to solicit more financing or to check on overseas investments. But when Sherm was in Brooklyn, he was the cock of the walk. He was as tall as Jack, but broader and meaner.

I'd been looking forward to meeting Sherm ever since Jack had grumbled the invitation a few days earlier. John Sherman Cutler Sr. was constantly in the business pages—browbeating foreign governments, bullying corporate boards to show better returns, and engaging in interminable litigation, both here and abroad. Yet almost all of what I knew about him had come from scuttlebutt. Jack rarely mentioned his father. And when he did, it was in a clipped and sarcastic tone.

About twenty minutes into dinner came my first surprise. Unlike her brother, Jack, who sat morosely at the table, C.C. had a light, teasing rapport with her father. C.C. was gushing about a birthday party her parents had thrown for her the week before—the girls in their lavish dresses, the boys in their awkward first tuxedos. Suddenly, Sherm starts channeling Ringo Starr: "You're sixteen, you're beautiful, and you're mine." Just like that, snap!, the two of them begin prancing across the parlor. C.C. had this vacant look in her eyes, while her mom and Jack exchanged a furtive glance. Then as if they had rehearsed the number—and who knows, maybe they had—Sherm and C.C. are white-breading Sam Cooke: "She was too young to fall in love / And I was too young to know."

More than thirty years later, that scene still creeps me out. I can only imagine how it made Jack feel. Here is Sherm, shimmying with his teenaged daughter to sixties ballads about girls on the cusp of adulthood. I wondered, then and now, whether Sherm's hands had been on his daughter's waist before. I do know this much, for whatever it may be worth: C.C. was married and pregnant at twenty, was divorced with two kids at twenty-four, and has never remarried.

The Cutlers served wine with dinner, though I took a pass. Jack drank nearly as aggressively as his father, and as the evening wore on, the Cutler clan was increasingly in its cups. Drink did not improve Sherm's disposition. All night long he badgered his son as if Jack had missed an interest payment on some foreign debt.

The worst of Sherm's onslaught concerned Jack's performance on an AP American history exam we'd taken a week before. The old man drew me into the fray, eliciting that I'd gotten an A+ on a quiz about Supreme Court justices. That just amped up the guy's outrage. Rising from the table, Sherm smoothed out a crumpled piece of paper he'd lodged in his jacket pocket and glared at his son.

"B plus? You got a B plus? I own bonds with a better rating than that, you dumb fuck."

Apparently, Jack had gotten two of the ten questions wrong.

"How the fuck do you not know who wrote *Brown v. Board of Education*? How do you not know it was that liberal prick Earl Warren? And I guaran-fucking-tee that your pal Robbie can tell us who the first Jewish Supreme Court justice was. Even I know that was Louis Brandeis, and all I do is make money all day."

Next came the Dartmouth crap. Like how would Jack get into Dartmouth, where Sherm had gone, with a B+ on an exam? How would Jack experience the pleasures of Hanover, New Hampshire, if he didn't ace every quiz?

I sprang to Jack's defense. "Jack's a great student," I heard myself say, "but maybe perfection is the only passing grade around here." Still, Sherm continued his diatribe unabated.

Meanwhile, you could see Jack's jaw tensing and his hands gripping the silverware ever more tightly. Suddenly Jack was on his feet, too, eyeball to eyeball with the old man, still clutching his dinner knife. I could have sworn he was going to slice his father in two. Sherm must have seen this coming—how could he not?—and took a step backward, giving Judith, Jack's mom, enough time to grab her son. Somehow we managed to finish dinner.

When I saw Jack the next day at school, he was pissed. "Would it have killed you to say a few words in my defense?" he asked. I reminded him what I'd said at dinner, but Jack, still blinded by rage at his old man, acted as if I'd just sat there in silence.

I never went back to Jack's house for seconds. And although I'd occasionally glimpse press reports about Sherm, I saw him in person only one more time, on a warm Saturday afternoon in the late spring of our senior year in high school.

The economy was teetering by now, a nasty year all around, especially for Jess's dad. His large S&L had cratered after Black Monday, scarfed up and resold by the FDIC for pennies on the dollar, and Avi Friedland had been unemployed ever since. Jess and I thought her parents might like to join us and the Cutlers for a home lacrosse match against Andover Academy, one of Briar's fiercest rivals. Jack was a starting midfielder, but he had a half hour or so to visit with us before the game.

Sherm had been "tailgating" since about ten-thirty that morning. "Tailgating," I gathered, meant sitting beside your Benz or SUV and slurping down pitchers of martinis, interrupted only briefly by modest picnic lunches. Sherm seemed to know Avi from what my dad used to call "the business world."

"So, Avi. Any nibbles from the job market these days?" Sherm asked.

"'Fraid not," said Jess's dad. "The financial markets are pretty tight. As you know."

"Leaves some great opportunities for the rest of us," said Sherm. "All the minnows, jumping into some bigger fish's mouth."

Avi took that jab in stride. "Sounds like your firm is thriving, Sherm. You're lucky."

"Luck has nothing to do with it, my friend. It's just data. Anyone watching the S&L market the last twelve months could've seen this coming. We sure did."

Jack broke in. "Dad, can we please leave the shoptalk for the shop?"

"For chrissake, Jack, don't have twins. Avi and I are just swapping war stories. Maybe I can even help him out a little."

"That's kind of you, Sherm," said Jess's dad, "but we'll be fine. How long can this cycle last?"

Sherm chuckled. "Tell that to the two hundred other S&Ls that went tits up this year. I bet those geniuses figured the high-yield lending bubble would never burst. Not us. We took the downside bet, bought some short swaps. Now we're in clover 'til the Second Coming."

I caught only the gist at the time: Sherm's firm had apparently hedged against the banking sector of the economy. Or, to put a finer point on it, Jack's old man was basically betting that Avi would fail. "Jack," I piped in, "how does the team look for the game?"

Jess squeezed my hand. Her guy had come to the rescue.

"Should be even steven. Tough players on both sides. My guess? The squad that commits the fewest penalties comes out on top. Which is my cue to get down to the locker room. See you all after we kick their ass."

The match itself was uneventful until the third quarter, when Andover scored three goals in quick succession. Sherm evidently thought that Andover had committed some infraction, and after the second goal he began to heckle the refs. Everyone in the stands, including his beleaguered son, could hear the dulcet tones of Sherm Cutler.

At a break, the senior ref came to the sideline and motioned—with admirable restraint, I thought—for Sherm to take it down a notch. That only egged the bastard on. Jack's dad got louder and more belligerent as the game clock wound down and Briar's chances grew slimmer.

With about six minutes left in the final quarter, Jack was called for a slashing violation and handed a three-minute penalty. In fairness to Sherm (who doesn't deserve it), the poke looked unintentional to me—Jack, perhaps distracted by his father's antics, lost his footing in a crowd of defenders and spiked an Andover player in the midsection. Sherm certainly saw the foul as accidental and called his views to the refs' attention. "Fucking this, fucking that," the usual.

Most of us had gotten used to Sherm's behavior by then. But not Jack. As he walked over to the penalty box, I could see venom in Jack's eyes.

And that's the moment Sherm chose for his coup de grace. This I remember clearly, Sherm hectoring Jack: "Hey, genius. Stick up for yourself, why don't you? Tell those fucks in stripes they work for you. We write their checks, for chrissake."

At the word *checks,* Jack was rocketing up the bleachers, his lacrosse stick hoisted over his right shoulder. The crowd parted as Jack vaulted to our row. In the time it would take Sherm to say *payment default,* Jack had speared the old man twice, sharply, one shot slashing Sherm's head, the other breaking his nose and drawing blood.

"Here you go, you useless prick," Jack taunted the old man. "He shoots, he scores," the future president roared, landing the first shot. "And Briar takes the lead, folks," as Jack's stick found a couple of Sherm's incisors. "Let's see how many credit default swaps you can buy now, you mother." Slash. "Fucking." Slash. "Waste." A final slash. "Of flesh."

Sherm fell backward and landed on top of the folks in the row behind us, blood spurting from his nose and two fewer teeth left in his mouth.

The rest of the afternoon is mostly a blur. I recall that a few of the parents grabbed Jack to stop him from inflicting further damage. Jess and I left with her folks and headed back to Cobble Hill.

So yeah, I could believe that Sherm, now eighty-nine, still touched a nerve with the former president of the United States.

"How about enemies?" I asked Jess. "Anyone you can think of with a motive to tar Jack with this killing?"

The first hint of a smile. "Gee, Robbie, I don't know. The last polling we did when Jack was in office indicated that 55 percent of the American public thought Jack fired the fatal bullet from the Texas Book Depository. But no, I don't know of anyone with a special interest in framing Jack, if that's what you're asking."

"I had to ask," I said, "and I'll ask Jack the same thing." Presidents collect enemies, it comes with the job. Jack was no different.

It was nearly two p.m., and I'd kept Jess long enough. "Jess, we'll do everything we can for you and Jack. You'll get through this. Count on it."

"I always have, Robbie."

I walked Jess to reception, gave her a long hug goodbye, and went back to my office to call the prosecutor. We set a time next week for me to come in and get briefed on the case. In the meantime, there was a trip out to the Maryland countryside I needed to make.

VII

*C*ome in, grab a seat. I'm Dr.—

I know your name. Nice office, by the way. Leather couch, soft pastel walls, inoffensive artwork. A whiff of air freshener—lilac, maybe. Not Park Avenue, but nice enough. You've got an eye for decor, Doctor.

It's important that you're comfortable here. Tell me how you've been feeling.

How I'm what? How I'm feeeeling?

I feel angry. For as long as I can remember, that's my only real emotion. The only thing that makes me come alive. As if I'm sleepwalking until the feeling washes over me.

How long have you felt this way?

Since I was a kid.

What's your earliest memory of this "coming alive" feeling?

I was maybe ten or eleven. There was this dog in our neighborhood, lived in an alleyway near our house. Barked all night, it was really quite appalling. None of us could get any sleep when that dog was hungry. One night I got sick of it. Someone had to take command, right? Someone had to lead the way. So I brought some food out to the alley after the owners had gone to bed. When that loud little scoundrel came for his last supper, I got a good look at him. Ugly little runt. It took ten seconds to wring his neck. Problem solved. As I said, someone needs to be in charge.

The anger is my body. It's my skin and bones. It's my gut. Sometimes I wonder, as President Reagan once wrote, "Where's the rest of me?"

Are you having any issues other than anger?

I also daydream and miss things. Basic things, you know. What people say to me. What I've said to them. Sometimes it just doesn't register.

I imagine that this all affects your relationships with others.

Listen, I have plenty of friends, as you can obviously tell. That's not the problem. But it's all surface bullshit. It's all what you therapists call *transactional*—you know, what do people want from me, and what can I get from them? I don't feel connected to anyone. Not in any fundamental way. Not even my family. Most people think they know me, but really they have only the dimmest sense of who I am. It's as if they don't see me, the real me, whoever that is.

I realize this may all seem surprising, Doc. Given the things I've accomplished in my life.

Even public figures struggle with mental health.

Is that why I'm here? So you can help me?

Robbie thought you should do some sessions with a psychiatrist. If you're not well enough to assist in your defense, you can't stand trial. That's why I'm here.

Well, if Robbie says so, Doctor, I guess that's what we'll do.

VIII

When you turn off the Clara Barton Parkway and go west to Potomac, Maryland, the yards get greener and the houses stand farther apart. On the Saturday following Jack's arraignment, I drove out past the stables and bridle paths, across miles of persimmon trees and summer honeysuckle, until the two-acre zoning finally gives way to farm country. At the end of a winding road, I came to an immaculately renovated eighteenth-century barn.

I had called ahead, and Jane Cashman, my former law partner, met me at the door in midsummer gardening gear. "Rob," she said, "so good to see you. I'll meet you in the den. Grab something to drink from the kitchen."

I poured myself some iced tea and found a seat. All around were pictures of Jane's children and grandchildren, and keepsakes from her long marriage to Philip, who had died of cancer only a few months after Jane's retirement from the firm.

Jane joined me as I was admiring her mementos.

"Kinder days," she noted. "There are still times I find myself talking to Phil, debating something that now seems so trivial."

"I'm sorry I missed the funeral, Jane," I offered. "Some issues with Josh." My son had suffered a bad episode that day.

"That's okay, Rob. It was mostly family. The kids and grandkids flew in. You could feel Phil's spirit. But something tells me you did not come all the way out here to pay a condolence call."

"You're right. Look, Jane, I'd like your help on the Cutler case. You can have any role at trial you want. I don't think I can win it without you."

I watched two beats go by before Jane answered. "Rob, I'm not sure I'm right for the job. For one thing, I'm no fan of President Cutler. I've never met him, and I didn't vote for him. You probably don't want a co-counsel who despises the client going in."

I hadn't reckoned with Jane's politics before heading out here. But I should have. Jane is a conservative Republican, an old-school type, cut from the now-ancient fabric of William F. Buckley Jr. and Edmund Burke, not the faux conservatism peddled by the Smith toadies on late-night cable.

"I don't get it, Jane. You and I never let political differences stand in the way of taking a good case. Remember Dylan Bradley? The hedge fund manager who gave millions to the Dems? You defended his fund when the investors cried fraud, and you never made a peep about his campaign contributions. And how about that ambassador Smith fired? She was an out and proud Democrat, but that didn't slow you down for a second when she asked for your help. To paraphrase my rabbinical fore-fathers, why is this case different from all other cases?"

Jane smiled. "It's pretty basic, Rob. I've been out of practice for a while now, and I'm not sure I can summon my A game for this client. Frankly, some of the 'sex slave' stuff makes me squeamish. I'm sure you've heard the same rumors that I have. Also, from what I've been reading, he sounds guilty. I have no interest in defending some liberal philanderer who also happens to be a murderer. But tell me why I'm wrong about your friend the president, Rob. Make your pitch."

I told her what I knew, including the fMRI results, but the puzzled look on Jane's face reminded me how much I still had to learn about the case. "I'm doing my first sit-down with the prosecutors the end of next week. 'Open files,' they assured me—they'll tell us whatever we want to know."

"I'd probably be that generous, too, Rob, if I had an airtight case against the president."

A fair point. "I just don't believe he did it, Jane, and the fMRI results confirm it."

"Come on, Rob. Science is fallible, you know that, especially new technology like this. Machines can be fooled. And Mr. Cutler is famous for his anger issues. He's your friend, but really."

"Jack can be a bit impulsive, I admit, Jane. But he's also got a big heart. Plus, I cannot picture him being violent with Amanda."

"That's the other thing," said Jane. "Amanda was our friend. I'm sure you've asked yourself what we owe her."

"Of course I have," I said, perhaps a bit too defensively. "But if Jack *didn't* do this, we owe it to Amanda to make sure the real killer gets charged." I paused to regroup. "Look, this is going to be the fight of my life, and I can't win it without you. It's that simple."

Jane shot me a look. "It's not that simple, Rob, and I think you know it."

I took a quick slug of iced tea. How much did Jane know? How did she know it? Amanda and I had always been so discreet. Or so I thought.

"What are you saying, Jane?"

"I'm saying that we were both close friends of Amanda's. And I think you may have been more than that."

She obviously knew about the affair—no point in demurring. "You're right, Jane. And I've struggled with this. I even told Jack I would find him another lawyer. But he pressed me, and let's face it, he and I have a long history, too."

"But the former president is not a lawyer, Rob. And lawyers have an independent duty to avoid conflicts. You know that as well as I do."

"What's the conflict? I don't see it."

"Rob, be serious here. I know you, and I knew Amanda. I know you were in love with her, and I know she broke your heart when she stopped seeing you. You've got to level with the president. And you've got to level with yourself. Can you really defend a man who may have killed Amanda? Can you really be a vigorous advocate for the man accused of choking her to death?"

I'd already asked myself that question a hundred times. And after the lie detector results, I'd made my peace with it.

"Yes, Jane, I can. As far as my 'independent duty to avoid conflicts,' that's between the client and me. And Jack wants me to do this."

"What if the government gets wind of your history with Amanda? Have you considered that the prosecutors may try to get you disqualified? Maybe even on the eve of trial, when there's no time to adjust?"

"The government won't learn about Amanda and me."

"You can't possibly know that, Rob. But one thing's for sure: If they *do* find out, the prosecutors will go right to the judge. They won't want to face the possibility that a month after conviction, Mr. Cutler will try to overturn the verdict because his trial lawyer had a conflict. The prosecutors are going to get the issue resolved before jury selection."

Jane was right, of course. If the prosecutors learned about my affair with Amanda, they wouldn't wait ten minutes before taking the issue to Judge Edgerton.

"All true, Jane. The government would have a fit—*if* they learn about it. But if we're lucky, they won't find out."

"That's a pretty big gamble, don't you think? This is a small town. With big ears."

"It's a gamble Jack seems willing to take. And even if the prosecutors get wind of my affair with Amanda, I won't necessarily get thrown off the case. Jack's Sixth Amendment right to counsel is pretty weighty, too. Bottom line: I explained the situation to the client, and he wants me as his lawyer. That's good enough for me. And I devoutly hope it's good enough for you to sign on as well."

"Okay, Rob," Jane said finally. "I'll give your proposal some thought. But I need your assurance that no matter what I decide, there will be no hard feelings. I'm not going to just be the Black lady lawyer in front of a D.C. jury, not for any client, and especially not for Jack Cutler."

"Jane, not for a second would I—"

"No, Rob, of course you wouldn't. But your buddy Jack? He would pimp me out in a heartbeat."

I told Jane that I hoped I could prove her wrong about Jack. Or that Jack could. As I drove back to D.C., I kept thinking how good it would be to pair up again with Jane at trial. Just like old times at the firm.

I was not a first-round draft choice at Lockyear & Harbison, LLC. Each recruiting season, as résumés pour in from law students hoping to work at the firm, Hiram Lockyear, still shambling about the office at ninety-three, renews his pledge that the law firm his family founded will never hire from outside the Ivies. It's bad enough, he tells us, to look beyond Harvard and Yale. Columbia and Penn are slumming, and heaven knows why anyone would consider a Fordham student.

But Fordham *night* school, my alma mater, was certainly a bridge too far. Never mind that I had little choice but to work during the day, or that I graduated first in my evening division class. When I got out of law school, firms like L&H wouldn't give me the time of day.

But I was used to being underestimated. Plus, I had no interest in being the lowest person on some Big Firm totem pole, the hapless drone who sits in a Topeka warehouse putting documents in chronological order. All so that some senior partner could use those documents at a trial I wouldn't even get to attend.

I wanted to be the guy trying the cases.

I grew up watching Perry Mason reruns with my grandmother in Borough Park, and from a tender age that's who I wanted to be. Perry seemed to handle only first-degree murders, and best as I could tell, he'd never lost a case. He cross-examined witnesses within an inch of their lives. He actually forced the real killers to confess on the witness stand. His clients were usually sympathetic, always grateful, and never seemed to carp about paying their bills. (Come to think of it, none of them ever seemed to *get* a bill for Perry's services.) I wanted to try cases like he did.

So I spent my first few years as a federal prosecutor in New York City, learning to try cases. It was a great job, but it was also a revelation to me. I found that I could cross-examine witnesses with a ferocity that felt foreign. It's still like that.

Where does that instinct come from? I really don't know. A type of possession—call it adrenaline, call it a spirit—simply comes over me. Suddenly the witness looks like prey and I become a hunter, armed with careful prep work, some provocative questions, and an overdeveloped instinct for sarcasm.

After I'd learned most of what government service could teach me, I sent my CV out to several dozen law firms, and to my considerable surprise, I was invited to interview at Lockyear & Harbison.

I donned my one Brooks Brothers suit and accessorized with a pale, spread-collar shirt and a yellow tie. (Someone once told me that yellow is an "approachable" power color.) On the train down to D.C., I tried to memorize the names and backgrounds of some of the L&H partners and associates I might meet, but that just reminded me how outclassed I was: the lone state school grad in a gaggle of Ivy Leaguers.

I arrived at Union Station, took the red line subway to Metro Center, and sprinted over to the firm's offices in Lafayette Square. The reception-ist on the ninth floor greeted me perfunctorily and handed me a schedule of the lawyers I would meet during the day. I tried to recall whether any of the names matched the list I'd memorized on the ride down.

Looking back, the interviews are mostly a blur. I remember being grilled by an assortment of partners ("tell me why you're qualified to work at a firm like ours") and treated to humblebrag from associates ("it's depressing to think that I've booked my entire calendar through next July"). At long last I was ushered into a large corner office over-looking the White House. Jane Cashman, a mid-fortyish partner with a short graying Afro, deep brown eyes tucked behind wire-rim glasses, and a conservative yet form-fitting pearl-gray suit, welcomed me warmly at the door and directed me to a comfy sofa by the side of her Harvard chair.

I have a few nervous tics—an array of oral fixations, like biting my knuckles or making small clicking noises with my jaw. Most of the time, they're not too dramatic. Over the years, I've found ways to compensate and conceal, especially in front of judges and juries. But the tics never totally go away, except when I'm asleep. I suppose they are a souvenir of my own special childhood.

I mention this now because the tics seemed to quiet when I nestled into the sofa and Ms. Cashman turned down the small speaker on the credenza behind her desk. Conway Twitty, to my surprise.

"Tell me what you're reading these days," Jane said. I still remember those opening words.

"I just finished Philip Roth's *I Married a Communist*," I said.

"You have good taste. I've read the entire Nathan Zuckerman series," Cashman told me. "For my money, *American Pastoral* is one of the five or six best American novels of the last century. So tell me your top five American novels."

I love list games. Best R&B songs, best Dylan covers, best vice presidents, you name it. I paused to make sure my list would impress. "Well, *American Pastoral*, for sure. Also *In Cold Blood* and *The Executioner's Song*."

"You go for true crime stuff. I like it. Must be your prosecutor's instinct. How about *Confederacy of Dunces*?" asked Cashman.

"One of my favorites," I said, and meant it. I love that book. "You know where the title comes from, right?"

"Jonathan Swift," Cashman answered. "'When a true genius appears in the world, you may know him by this sign, that the dunces are all in confederacy against him.' Basically, my mantra for life."

A libertarian's credo. I was surprised at the time and tucked that nugget away for future questions.

We spent the next half hour talking about *Confederacy*. Ms. Cashman turned out to be something of a scholar on the main character, Ignatius J. Reilly. She even knew that a bronze statue of him greets pedestrians on Canal Street in New Orleans.

"So you've passed the test, Rob," Jane announced finally. It was Jane and Rob from then on. "I ask every L&H applicant what they think of *Confederacy*. The ones who have read and loved the book get hired. The others, not so much."

I started at L&H about two months later. Jane was a rising star in the litigation department. Like all her lit partners at the time, Jane handled civil cases, mostly for corporate defendants, and almost always with high-dollar stakes. Because I joined the firm from a prosecutor's office, I knew the penal code, but next to nothing about civil litigation. Jane was my teacher.

"Don't peak too early," Jane instructed the young lawyers who worked with her. "The first hour or so of an examination should be spent laying groundwork. Get the witness to agree or disagree with certain broad propositions. Dig him into his story. Discover and develop information. But don't ever, ever go in for the kill too soon. The rule is 'plant seeds and get leads.' The punch line may not come until the end of trial, when the witness has already committed himself to a point without realizing why it matters. By the time he figures out how you intend to capitalize on his earlier answers, it will be too late for him to do anything about it."

Jane and I worked together regularly over the ensuing years. We tried at least a dozen cases together. Like an old married couple, we learned each other's moves. Before Jane officially retired two years ago, I watched her give that same "seeds and leads" speech to countless new associates. She could have written a book about her trial tips or even her memoirs. But she was never that kind of showboat.

All of us counted ourselves lucky to have practiced with Jane. And that includes the rock star who joined us some fifteen years after I became a partner.

IX

Amanda Harper joined L&H with one of the most dazzling résumés I'd ever seen. Yale College (where she rowed varsity women's crew and had an Olympics tryout), *Harvard Law Review*, a clerkship with a prestigious federal district court judge, fluency in three languages. The firm was lucky to get her.

Right from the start, Amanda's time was in huge demand, but she had a prodigious work ethic. Amanda was in the office before our receptionists and left when the cleaning crew was unplugging the last vacuum. She had no apparent concept of "weekends." Unlike some of our peers—who suck up and piss down—Amanda lacked sharp elbows or callous edges.

She also had balls. The firm had this one partner—I won't name names—who habitually assigned work to associates, then waited until the very last minute, often just before the court filing was due, to look at the associate's draft. If there was a single blemish in the work, real or imagined, this jackass would explode in a torrent of abuse.

One day this partner assigned Amanda and a more senior associate—let's call him Jim—a complex motion to draft. Amanda did the initial draft and gave it to Jim to edit. The two of them then gave it to the partner, who, as usual, left the papers in a disheveled pile on his desk until shortly before they were due.

What happened next became L&H legend. The partner summoned Amanda and Jim and berated them in a voice you could hear from a casket in Baltimore. Jim was understandably on the verge of tears. Amanda, by all accounts, was unfazed. She turned to the partner and said, "Jim and I are walking out now. I'll be in my office. If you'd like to have a civil conversation about this motion with my colleague and me, we will be glad to come back. Otherwise, I respectfully suggest that you go fuck yourself."

What could the partner say? He turned various shades of red, puffed himself up like a blowfish, and bitched about the incident to every lawyer within earshot. No one gave a shit. Years later, Mr. Go-Fuck-Yourself found himself standing before a disciplinary panel answering questions about his unconventional billing practices.

Amanda was a stunner, but casually so. Curvy yet crew-chiseled, slightly shorter than me, with lush, flaming red hair and a minor constellation of freckles scattered off the bridge of her nose. Amanda seemed to have only two basic outfits, which she mixed and matched from one day to the next. She was comfortable in her skin, or so I thought at the beginning, and much smarter than I am, which I've always found irresistible. In women, anyway.

I should also confess, given how events unfolded, that I was starved for female attention at the time I met Amanda. My wife, Nan, and I were going through a period too protracted to call a "bad patch." We were barely even speaking. I told myself it was because of the long hours I was putting in at the office, but if you'd asked Nan, she'd tell you that I had erased her from my mental hard drive. There was probably some truth to that, more than I acknowledged at the time.

About eighteen months before she left the firm, Amanda and I were working on the Bronstein case. Margi Bronstein was a pain doctor in Bethesda, Maryland, who'd been charged with federal narcotics violations. The government claimed that Dr. Bronstein had overprescribed opioids to many of her patients, some of whom then resold the prescriptions for profit. The prosecution alleged that Margi must have suspected the reselling but had turned a blind eye to it.

By then, Amanda had been with the firm for three years, and had become one of our toughest litigators. She was imaginative and fearless. And funny. Judges, especially older male judges, loved her, and juries usually did, too. As my frequent second chair at trial, she had no compunction about telling me when she thought I was wrong.

We were in our third week of the Bronstein trial, and the government's star witness, a former patient of Margi's named Tom DeAngelis, was on the stand. DeAngelis, having been arrested reselling some of Margi's pain medications, had agreed to wear a wire during his visits to her clinic, and the government played snippets of those tape-recorded conversations at trial. But the centerpiece of DeAngelis's testimony, which he recited in response to the prosecutor's faux-dramatic questioning, was that he had lost seventy pounds, quickly wasting away under Margi's care. To make matters worse, said DeAngelis, Dr. Bronstein had never even weighed him during his appointments, and instead had falsely entered the patient's weight as 225 on his chart. His actual weight as of his last appointment, DeAngelis swore, was a skeletal 155.

This gripping performance ended the morning session, and so the jurors took DeAngelis's unrebutted story with them into their lunch break. At two p.m. sharp, Amanda began her cross-examination. Mind you, Amanda was about five-seven, maybe 125 pounds dripping wet. De-

Angelis, although some distance away on the witness stand, was a hulking six-four and newly jacked with prison muscle.

Amanda started by planting seeds, as Jane had taught her. She reminded the jury, at the outset, of DeAngelis's basic accusation.

"Mr. DeAngelis, when you went into your appointments with Dr. Bronstein, there were just the two of you present, isn't that correct?"

"Yeah."

"So the jury has only your word for the fact that you lost seventy pounds under Dr. Bronstein's care."

"Yeah, but it's the truth."

"And the jury has only your word for the fact that the doctor never weighed you."

"Yeah," said DeAngelis, "but like I said, it's all true. She never put me on a scale, and I didn't weigh 225 the last time I seen her."

"Well, gosh, Mr. DeAngelis," Amanda asked, feigning bewilderment, "what kind of a doctor would watch her patient lose a third of his body weight in a few months' time, and not even do a weigh-in?"

"A drug-dealing doctor like your client. That's who," said DeAngelis, sounding emboldened.

"And what kind of doctor would make up the number 225 and falsely put it down on your chart?"

"Only a drug dealer like Dr. Bronstein."

Then came the punch line.

"Mr. DeAngelis, do you think it would be helpful to the jury if there were some way to verify your statement that Dr. Bronstein never put you on a scale and simply made up 225 as your weight?"

The witness hesitated, apparently trying to determine what Amanda was up to. "I guess so," DeAngelis said at last.

"Well, maybe there is. When you went to your appointments with Dr. Bronstein, you were wearing a wire, were you not?"

"Yeah."

"That wire recorded your appointments with Dr. Bronstein, from the moment you walked into the examining room until the moment you left the office?"

"Yeah," said DeAngelis, a bit more meekly now.

"In fact," Amanda continued, shooting a withering glance at the government table, "the prosecutors played portions of the tapes they liked for the jury, right?"

"Yeah."

"So, Mr. DeAngelis, I listened to *all* of the tapes, and would you like to guess what the government neglected to play for the jury?"

The next thing the jurors heard were the recorded sounds of DeAngelis stepping on the doctor's scale, the clinking of the metal weights as the final number was set, and DeAngelis's own voice announcing that he weighed a robust 225, just as Margi had recorded in the chart.

Amanda sat down, having shredded the credibility of the government's lead witness. The prosecutor attempted a comeback on redirect, but everyone in the courtroom knew the damage was done.

Amanda and I met with a grateful client after court, then headed back to the office to prepare for the next day's testimony. The hallways at L&H were already dark as we ducked into my office. One of us locked the door.

Whether it was the giddiness of the moment, Amanda's sense of triumph in battle, or just libido, the two of us were screwing five minutes later. It was thrilling, though that first time was surely better for me than it could have been for her.

I've thought about those moments almost daily, in the months, now years, that followed. I still picture the soft curve of Amanda's neck and that small birthmark at the top of her spine where I first placed my tongue. I remember, with some embarrassment even now, how hungry I was for her, and how quickly that first time came to its natural conclusion.

I won't deny the frisson of guilt I felt each time we slept together. She was, after all, my subordinate at the firm. That could be a firing offense at L&H, except for the fact that several of the senior-most partners had their own romantic skeletons in the closet. Amanda was also some twenty-five years my junior. I was reminded of our generational difference every time we were intimate.

But I would be lying if I denied my excitement as well, and my amazement that she had chosen me. By the second week or so of our affair, I'd become the most pathetic of midlife clichés. I longed for our trysts at the end of court days. I dreamt of liquid lunches that spilled into hotel afternoons. I fantasized about Amanda when we were apart and felt a quicksilver of energy when we were together.

Amanda was also calming. There were nights we just lay in bed as Amanda read to me, mostly poetry. She was reassuring. My tics never seemed to frighten her. We'd be sitting at the table after a home-cooked meal, and Amanda would gently, quietly, not even meeting my eyes, place her right hand over my left, the one with the calloused knuckles, and stroke. Stroke the bruising, over and over, until I calmed. She gave me consolation I could never find for myself.

Where's that consolation now?

One night at Amanda's place, after we'd finished supper, she emerged from her bathroom with two small white pills.

"Ecstasy," Amanda announced. "Ever tried it?"

No, I told her. Of course I hadn't.

"Well, you'll love it. It puts the *x* in *sex*. Give it a try," and with that, she swallowed hers.

I took a pass. Sex with Amanda was thrilling enough without my having to violate Title 21 of the United States Code. I have to admit, however, that Amanda was more energetic than ever that night. And, I suppose, I was relieved to have a helpmate in the bedroom.

The next time we were together, Amanda upped the ante. She pinned her hair in a tight bun, leaving the thin outlines of her face and neck exposed. Maybe it was the E she'd taken, I have no idea, but a few minutes after I'd entered her, Amanda asked me to cup my hands around the sides of her neck, just below the jawline, and lightly squeeze.

"You're kidding," I muttered.

"C'mon, Robbie, it's just some basic breath play. Stay away from the windpipe and push up gently. I'll tap you twice on the thigh if it ever gets uncomfortable for me."

"It's already uncomfortable for me," I told her.

"Haven't you ever wanted to give up some control? Get a sense of what powerlessness and trust feel like? I know what I'm doing here, you won't hurt me. Try it, lover."

As I put my hands on the sides of her neck, I felt myself soften inside her.

"I can't do this. I'm sorry, honey."

Amanda assured me it was okay. At the time, I believed her.

Six months later, I'd moved out of my house. Nan and I had been all but strangers for months—I wasn't sure she'd even notice. In fairness, Nan would've said the same about me, and did. She thought I was sleepwalking through our marriage, impersonating a partner, not actually *being* one.

By early 2021 Amanda and I were seeing each other regularly, some nights in her garret in Northwest, and others in my rental along the red line. But we tried our best to keep things on the down-low. Neither of us wanted our colleagues to think that Amanda's success at the firm owed anything to her sleeping with a senior partner.

In chronological order, here are my top three romantic breakups (actually, there are only three to choose from).

First, there's Jess. The end arrived at 3:36 p.m., February 14, my sophomore year in college. Exactly—Valentine's Day.

I'd come home that week to take Jess and her sister, Madeline, then eight years old, ice-skating at a lake out on Long Island. Jess and Maddie had gotten new skates for Hannukah. It was an icy-bright Wednesday afternoon.

When we finally got to the lake, I had the idea to play a game of ice tag. I skated ahead, daring Jess to catch up. As the two of us tried to outdo one another, Maddie, determined to do whatever her big sister was doing, raced after us. Jess's sister was more enthusiastic than skillful on her skates. As she wobbled toward us, you could hear her shrieks of joy.

In the blink of an eye, the shrieks turned desperate, and to this day I blame myself. I swept Jess toward me for a quick smooch, and as I did, you could hear the crack. It spidered across a thinning layer of ice, dragging Maddie into the waters below.

Jess bolted after her sister and jumped into the expanding pool of water. She submerged four times, each time gasping for air and screaming out to me. A few adults on the ice rushed over and tried to assist. No luck. Someone must have called the police, for soon there were sirens and flashing lights.

Where was I? What did I do? Not a damn thing. I just stood there, rooted to the surface like some pathetic ice carving. I felt boxed in. I could have, should have, done *something*. I could hear Jess gasping, then plunging, screaming, then plunging. Meanwhile, some force field was holding me back, as if to stop me from falling in, too. By the time I finally got to the break in the ice, Jess's sister had drowned, and Jess was shivering in a stranger's overcoat. I could not bear to look at her. And I cannot recall how we managed to get home. Maybe in one of the cop cars.

Maddie's shiva was the last time I visited Jess at her parents' place. I still recall those close, still rooms, half lit by standing lamps draped in black lace. The walnut furniture, the faux antiques, the sofas from another generation still covered in plastic. A shtetl's worth of aunts and uncles, wearing their torn black ribbons, whispering and sneaking accusatory looks in my direction.

Jess and I did our best after that. She assured me that Maddie's death wasn't my fault. What could I have really done, after all? Still, Jess could never see me without thinking of Maddie. *Choshek*—the plague of darkness visited on the Egyptians, according to the Book of Exodus—settled into our relationship for good. By my junior year at Albany, we were finished.

How did she wind up with Jack? you ask. It began with politics, of course. During his last two years at NYU (Jack has the Dartmouth rocker, but not a diploma), Jack interned in the Manhattan office of the local assemblywoman. In 1994, when his boss was elected to Congress, Jack threw his own name in the ring to replace her. No one gave this upstart, only two years out of college, much chance of winning.

Jess and I had split up a few years before, but we worked closely with Jack on that first campaign. Jess and I wrote speeches and helped craft Jack's platform. But Jack was the glue. History will record that John Sherman Cutler Jr. was born for politics. No one I'd ever seen—before or since—could hold a room like Jack. He had a kind of street smarts, a sixth sense for what would and wouldn't play before a given audience. He was also completely comfortable with the nip and tuck of political jousting.

When the votes were tallied on election night, Jack had eked out a 22-vote margin. I remember sitting glued to the headquarters screen as the last votes came in from the West Village precinct, putting Jack over the top for good.

A raucous crowd squeezed into the Warren Street Community Center for Jack's victory speech. There were kegs, balloons, and makeshift streamers; lots of noise filled the hall. As Jack walked out to the mic, Jess and I looked on from the wings until Jack, ever gracious, called us onstage. As he finished thanking his supporters, to sustained whoops and applause, Jess clasped her right hand around Jack's left.

I froze for a moment, then figured: Sure, it makes sense. Jess had known Jack almost as long as I had. They were a handsome couple. Jack had charisma I could only dream of. He was capable of sweetness, even if that wasn't his long suit. And what could I do about it anyway? I'd obviously lost Jess for good.

Jack served two terms in the state assembly, and two more in the state senate. By early 2000, the name State Senator Cutler was a regular feature in the New York press. Journalists, like everyone else (but his father), adored Jack. He was great copy. He answered questions in a disarming, self-effacing manner, with a wicked sense of humor, at least when he was off the record. He gossiped. He charmed. He could talk policy and politics but never lose the twinkle that said, "I know this is mostly bullshit."

And it didn't hurt that Jess Friedland, now Cutler, was by his side. Jess sanded Jack's harder edges. If she regretted the full-time role of political spouse, she never showed it, not to me anyway. "It was just a matter of time," so the pundits said, before the two of them moved up the political ladder.

And that's just when circumstances conspired to give "a matter of time" a shove. Around Memorial Day 2002, U.S. Senator Fletcher Pritchard (D-NY) was arrested in a Penn Station men's room when, according to undercover detective Ernest Miranda, Pritchard's right hand somehow migrated to the detective's left thigh. Senator Pritchard tried to plead the case out, quickly and quietly. But nothing could squelch the story once "Fletch the Letch" went viral.

Six months later, Jack and Jess were on their way to Washington, D.C.

———

My second breakup was Nan. The ending with Nan arrived like Hemingway's bankruptcy: "gradually, then suddenly."

Nan swore that I'd just stopped hearing her, but nothing is ever that simple. I may have missed things, sure, but so did she. Nan couldn't have named any of the clients I represented, and I don't recall her ever attending any of my trials after we got married. My work just didn't register with her.

But I may have been responsible as well. Nan had an active architecture practice, mainly restoring historic houses. If you drive through North Chevy Chase toward the Beltway, you'll pass a half dozen of Nan's restorations. But I couldn't have told you what project she was working on at any given time. Sometime later, Nan might mention Palladian windows or articulated doors or shingled gables, as if I knew what she'd said about them. I never did.

And then there were the Josh issues. When our son, Josh, entered his teens, he became more distant, a bit listless, and seemed to have some trouble sleeping. To me, this was just Josh being a teenager—I thought that Nan was exaggerating the problem.

Take the night we all had dinner together when Josh turned thirteen. I thought we had a lovely evening—our favorite Chinese place in Dupont Circle, a nice, civil conversation, lots of back-and-forth with Josh, a real sense of bonding. On the drive home, however, Nan asked Josh and me why we'd been so quiet at dinner. I hadn't seen it that way at all.

Nan thought I was oblivious, and maybe I was. I can be absent-minded, I know that. But I also thought that Nan was too quick to draw the worst possible conclusion. In the end, though, her fears about Josh turned out to be justified. After we'd consulted a series of specialists, the diagnosis proved worse than even Nan had imagined: our son had the onset of schizophrenia. This boy whose hand I had held in mine, whose sunniness had once filled our home—our boy now faced a lifetime of unimaginable troubles.

I blame myself. Mental illness runs in my family, not Nan's. There must have been a genetic predisposition that landed with Josh.

Nan and I split up when Josh was nineteen.

Finally, there's my breakup with Amanda. Until much later, I had no fucking clue why she split with me. Here's all I knew at the time. Late in her fourth year at the firm, Amanda stopped by my office. Seems she'd gotten an inquiry about joining the White House Counsel's Office. She was certainly qualified for the job, and my friendship with Jack wouldn't hurt her chances. Amanda left the firm right after New Year's.

We continued to see each other for the next few months, although Amanda's work obligations caused several last-minute cancellations. In mid-June, on the second anniversary of her DeAngelis cross, I surprised Amanda with a pair of third-row tickets to see the King's Singers at Wolf Trap. She told me she had a nomination memo to get out that night and couldn't make it.

Two days later, she called to say that it would be best if we cooled things for a while. She cleaned her things out of my apartment that weekend. I never got a straight answer why. "Sure, you're busy. I'm busy. We're all fucking busy. But we can make the time. I know that we can."

Amanda didn't think so.

I helped myself to all the usual suspects: liquor, Xanax, stronger dope than I was used to. Nothing worked. There's a hole in my heart you can walk through to this day.

Eight months later, in early February, following Jack's reelection defeat, I was driving back from a client meeting in Northern Virginia. I had just gone over the Key Bridge, the snow was banked on the side of the highway, the Magnetic Fields's chestnut "Book of Love" finished on the radio, and the News at 5 began: "D.C. police announced this afternoon the discovery of the body of Amanda Harper, former assistant counsel to President Jack Cutler, in Rock Creek Park."

I swerved into oncoming traffic on Canal Road. I damn near hit a small red van heading toward me in the opposite lane. "Oh, Jesus. Oh, Jesus." I switched channels to get more details. No luck.

I was sucking in air. My eyes were puddling. There was no shoulder to turn onto.

Several dozen emails awaited me when I got home. L&H colleagues had heard the news. "What was she doing in the park in February?" "Who could have done such a thing?"

I spent most of that night in front of the TV trying to drown myself in infomercials and porn. When I'm this upset, my sobbing somehow operates in reverse. I suck the cries *in,* one after another, and only after a series of them do I expel them in a single whirlwind. Then, finally, having let the air burst out, I stop to catch my breath. Until the cycle starts over.

I thought about calling Amanda's family but couldn't face up to the task. It was too late to call Jane. No one else came to mind.

I have no idea how long I stayed up that night. Eventually I put Monteverdi on the Sonos, took two Klonopins, and waited for sleep to arrive.

Two months later, I filed into a Quaker service at the Friends Meeting House just off Dupont Circle. A simple sign outside the brick facade announced the celebration of Amanda's life. The room was packed that morning, but I didn't recognize any of the congregants. Candidly, I didn't even know that Amanda was a Quaker. How well did I know her? What else had I missed?

A few minutes after ten, a rail-thin man with a shock of white hair—one of the church elders, I suppose—rose from the hardwood pews and addressed the congregation.

"For those of you who are new to Quaker worship, welcome. My name is Alan Evers, and on the premise that old age confers some blessings, I've been asked to give you a sense of our service this morning.

"Today's memorial will last about an hour. As you will see, we have no altar, no pastor, no hymnals, and no prepared agenda. This is a place for quiet reflection where all can come and listen for the word of God.

"Today is also a celebration of the life of one of our congregants, Amanda Harper. So if there are those gathered among us today who wish to speak about our Friend Amanda, please let the spirit move you. The service will conclude when I shake hands with the Friend sitting to my right."

We sat in silence for what seemed an eternity, but a glance at my watch showed that only twenty minutes had passed. Then a short woman with half-moon glasses rose from the middle of the facing pews.

"My name is Lucy Macalester. I grew up with Amanda in Rapid City, South Dakota, but now live with Greg, my husband, and our four children in Pierre, our state capital. Mandy Harper was my best friend from elementary school till the day we both left for college."

Mandy? I thought to myself. I'd never gotten a whiff of that nickname.

"But there were parts of Mandy I never got to know. Some veil I could never pierce. No matter how many people gravitated to Mandy, she was mostly alone.

"Mandy also had a thing for bad boys. Boys who were rough and sometimes mean to her. I never understood that, either. There were great guys who would have given anything to get close to her. But they never could.

"Mandy loved a Joni Mitchell song called 'Cactus Tree.' The last few words capture so much about my friend, how she loved others but could never truly give herself completely to anyone:

And her heart is full and hollow
Like a cactus tree
While she's so busy being free.

"This is why I knew I had to get on a plane to be here today. Mandy Harper meant to please others, but we'd lose her if we tried to follow. I was her best friend, and yet I could never get close enough to her. Maybe one of you did. I hope so. She deserved it."

A minute or two passed as congregants soaked in Lucy's remarks. Some were softly crying in their seats. Then a dry-eyed woman in tweeds, who looked to be in her early sixties, stood up a few rows ahead of me.

"I'm Willa Harper, Amanda's mom. I want to start by thanking Lucy for her touching remarks about my daughter. And I'm here to assure you all that I was always close to Amanda.

"Amanda was the best daughter a parent could hope for. You never had to ask her twice about anything. Did she finish her studying? Was she prepared for the midterm exam? Did she check her work before handing in an assignment? Did she ace her finals?

"I like to think that my husband Vaughn and I modeled what hard work and a good attitude can achieve in life.

"Some of you may know that Vaughn and I worked on several of the most important archaeological finds of the last thirty years. But what you may not know is how much joy Amanda took in her parents' achievements.

"In 2005, for example, when Amanda was maybe seven or eight, I forget which, Vaughn and I took her to Mexico City to see the newly discovered child sacrifice to the Aztec war god."

This was Amanda's *mother*? First of all, Amanda was twelve in 2005, for chrissake. And "child sacrifice"?

"The small, sacrificed child had been unearthed that year, but CT scan technology, which Vaughn had been perfecting for several years in our local lab, allowed archaeologists to date the skeleton to about 1450. I remember showing Amanda the five fingers on each of the child's two hands.

"Amanda spent much of the next year with her grandparents in Wall, South Dakota. That was the year Vaughn and I went to Italy to work on the Tomb of the Roaring Lions. My husband and I helped unearth two of the four fresco paintings showing the feline-like creatures that accompanied the Etruscan burial.

"Those were amazing years for archaeology. I always thought, and hoped I guess, that Amanda would carry our torch to the next level. But to our disappointment, she had other plans. Amanda took up sculling on Rapid Creek. Every morning around five a.m., she'd take her boat out and push herself upriver. Personally, I never saw the point. How does rowing increase anyone's knowledge of history or culture?

"But Vaughn and I told Amanda: 'If you must take up this silly hobby, then be the best at it you can. Push yourself harder.' And you can see what happened as a result: Our little girl got an Olympics tryout. She came *that* close to success.

"That's what good parenting can do. It's like any other kind of science. Establish your principles, apply them consistently, and the proof is in the pudding. Vaughn and I couldn't be prouder of what we achieved with our daughter, just as Amanda was always so proud of us."

There were a few moments of silence—embarrassed silence, I suspected. Then I could hear a low, guttural moan, which to my surprise was coming from me. I thought about saying something to the congregation. Like how I was beginning to understand why there were parts of Amanda I could never reach. Like how painful it must have been to be raised by parents like these. Or how I still couldn't get Amanda out of my heart. But no, I sat there and said nothing.

You may therefore be asking yourself the same question Jane asked me at her Maryland farmhouse: How could I defend the man who may have killed Amanda? I could say that I didn't believe Jack capable of doing something so heinous, especially after the lie detector results. And yet I knew that Jack was capable of cruelty. I'd seen it up close.

The truth, as it is so often, is more unpardonable. Whatever excuses I told myself or others, I took the case because I *wanted to*. I wanted to occupy center stage. I wanted the press attention. I wanted my old friend to depend on me in his hour of greatest need.

I wanted to defend the former president of the United States, even if he'd murdered the woman I loved.

X

Toward the end of July, a couple of weeks after arraignment, I went in to see the prosecutors. For those of you who don't defend criminals for a living, *you* go to see the *prosecutors*—they don't come to see you. The government always meets you on its own turf. It's the prosecutors' way of reminding you that they hold all the cards, at least at the beginning of a case. As a defense lawyer, you are a supplicant, trying to learn as much as you can about the government's case.

The next thing you need to know is that prosecutors begin cases with a big advantage. Almost all judges, even the most liberal-minded, favor the government in criminal cases. Don't get me wrong—most judges let defense counsel do their job. But a prudent defense lawyer never forgets that the government usually gets the benefit of the doubt.

How come? Well, for one thing, prosecutors appear before these judges much more often than most defense lawyers do. In a busy DA's office, prosecutors juggle dozens of cases at a given time. They're running in and out of courtrooms all day long. Over time the judges get to know the prosecutors and trust them. They see each other in the hallways and on the elevators. The judges start calling the prosecutors by their first names. It's a club that defense lawyers rarely get to join.

Then, too, there's the secret no self-respecting judge will admit out loud: Most judges assume that the prosecutor would not have brought charges unless the defendant was guilty. So when your average judge looks up from the bench, he sees a prosecutor valiantly seeking the truth and a defense lawyer paid to thwart it. Of course, the best judges try to keep that prejudice in check. But I have little doubt that, in their heart of hearts, most judges believe that the defendant on trial is guilty as charged. Some of them continue to think so even after a jury has said otherwise.

The first time you meet with the prosecutors in a case, your job is to listen. Take down every word the prosecutors say, in case you ever need to quote it back to them. Feign interest, even appreciation, when the prosecutors tell you what a scumbag your client is, how atrocious his crimes were, and how devastating the evidence against him will be. By doing so, defense lawyers encourage the prosecutors to spill the beans. The goal is to extract as much information as you can.

Armed with legal pads and a few ballpoint pens (yes, I'm a troglodyte about technology), I entered the Municipal Building and took the elevator up to the fifth floor. Like most government quarters, the Homicide Division is cramped, habitually understaffed, and littered with well-thumbed case reporters and statute books. A security guard escorted me through the library, where half-filled coffee cups and water bottles dotted the basic brown government-issue research tables. Finally we arrived at a small, windowless conference room flanking a corridor of secretarial bays.

Three lawyers in navy blue business suits stood up from the far side of the table to greet me. The lead prosecutor, Katherine Hannigan, looked to be in her late thirties, short and intense, but projecting a friendliness that told me, always wary, that she hoped I would plead out the case quickly. She introduced her two colleagues: Sam Parker, African American, perhaps a few years younger than she, and reserved; and Gary Shapiro, mid-fifties, I'd guess, whom Katherine identified as the team's "law guy" (meaning that he'd be drafting and arguing the legal motions in the case).

The three prosecutors had obviously arranged their speaking roles in advance, and Katherine led off.

"Rob, thanks for coming in. I've been a fan of yours for years. I saw you lecture on cross-examination techniques at a continuing legal education seminar some years ago. It will be an honor to work with you on this case."

Notice the phrase *work with you*. As if we were all on the same team, trying to solve Goldbach's conjecture, rather than implacable adversaries, which is what we actually were. But I played along.

"Thank you, Katherine. That must have been quite some years ago indeed, since I haven't taught one of those CLE classes for at least a decade. Anyway, I'm glad to have a chance to sit down and hear something about the case. I'm really just starting to get my feet wet."

Which had the virtue of actually being true—all I knew about the case were the scattered news reports and Jack's denial. Barely a start.

Katherine smiled, then began in earnest. "As I mentioned when you called the other day, we'll be making our entire files available to you, starting the end of the week. You'll get witness statements; all the forensics, police, and CSI reports; autopsy results when they're completed— the works. What I hope to do today, however, is give you the highlights. The greatest hits, so to speak."

"That'd be great, Katherine," I said. "Thanks."

"Let me start with a caveat," she began. "We're still investigating. We're at the tail end of our forensic work, but we still have a little ways to go. So I'll tell you what we know to date, and we'll fill in the rest in the coming weeks."

"That's fine," I said.

"So here's the overview. Ms. Harper was choked to death in late January. Based on the condition of the body and some other evidence, we believe Ms. Harper was killed in her apartment, then moved to the park, where she was discovered a few days later. And I'm afraid some of the more lurid stories are true. There were lacerations on Ms. Harper's wrists and just above her ankles, consistent with some history of rope restraints."

As Jack had told me. "Were the ropes used in any way to commit the crime?"

"Not as far as we can tell. Ms. Harper appears to have been manually strangled. We suspect that the ropes were used for sex play, probably well before the murder itself."

"Did you recover any rope fibers from the body?"

"No," said Katherine. "But we've been able to recover a wealth of other evidence, all of which points to Mr. Cutler as the killer."

With each piece of evidence she described, Katherine counted off a finger, in case I couldn't do the math in my head.

"Let's start with some of the physical evidence. First, we found the president's DNA on parts of Ms. Harper's body, including her neck. We also found his DNA on the victim's collar and other parts of her clothing.

"Second, we recovered a White House dinner knife, part of the James Monroe collection, wedged into Ms. Harper's briefcase. We believe that Mr. Cutler may have been trying to jimmy open the case."

"Wedged how?" I asked.

Sam Parker demonstrated. "The briefcase opens at the top, with a latch that catches when the briefcase is locked. The Monroe knife was stuck partway into the opening, next to the latch."

"I take it that whoever used the knife was unsuccessful in trying to pry it open."

"Correct," said Katherine.

"So no materials were actually taken from the briefcase before the police arrived?"

"Not as far as we know," said Katherine. "As Sam said, the briefcase was still locked when the police found it."

"What did you find inside the briefcase?"

"There were some loose papers and memoranda from Ms. Harper's time at the White House," Katherine answered. "We'll provide you with copies of all that, of course."

"Do you have a theory as to what, if anything, the assailant was trying to find in the briefcase?"

"Not yet," said Katherine. "But we're working on it."

Katherine then resumed her finger counting.

"Third, a partial thumbprint from your client was lifted from the victim's shirt collar.

"Fourth, a few strands of curly gray hair, which look like the president's and nothing like Ms. Harper's, were found on the outside of the victim's clothing, as well as in her undergarments."

I interjected again. "I don't mean to interrupt the flow, but have you already done DNA testing on the individual hairs?"

"Can't be done," Parker broke in. "The hair had no follicles, and a strand of hair without a follicle can't be tested for DNA."

"But," Katherine resumed, "coupled with the rest of the evidence, physical and otherwise, we're confident that a jury will see the hair strands the way we do."

"Anything else?" I asked, hoping we were nearing the end.

"Yes. Fifth, we downloaded Ms. Harper's cellphone. Turns out she made a number of calls to your client in the six months before her death.

Ms. Harper's phone also contained a locator function, which records the owner's precise location at every five-minute interval. Ms. Harper was in the Oval Office on at least nine occasions during the last two months of the Cutler administration."

So what? I thought. "Ms. Harper worked for the White House Counsel. I imagine that members of the president's legal team are in and out of the Oval several times a day."

"And that's the sixth piece of evidence I want to tell you about. I assume you know that your client talked at some length to our investigators."

I struggled to keep a poker face on that one. Jack hadn't mentioned this little nugget. Katherine continued.

"Mr. Cutler came into our office and denied that he'd ever spoken with the victim, apart from greeting her when she started in the office. He also denied that he'd ever touched Ms. Harper, denied ever being in the Oval Office with her, and of course denied having killed her. The president couldn't account for any of the physical evidence—the hair, the knife, the DNA, the phone records, or the fingerprints. We plan to argue to the jury that your client's statements to the police were false, and that his lies confirm his guilty mind."

I sat silent for a few seconds that seemed longer than that. "Have you checked your theory with President Cutler's security detail? Have they confirmed that he was in Rock Creek when you say he was?"

Katherine smiled. "We would have loved to, Rob. Unfortunately, your client relinquished his Secret Service protection the day he left office. It was in all the papers. Too bad for us."

Too bad for you? I thought. Those security folks could also have provided an airtight alibi for Jack. I now recalled having read that Jack terminated his Secret Service protection, the first president since Nixon to do so. Maybe he and Jess just wanted a semblance of private life again.

"May I ask why the president would commit this crime? What's his motive?"

Now it was Gary Shapiro's turn to answer. "As I'm sure you know, the law does not require the prosecution to prove motive. *Why* someone commits murder may be nice to know, but it isn't an element of the offense we have to prove."

For chrissake, I remember thinking. This asshole thinks I skipped Crim Law 101. *Rein it in, Robbie.* "I appreciate that, Gary, but all the same, won't a D.C. jury wonder why a man most of them voted for would kill a woman he barely knew?"

Katherine took over again. "I agree, Rob. They *will* want to know your client's motive. And I'll be candid with you: We don't know yet why the president did what he did. I can tell you that your client had several affairs when he was in the White House and that Amanda Harper could well have been on his hit parade. We're still investigating—we have all kinds of leads and witnesses banging on our doors. But in the end, if we can't show motive, then Gary's right, of course. The case still goes to the jury, as you know."

I started to get up from the table, but Katherine motioned me to stay put.

"There's one more thing, Rob," Katherine said, looking up from her notes, then pausing a few beats. "Ms. Harper was six weeks pregnant at the time of her death."

Good Lord. "With whose child?" I asked, trying to maintain my composure.

"We're still working on it. The autopsy is taking more time than we anticipated. In the meantime," the prosecutor continued, "my door is always open. A case like this doesn't have to go to trial."

I left the Municipal Building and headed for my office. It was come-to-Jesus time with the client.

XI

*C*ome in. Tell me how the trial prep is coming. Have you been able to participate?

I leave that to Robbie. I try not to play lawyer. Fool for a client, isn't that what they say?

But you're at least talking to Robbie, helping out in prep?

Sure. Do you have a spare cigarette?

Sorry, I don't permit smoking in my office.

That's fine. So what's next on your agenda?

Let's start with that violence against your father.

Oh, you've heard about that. There's nothing much to tell. I'd just had enough.

Can you say more?

You can take only so much. I was just tuning him up a bit.

Seems as if you did more than tune him up. From the accounts I've read, there was a fair amount of blood loss.

Not my blood.

How did you feel when you finished beating him?

I honestly don't remember. I know I had the stick in my hands, at least in that moment. All I could feel was the anger. My body was somewhere else. The rest of the day is a great blank. I can tell you one thing, though.

What's that?

The level of abuse at home went way down after that. Way, way down.

XII

I was three cups of coffee into my morning before Jack arrived. Was he the father? Jack hadn't said squat about a pregnancy when we met in his study. Nor did he share with me that tidbit about talking to the cops.

I'd asked Jack to meet me at my office. I was tired of playing patty-cake with the press occupying his neighborhood. Plus, a change of venue might convince the client that I was done being lied to.

Jack showed up about twenty minutes late, sashaying into reception, where he was quickly mobbed by a dozen of my associates and a couple of star-fucking L&H partners. When Alec came to tell me that Jack had arrived, the former president was twenty paragraphs deep into his set piece about winning Wisconsin in the first election. I asked Alec to fetch the client so we could get to work.

I dispensed with small talk. "I met with the government yesterday," I began.

Jack stiffened. "You don't look happy."

I described the physical evidence, more or less as Katherine had itemized it. Jack feigned disbelief as I ticked off each piece of proof, as if the prosecutors hadn't already given him the same speech. "But that's not really why I asked you to come in, Jack," I said. "I told you on day one that I needed the complete and unvarnished truth from you. No surprises. I thought I was pretty damn clear about that."

Jack acknowledged that I had indeed been pretty damn clear.

"So imagine my surprise, Jack, when the lead prosecutor told me that Amanda was pregnant at the time of her death."

Jack looked genuinely stunned. "Robbie, I swear to you, I had no idea. Pregnant? How far along?"

"Six weeks, the prosecutors said. You really didn't know?"

"Amanda never said a word about it to me. Even our last time . . . in January. When we . . . Do they know if I'm the father?"

I glared at the client. "Not yet. But who else's do you suppose it is, Jack? We obviously need to prepare for the likelihood that the baby was yours. Which brings me to the next item, Mr. President: You sat for a *fucking interview* with the cops. When were you planning to mention that to me?"

Jack took a first pass at an excuse. "I had nothing to hide, so why not answer their questions? Asking for a lawyer would only have added to their suspicions, right?"

"Wrong. Wrong. Totally, mind-numbingly wrong. There is almost *never* an upside to meeting with cops. And if you're planning to do something as boneheaded as that, for Christ's sake, *tell your friggin' lawyer.* How else am I supposed to do my job?"

Jack tried another tack. "Look, the interview went fine. The cops told me about the DNA and the fingerprints, but now you know what I know. No harm, no foul."

Now I was on my feet, trying to steady a mug of coffee as I paced. "Not telling me about the interview is the least of your problems, Jack. You also lied your ass off to the cops. Like how Amanda was never in the Oval Office. Like how you'd barely ever spoken to her. For god's sake, Jack, we both know that's bullshit, and what's worse, the government knows it, too. They will toast you with those lies at trial. I can't protect you if you won't tell me the full truth."

Jack seemed to waver. "How can the cops possibly know whether Amanda was ever in the Oval?"

I tried hard to mask my rage—Jack was trying to play me like some precinct captain at an Iowa steak fry. "They know Amanda was in the Oval because the locator function on her phone says so. And you and I both know that you've talked to her plenty of times. So stop telling me otherwise, or you can expect to spend the rest of your life telling electoral college stories to the former voters in Allenwood."

"All right," Jack said after a pause. "But I'm innocent, and I need you to believe me."

Time to push the client harder. "How many affairs have you had during your White House years?"

"Amanda. Just Amanda."

"The prosecutors believe otherwise. They talked about a 'hit parade,' Jack. They may even try to call a few of your honeys to the witness stand. Let's face it, Mr. President, your reputation precedes you."

"It's all just talk. I'm a big fat target. Always have been."

"Jack, it's me you're talking to. I *know* you."

"Just plain crap, Robbie. Right out of the New Nationalist playbook."

Oh, for chrissake.

"Jack, the White Suit interview? The pied-à-terre in New York? Do you think I've forgotten? Do you think I wasn't watching *60 Minutes* that night?"

"All horseshit, Robbie. Just a bunch of fake news." Jack's face was bright scarlet by now.

I took a long cleansing breath, then walked over to the sofa and stopped three inches or so from my client. I grabbed the lapels of his blazer and forced Jack's face up to mine. "Do. Not. Treat. Me. Like. A. Goddamn. Stooge. What else do I need to know?"

Jack looked up at me with something approximating fear. "Jesus, Robbie, what's gotten into you? Where's my old friend?"

"I'm right here, Jack," I said more gently. "Same guy who stood up to your old man at dinner once upon a time."

Jack looked at me quizzically, as if he'd forgotten that evening. Then he said with conviction, "Well, there's nothing more to tell. No more affairs and that's the truth."

About a week later, after hours, the actual truth came waltzing into my office.

XIII

It was a few minutes after nine p.m. when the buzzer rang and a statuesque blonde in her late thirties stepped into reception. Caroline Morgan, she called herself. To this day, I can't tell you if that was her real name. We walked back to my office, where I had some coffee brewing.

Ms. Morgan had called a few days earlier and insisted on seeing me alone. That's almost always a bad idea for a defense lawyer. Without an extra witness in the room, an informant can later make all kinds of accusations, and it'll just be your word against hers. Still, my assistant had sworn that Ms. Morgan sounded on the level.

Now, sitting on my office sofa, she came right to the point.

"Mr. Jacobson, I'm sorry for all the cloak-and-dagger, but I have no interest in getting drawn into this shit show. I got some info, which you can take for whatever it's worth."

I told Morgan that I would try to keep her visit confidential, but that I might need to disclose what she told me to my client.

"That's fine," she said. "Your client already knows what I have to say."

I guess I knew what we were about to discuss.

"I read in the *Washington Examiner* that Jack—President Cutler—claims to be a happily married man who would never have fucked around with the victim. Well, I can't tell you whether he ever poked Ms. Harper, but let me tell you—he's not a happily married man."

More or less what I'd guessed. But I needed the corroborating details. "How do you know that?"

"How do you think? I'm a registered lobbyist for the Distilled Spirits Council. I'm up on the Hill all the time and used to have drinks with Jack when he was the junior senator from New York. When he moved down the street to the White House, we had more than drinks together. Your client is no angel, and the first lady knows that."

"How so?"

"Because the last time Jack and I were in the Oval, your client called his wife while I was, let's just say, otherwise occupied. The phone was on speaker, and I have no doubt she could hear me at work. Just ask her."

Jesus. I tried to imagine Jess's reactions as she listened in. It was too atrocious to conceive. Must have been Ms. Morgan's idea, I suggested. But no, said the witness, it was all Jack's doing. He was apparently checking in on the kids while getting serviced. Good god.

"Did Mrs. Cutler say anything during this . . . escapade?"

My informant thought for a moment. "I could only make out a few words," she said finally. "A phrase that sounded like 'your legal eagle.' It was pretty faint, I can't be sure."

Did Jess suspect an affair with Amanda? Some other lawyer?

"Is there anything more you can tell me about your time with the president?" I asked.

"Only that Jack was into some rough stuff, not just with me but with lots of other women in town. Check around."

"Rough stuff?"

"Put it this way: your client likes to dominate—loves it, really. I'm guessing most presidents do, but Jack is off the scale. And that's where I draw the line. One night, out of the blue, Jack gives my neck a little squeeze. Then he slaps my face hard, with the back of his hand. I had markings from his wedding ring for days. I'm no prude, Mr. Jacobson, but I'm not into that shit, and I let your client know that in a way his nutsack will remember."

"You're talking about choking and hitting during sex?"

"Fucking right. Your boy just grabbed my neck and pressed up. I had to land a sharp knee to Little Jack to end it. Then I got smacked around for my trouble."

"You say there are other women in town with similar stories. How do you know that?"

"Word gets around, Counselor. We actually have an informal alumni association called the Rope Line. Wanna guess why?"

I could imagine, I told her.

My informant assured me, one last time, that she had no intention of telling her story publicly. A lucky break for us, as there were tabloids run by Jack's political enemies that would pay dearly for Ms. Morgan's story, even without corroboration. I thanked her for coming in.

After the witness left, I called Jess's cell, which went straight to voice mail. I left a message asking her to stop by my office in the morning.

XIV

Jess stopped in after dropping the kids at school. She wore a brown bomber jacket over sweat gear, and large dark sunglasses against a bright August sun.

We met again in the conference room, although this time I'd taken some technological precautions.

Jess and the kids had moved out of the Georgetown house and decamped to a small rental in Bethesda. "I'm still digging out of boxes and figuring out the new neighborhood," Jess said. "It's been a tough slog. The kids are struggling."

I offered my condolences. "If it's any consolation, Jack's having a pretty rough time, too. I don't think he's sleeping much. At some of our meetings at the house, he's still in boxers and stubble."

"It's not any consolation at all, Robbie. I'm pissed as hell, sure, but he's still my husband, at least for now, and I'm rooting for him. You know that, right?" Jess searched my eyes for reassurance, which I gave her. I then turned to the reason for the meeting.

"Jess, I received some information last night that makes me wonder about our last conversation. I don't want to say more until I've had a chance to talk to Jack, but I need to ask—are you really sure he hasn't been involved with other women?"

Jess paused two beats before speaking. "I'm not like Jack, you know," she said finally. "I put up with the media blood sport when Jack was president. Had no choice, really. But I hated it then, and I hate it more now. I try to keep my pains and pleasures to myself. But the rumors were always true. Jack found other women most of our married life. I've stopped counting, Robbie. You know your friend—he has his appetites, and he will be served. It used to be painful. Now it's just another day."

"Jess, I'm sorry. I wish I could say I'm shocked to hear it."

"And I wish never to have to discuss this again, Robbie. The public humiliation would be worse than the betrayals themselves."

"I understand this is unpleasant, Jess, but I have to press. You say Amanda was not among his companions. How can you be sure?"

Jess paused again. "Well, I suppose I'm not sure. It depends on, well, what she's into. Jack likes to be commander in chief wherever he is. He goes for willowy types who cater to him. Even politics rarely separates him from his conquests. Remember that blond fräulein who did commentary on OAN? The one who convinced Smith to dis NATO?"

"Who could forget her?" I responded.

"She and Jack had a few trysts while we were still in the White House. I heard from a staffer that the Secret Service used to smuggle her into the Oval. The bitch actually called Jack on his personal cell at two a.m. and threatened to go public unless he left me. I was right there when she called. She shouted something about 'handcuff sessions.'"

I took a breath, then let it out slowly. "Did you ever walk in on Jack in the act or somehow get a firsthand look at his screwing around?"

Jess looked pained, then appalled. "There was this one time. In the White House. I was actually upstairs in our bedroom, while Jack was with one of his . . . his *women*, in the West Wing somewhere. The bastard actually called me, and I could hear . . . a slurping noise . . . in the background." Jess's voice cracked.

"Jesus, I'm so sorry." Story confirmed.

She continued. "This is also why I cannot help you with an alibi. Jack and I have led pretty separate lives since we left the White House. I cannot tell you where he is or where he goes from one day to the next. I've considered divorce, and sometimes still do. But lately . . ." She trailed off. "I've spent some quality time in therapy. And I've found some companionship of my own."

"I'm relieved to hear that, Jess." And I was, I suppose, although I also had the usual jealous twinge. "You understand that I may need to discuss this with Jack."

Jess said that she understood and gathered her gym bag. But as she got up to leave, Jess dislodged the glasses she'd been wearing. There was purple bruising around her right eye that her makeup could not conceal. I froze.

"It's not as bad as you think, Robbie. You should see the other guy."

"God, Jessie, what happened?"

Jess came back to the conference table. "When I told Jack that the kids and I were leaving, he exploded. I've never seen him like that. It's the pressure, of course, worse than anything during his presidency. He's just so scared. I went to calm him, just to hold him for a moment, and . . . it just happened."

I let this settle for a moment. "Has he hit you before, Jessie?"

"Never. Well, not since Bishop's Gate. You remember," Jess said with a blush.

I did remember.

During Jack's second year in the New York state assembly, he and Jess lived in a small one-bedroom apartment in the Bishop's Gate neighborhood in Albany. Just before New Year's, I took the train up from the city, planning to crash for the long weekend on their living room pullout. It was cold in upstate New York that night, maybe 15 degrees, with winds that got your attention. I arrived at the Cutlers' building around seven p.m., only to receive a text from Jack that said something like "Hey, Rob, Jess and I ran out to pick up some beers, see you in a minute."

That minute became an hour, then three hours, as I sat on the third-floor landing, growing colder and angrier. My long history with Jack came flooding into my mind, and all I could think of were times like this. The sly put-downs. The high school pranks at my expense that Jack found hilarious. Like the time he announced my untimely death to the whole school over the morning intercom, sending Jess into shock until she could find me in the hallway. Or the time he replaced my bow rosin with a mild caustic that temporarily numbed my fingers when I played my bass violin at rehearsal. Or the graduation-day prank when he and some confederates filled the faculty parking lot with chairs at eight a.m., scattered to the four winds by eight-thirty a.m., but told me to arrive at the lot at nine, so that I alone got blamed for blocking all the room for teachers' cars.

Four long hours had passed before Jack and Jess returned to the apartment. Turns out Jack had run into some of his assembly buddies and decided to have a drink or three with them before heading back home.

I was livid. I grabbed my backpack and announced that I'd be staying at the Westin around the corner. I glanced at Jess on the way out. She looked stricken but did not meet my gaze.

A little after midnight, there was a knock at my hotel door. It was Jess. She was shivering, dressed only in a thin sweater and leggings and carrying an overnight bag. There was some redness newly splayed across her left cheek.

Jess never said a word, but I knew what must have happened—we read each other so well. I draped my winter coat over Jess's body, tucked her into the right side of the queen-size bed, and slipped back into the other half of the bed. After a few tense minutes, I reached over to hold her, but Jess didn't reciprocate. We slept together chastely until early morning. Jess was gone when I awoke.

———

"Jess, I hope you're getting the help you need. Jack should do the same. I'm going to insist that he see a therapist friend of mine. He clearly needs to talk to a professional." And if nothing else, I said to myself, maybe it will give us a mental health line of defense at trial.

"Good luck getting Jack to agree to therapy, Robbie. If he's barely getting through the day as it is, I don't see him adding an hour of shrink time to his docket."

"I have to give it a try, Jess. In the meantime, you did the right thing getting out of the house. I'm Jack's attorney, but I'm here for all of you if you need anything. Anything at all."

XV

In late August, I received the list of potential jurors, along with their ages, addresses, marital statuses, and occupations. In Perry Mason's day, that's about all you learned about the jury pool—until trial, when you got to ask them a few questions.

But progress, such as it is, advances in only one direction. Over the past year, the Department of Justice had launched a pilot program called the Government Data Mining Network, or G-DaMN for short. G-DaMN, now available for free to prosecutors and to defense lawyers for a subscription fee, gives you access to the purchasing history of all Americans, including potential jurors. Appalling? Maybe. But what defense lawyer can go without it, knowing that the prosecutors will certainly be using the service? Plus, how could I properly defend a former Democratic president without some sense of the political persuasion of the twelve men and women who'd be judging him?

G-DaMN made available vast swaths of data. What TV shows and movies did the potential jurors watch? Did they order *The Simpsons,*

Modern Family, and *The Office*? Did they download *Brokeback Mountain* and *Newsworthy*? If so, they were probably Dems, and we wanted them on the jury. Did they watch *Duck Dynasty* reruns or Mel Gibson crucifixion movies? If so, they likely leaned right, and Jack was better off without them. Did they shop at Whole Foods, where 1 percent of every purchase these days was donated to rainforest protection? If so, they were probably libs. Did they buy power tools at Mirage Garage, which had gone to the Supreme Court to defend its right to fire atheists? If so, they were probably wingers.

When I wasn't studying potential jurors, I was examining evidence. The government had turned over, among other things, copies of the materials recovered from Amanda's briefcase. Some of it was innocuous—two legal pads with doodling on a few pages, some ballpoint pens, a couple of chargers for a laptop or an iPhone. But within a separately sealed compartment, arranged in chronological order, were copies of the memoranda Amanda had written during her time as assistant White House counsel. She must have printed them out before leaving office.

They were apparently still with her at the time of her death.

As if prepping for a president's trial weren't demanding enough, I was fielding a relentless barrage of press inquiries. Jack's case was media catnip—only one former president had ever stood trial for *anything,* and it wasn't for murder. I would have loved to share the press burdens with Jane, but as of late August she had not yet agreed to take the case. And I was never much for media chitchat. I couldn't bear the thought of being one of those cable TV lawyers, none of whom has an actual law practice to go home to.

By Labor Day, however, Jack's PR folks had begun to fret that we were "losing control of the narrative." After resisting for as long as I thought prudent, I agreed to do an interview about the case. And not just any interview—the belly of the beast: a one-hour sit-down with Ryan MacGregor on Smith Universal.

MacGregor hosted the ten p.m. slot on weekdays, reaching nearly five million viewers each night. Needless to say, I'd never appeared on his show. But I'd seen *The MacGregor Solution* while channel surfing. MacGregor made no pretense of objectivity. He was a flamethrower and a far-right activist. He regularly appeared at Republican campaign rallies, sometimes as the MC firing up the crowd. He'd written a bestseller proclaiming that President Smith was anointed by God. And he was no friend of Jack's.

In the run-up to the interview, I spent a couple of hours watching clips of MacGregor's show. The prep time was painful but worth it. MacGregor usually booked fellow travelers who would say exactly what he wanted. On those rare occasions when he invited a political opponent, he bullied them with interruptions, filibustered their allotted time, and if all else failed, disconnected their mics. His interview style reminded me of a certain Yankees pitcher I'd seen in his declining years. He threw every pitch at your head, but at least you knew which pitch was coming.

MacGregor was no genius, that much was obvious. But his everyman style was key to his appeal. He spoke in simple sentences packed with emotion. He reduced complex issues to seductive talking points. He deployed lots of red, white, and blue graphics. And it would be a mistake to underestimate his charm. He had an engaging manner, an easy smile, and of course an adoring, nearly cultlike fan base with the attention span of a fruit fly. To make matters worse (for me, anyway), MacGregor also sported a full head of salt-and-pepper hair.

We offered the network a set of take-it-or-leave-it terms. First, the interview had to be in person. I didn't want to be some disembodied figure on a screen somewhere, or worse yet, just a voice on the phone. Next, there could be no edits to the tape—MacGregor's network had to broadcast every word of the interview, just as it had been conducted, no matter how long it ran. Finally, I insisted on no interruptions—no commercials, no commentary spliced in between the Q&A, no voice-over, nothing. Just Ryan and me, chatting it up, for as long as it lasted.

To my surprise, SMUT took the deal, and the interview was scheduled for the following Thursday night. In the meantime, the network promoted the show around the clock. Chyrons advertising the interview ran continuously during prime-time telecasts. I even spotted a few D.C. cabs with top ads hyping what promised to be a slugfest between MacGregor and Jack Cutler's lawyer.

When I got to the studio on Thursday, MacGregor met me in reception and pretended to ask after Jack's well-being. Surrounding us were floor-to-ceiling photos of the entire prime-time lineup. The smarmy prepster who fancied himself an intellectual but was little more than a Klansman without the charm. The willowy brunette who'd remade herself as a Smith fangirl when she wasn't working her way through married men. And my host, Ryan MacGregor, all hat and no cattle.

After a dab of makeup, we took our seats, MacGregor ensconced at his familiar glass table, me to his right in an ergonomic desk chair.

MacGregor opened the interview with his usual haymaker.

"This is the first press interview you've done, Mr. Jacobson. Is that perhaps because the evidence against President Cutler is so overwhelming?"

"First of all, Ryan, let me thank you for hearing me out. I realize that giving me a fair opportunity to speak to your audience is not your forte. As for President Cutler, it's my honor to represent him, and I fully expect him to be vindicated at trial."

"You can't really be that confident, can you, Counselor? From what I've heard, the physical evidence squarely places the president at the scene of the crime. Isn't that correct?"

"No, that's not correct. While I obviously cannot divulge our defense strategy, Ryan, you can rest assured that we will easily be able to account for every shred of evidence in the case."

"Does that include the rope burns and the shackles we've all been reading about? I'm surprised the former president of the United States walks on the wild side. Plus, rumor has it that Ms. Harper was pregnant when she was murdered. Care to confirm any of this, Mr. Jacobson?"

"Ryan, I'm not going to dignify your speculation with an answer. But I'll be glad to tell your audience what they *should* be concerned about."

Ryan hesitated, then bit. "What's that, Counselor?"

"Your viewers should wonder about a justice system in which the police focus only on a single suspect. What if a member of your audience were on trial? What if he or she learned that the prosecutors had never looked at anyone else for this crime? Never asked themselves whether the victim's own past might help identify her real killer? I realize that most of your viewers aren't fans of President Cutler. But I bet they think the justice system ought to treat everyone fairly."

MacGregor's face darkened briefly. "That's a lovely speech, Mr. Jacobson," he said finally. "But from where I sit, there's so much evidence against your client that the cops would've wasted their time looking elsewhere."

"Have you seen any of that evidence yourself, Ryan?"

"No, of course not."

"Yet you are already convinced that the president is guilty as charged? Is that how you would expect an objective person to make up his mind? Convict first and examine the evidence second?"

"I don't claim to be objective, Counselor. This is a commentary show, not a news broadcast."

"I'm glad to hear you admit that, Ryan. I worry sometimes that your audience may mistake your opinions for the truth."

"My audience is fully able to make up its own mind, thank you. You know our network's motto: 'We conclude. You concur.'"

"Ryan, you're the guy who told viewers that Muslim Americans were celebrating the attack on the Twin Towers. You're the guy who said that the Russians never interfered in our presidential elections. You're the guy who said that the coronavirus was a scam invented by Democrats to tarnish your favorite former president. Do you intend to apologize to your audience for any of those whoppers, Ryan?"

"Right after Jack Cutler apologizes for pardoning illegals who go on to commit murder."

"C'mon, Ryan. Haven't you worn out those bromides?"

"Let's get back to your client," Ryan countered. "We did an instant poll of our viewers. Seventy-nine percent of them think Jack Cutler is guilty. Seventy-nine percent. That ought to worry you, Mr. Jacobson."

"Ryan, I've seen some polling, too—polling about your viewership. Eighty-five percent of them think that President Cutler stole his election four years ago; eighty-nine percent of them believe that evolution is a myth; and ninety-two percent of them are convinced that windmills cause cancer. Compared to those numbers, I'd say that Jack Cutler is doing pretty well."

It went on like that for a little over an hour. By the end, I thought MacGregor looked like Foreman in Zaire. And the network was true to its word—the entire interview ran, with no commercial interruptions, at the ten o'clock hour that night. Score one for the good guys.

Elsewhere in town, my son was paying the price for the hours I was spending on Jack's case.

XVI

After Nan and I split up, things got rough between Josh and me. Looking back, I can see that my affair with Amanda had only made matters worse.

One spring weekend, Josh and I made plans to ride the horse Jack stabled at Rock Creek. I figured that since I was no longer married to Nan, I'd invite Amanda to come along. A really dumb idea, I get that now. But I was caught up in a romance and wanted to share it with my son. The three of us headed out that Saturday morning for the Horse Center. I had high hopes for the outing.

But it did not go well. Josh, in the front seat next to me, was sullen for most of the drive out. Just before we reached the barn, Josh turned to Amanda.

"How old are you?" he asked.

"I'm thirty," Amanda answered.

Josh was silent for about a minute. "You're not much older than me. What are you doing with my dad?"

Amanda tried to laugh it off. "Oh, you know what they say, Josh. Age is just a state of mind."

"Who says that?" Josh asked.

"Well, I guess I say that, Josh. Your dad seems young to me."

"Well, he isn't," Josh replied, now in a higher register.

I smiled. "C'mon, Josh, I'm not that old. I can still ride a horse pretty well, right?"

Josh turned to Amanda again. "Do you know my mom?" he asked.

"I don't," said Amanda. "But I would love to meet her sometime."

That wasn't going to happen, of course. As far as I knew, Nan had never met Amanda, but she held Amanda responsible for our split-up. Which was horseshit, but there was no persuading Nan otherwise. And she'd evidently shared her judgment with Josh.

Ten more minutes passed in silence, and by now we were at the stables. Josh looked at Amanda for a few seconds and said, "No."

That was his last word to either of us that day. Believe me, I tried my best to draw Josh out. He and I walked, without Amanda, to the stall that housed Jack's horse. Nothing but crickets.

It would be weeks before he spoke to me again.

Nan, by contrast, has always been able to connect with Josh. My ex has this soft voice that puts Josh at ease, even when he's at his worst. I used to watch Nan when the three of us were together. She embraced Josh on his own terms—never a hint of judgment or disappointment in her face or voice. Josh knew that he was in a safe place.

I lack Nan's skills. I've tried, don't get me wrong. On the rare occasions I saw Josh, I'd ask him about his day, his friends, girls, anything he was willing to share. Sometimes, maybe when his meds were more effective, I could break through. But without warning, Josh could vanish to some other mental place, you never knew when or why. Or where. And I couldn't shake the feeling that Josh's illness was my fault.

It wasn't just the guilt talking. Josh's doctors explained that my mother's mental illness almost surely had a genetic component. The professional literature confirmed that psychiatric disabilities may lie dormant for a generation or more, only to resurface suddenly. And it hardly took the *DSM-5* to persuade me that Evie and Nathan were a gift that kept on giving, even many years after their deaths.

As Jack's case demanded more and more of my time, I scarcely saw Josh at all. I told myself, and I suppose it was technically true, that even my full attention would not cure my son. His disability was about chemicals and genetics, two things not even the best parent (or lawyer) can control.

But it was a bullshit excuse, and I knew it. Here's the nasty little truth: I wanted the case more than I wanted time with my son. I craved Jack's neediness. I craved the limelight. I loved keeping score. Josh couldn't give me any of that.

A few weeks before trial, Josh and I did manage one lunch together, at a diner near Chevy Chase Circle. Josh ordered his usual—a tuna melt with Swiss cheese, not American—too orange—and an extra-large helping of fries. I always try to avoid shoptalk when I'm with my son, especially if it's just the two of us. So I was surprised when Josh asked about Jack's case.

"Is it hard to be working for him, Dad?"

"In some ways, yes," I said. "It's not an easy case. But what makes you ask, Josh?"

"Well, the TV reports say that Jack may have killed your friend Amanda. I remember when the three of us went to the stables. I thought you might be sad helping someone who may have hurt her."

"It is hard, you're right. I miss Amanda. But Jack is also my friend, right? And he's your friend, too. Remember all the times we've spent together, you, me, and Mom, and the Cutlers and their two kids? The times Jack showed you around the Horse Center? That speckled pony he picked out for you? The two of you always had fun together."

Josh looked off somewhere and smiled, twirling one of his fries.

Just like that, I lost him for the next few minutes. Finally Josh gave me the most curious look, then said, "You don't need him. You have other friends."

"I do have other friends, Josh, but Jack is one of my oldest."

Josh smiled. "Sure, but he's not really your *friend* friend, is he, Dad? Someone who knows you inside and out. Someone who's always there for you. Who never leaves."

"Do you have a friend who never leaves?" I asked.

"Of course. Don't you? I talk to my friend all the time. Except when he gets angry. Then I need to stay out of his way."

Josh's doctors had warned us about this. Evidently, it's common among schizophrenics to have imaginary friends who seem entirely real to the patient. It's their own form of *choshek,* the kind of darkness the rest of us cannot truly fathom. The best we could do, or so the doctors advised Nan and me, was to accept Josh's friends as real, at least to him.

"What kinds of things make your friend angry?" I asked him.

"When people get mad at me. Or I get scared. Then my friend stands up for me. Doesn't yours?"

Play along, I told myself. "I guess that sounds like a good kind of friend to have, Josh. I think you're lucky."

Josh sat silently for a few moments, smiled at some unknowable thought, then emerged from the darkness.

"I think you'll win the case," Josh announced finally.

"Why's that, Josh?"

"I just think Mr. Cutler didn't do this. He didn't kill Amanda."

XVII

We were talking about your anger at Amanda. What can you recall about that?

Last year of the administration, Christmastime. I remember because folks in the office were dressed up for the White House holiday party.

And you saw Amanda that day?

Yes, that was the day she told me she was pregnant.

Can you say any more about that meeting?

She just blurted it out. I'd stopped in after lunch. Why the hell did Amanda seem so excited? I wondered. We'd just lost the campaign—what was there to be happy about?

How did you feel about Amanda's news?

I was floored. And betrayed. "Didn't you take precautions?" I remember asking. "Yeah," she assured me, "but nothing's perfect. And maybe this is for the best."

"How could this be for the best?" I asked her. "How the hell could this possibly be for the best?"

How did Amanda respond?

She said she looked forward to being a mom.

Do you recall your reaction?

I could feel my heart race. The room grew silent; then my ears filled up, quickening blood, I guess.

I told her: "You are fucking kidding me. You cannot be serious." Jesus, how pathetic I sounded. How angry.

Did Amanda answer?

Yeah. She said, "This is none of your business. I'm the one having this baby, not you. And I'm doing this alone. I don't need help, yours or anyone else's." I was stunned and furious.

What happened next?

I must have said something else in anger, I'm not sure. Amanda looked shocked. "What is wrong with you? It's like I don't even know you." Those were Amanda's exact words. She was frightened, of me, I guess. "You need to leave now," Amanda said.

So I did. I paced back to my office and replayed the scene in my head. I had a lot to figure out.

XVIII

Judge Edgerton had set aside a half hour of courtroom time, two months before trial, to hear argument on the parties' legal motions. I hadn't filed any. I always prefer to keep my powder dry and then ambush the opposition at trial.

Jack's prosecutors evidently felt differently. They flooded our in-boxes with all kinds of legal motions, but only one actually worried me. The prosecutors wanted the Court to permit them to put in evidence of Jack's extramarital affairs while he was president. Their theory was simple, if audacious: if Jack was willing to cheat on his wife—many times—then he was also capable of sleeping with Amanda, and later killing her for reasons the prosecutors had yet to articulate.

I doubted that Judge Edgerton would go for this. But the government was swinging for the fences. If they could get this incendiary garbage into evidence, particularly in front of the churchgoing folks likely to be on the jury, the prosecutors might convict Jack just for being a letch, not for being a *murdering* letch. This was a motion we couldn't afford to lose.

So I called Jane again and asked if she was ready to join the team. When losing is not an option, you call Jane Cashman. I explained what the government was trying to do, trying to appeal to her sense of due process.

It worked. Jane was as appalled as I was by the government's over-reach. Despite her low opinion of our client, Jane fundamentally believed in the system. Even a first-year prosecutor would know not to offer this kind of peripheral yet incendiary testimony.

Before the hearing, Jane and I asked Judge Edgerton to close the courtroom to the press and to seal the motion papers. If the allegations about Jack's affairs got out, they might taint the potential jury pool. The judge agreed. It would be just the lawyers and the judge in court that day.

A minute or two after ten, Judge Edgerton called the case. "We're here on the government's motion to permit proof of prior acts of infidelity by the defendant. Mr. Shapiro, I understand that you will be arguing for the government. Each side will have fifteen minutes."

Gary Shapiro approached the podium. He had not gotten far beyond "May it please the Court," when the Court, not much pleased, began its onslaught.

"Explain to me, Mr. Shapiro," Judge Edgerton growled, "how a bunch of extramarital screwing around tends to prove that the defendant had an affair with *Ms. Harper*, in particular?"

Shapiro was ready for that one. "It's the defendant's modus operandi, Your Honor. It's the way he does business—he seduces women. He isn't constrained by his marital vows. Because he does not think that conventional morality applies to him, he is more likely to have had an affair with Amanda Harper. We think that is enough to make the evidence relevant."

The judge pressed. "Isn't it the most basic principle of evidence, especially in criminal cases, that a defendant's prior bad acts don't get admitted? Why shouldn't I be concerned that this kind of prurient stuff will distract the jury from its real task? Isn't there a high risk that the jury will convict Mr. Cutler simply because they find his personal life distasteful?"

Again, Shapiro had an answer. "You can instruct the jury that the proof of extramarital affairs is being offered only to show that the defendant is more likely to have had an affair with the decedent. You can tell them not to use it for any other purpose. We'll be happy to submit a proposed instruction for the Court to consider."

Judge Edgerton was just getting started. "Well, tell me this, Mr. Shapiro. Are we really going to have a parade of women testifying about their affairs with the president? If what you're telling me is true, we may have days, if not weeks, of kiss-and-tell stories. Then, each time, the defense will have to cross-examine the woman. How long do you want this trial to last? Until I'm dancing at my great-grandson's wedding?"

The judge shot Shapiro the Full Eyebrow, but Gary must have missed the signal. "Your Honor, the prosecution shares the Court's concern about creating a sideshow here. We're prepared to limit the number of such witnesses to fewer than a half dozen."

That's when the dam broke. "Mr. Shapiro," Judge Edgerton began, "I'd like to believe that the government will keep this proof to a minimum. But I still see two big problems.

"First, the *fewer* women you call, the *less* probative this line of evidence is. Do you see that? If you cut down the number of women to three or four, instead of twenty or fifty, it starts looking less like a pattern and more like behavior engaged in by countless married men and women the world over. By cutting down the number of witnesses in order to avoid a sideshow, you'd also be undercutting the rationale for admitting that evidence in the first place.

"But I've got an even bigger problem. No matter how few women you haul into my courtroom, this kind of proof will inevitably create a spectacle. You and I both know that such salacious evidence, assuming it's evidence at all, will overwhelm the jury. Every reporter will pick it up. The cable networks will run, rerun, and then re-rerun every last detail. Some of these women may start appearing on late-night TV, which none of us can prevent. Then I'll have to poll the jurors each morning to make sure they haven't violated their oaths by tuning in.

"I won't let my courtroom devolve into a soap opera. And frankly, I don't see how I can avoid that if I let you start down this road. But I'll reserve my ruling until the defense has had a chance to speak. Ms. Cashman, I understand that you are arguing for the defense."

"That's correct, Your Honor," Jane said as she approached the lectern. "May it please the Court. Jane Cashman, Lockyear & Harbison, for defendant John Sherman Cutler.

"Your Honor, there is a typographical error on page 13 of our brief. The fifth word on the last line of the page should be *poison,* with one *s,* not *poisson,* the French word for fish. Otherwise, unless the Court has questions for me, I propose to sit down." That was it, Jane's entire argument.

Judge Edgerton suppressed a smile. "As Justice Felix Frankfurter is reputed to have said about a similar argument in the Supreme Court, 'I've heard learned arguments, I've heard powerful arguments, I've heard eloquent arguments. But I've heard only one *perfect* argument.'

"The government's motion to admit instances of marital infidelity is denied.

"See you all for trial in sixty days."

———

I now had my longtime law partner at my side. Time to start uncovering some evidence of our own.

Time to go on offense.

XIX

A good defense lawyer can't simply rely on the evidence the government turns over. That's where trial subpoenas come in. Defense counsel, just like the government, may subpoena individuals or businesses and require them to produce evidence the defense needs for trial. Jane and I issued a batch of subpoenas, then waited for the materials to trickle in.

Among the documents we subpoenaed were Amanda's financial records. Jane was poring over the bank statements one afternoon when I stopped by her old office, which Jane had reoccupied until the trial concluded.

She looked up from the stacks of paper.

"How well did you know Amanda's habits?" she asked.

"A little," I admitted, "although I saw her only a couple of times toward the end. Have you found something in the records?"

Jane frowned. "Well, it may not amount to much, but I notice that one Saturday every month, Amanda went to an ATM and withdrew a thousand dollars in cash. Always a thousand, not a penny more or less."

"That could be anything," I said. "What's the big deal?"

"Just getting to it," said Jane. "If you look closely at the records, you'll see that every time Amanda withdrew the thousand, the very next day she made a series of purchases at a particular pharmacy. A place called Overdon, in Southeast. Nowhere near her apartment. And she always used her credit card at the pharmacy, even though she'd just gotten a grand in cash the day before. Doesn't that seem peculiar to you?"

Maybe. It had occurred to me that Amanda bought her Ecstasy *somewhere*, and maybe other drugs, too. But I kept that to myself. Bad lawyering, I know, but the notion of blaming the victim, especially *this* victim, made me want to puke.

Still, we had to look into this pharmacy business. And I knew just the guy for the job—Hummer.

Humberto Mercado—Bert to his friends, and Hummer to anyone willing to use that nickname to his face—was my private investigator. I met him twenty-plus years ago when I was still a young prosecutor and Hummer was an ATF agent with a bad temper. If you needed someone to execute a warrant in a gnarly neighborhood or to flatten a door that could have an armed perp behind it, Hummer was your man. He was fearless. I remember how it felt to be around him in those days. It gave us dweebs with a JD the vicarious sense that we, too, were tough law enforcement officers. Instead of the pantywaists we actually were.

When I left the government for the defense side, Hummer was getting close to retirement and was looking for a soft landing. He got in touch, and his timing was perfect. He's been my main PI ever since. While Jane and I were still in her office going over the bank records, I called Hummer and asked him to stop by.

———

Not five minutes later, Katherine Hannigan called. "Rob," she said with a note of triumph in her voice, "the paternity results finally came in this morning. Your client was the father of Amanda's baby."

XX

I wasn't totally shocked by the news. Indeed, some part of me had always known. At trial, we would now have to concede that Jack and Amanda had an affair—the pregnancy left us no choice. The pregnancy also raised the stakes. Whoever killed Amanda had also killed her unborn child. The jury would be unforgiving.

Jane and I needed to regroup. I stopped by her office to share the government's latest revelation. "It's 5 O'Clock Somewhere" was playing on the Sonos, while Jane mimed a country dance of some kind.

"Just a Texas two-step, Rob. Come on in, I'll teach you the basics."

"Maybe some other time, Jane," I said, and told her the news.

Jane turned off the music. "Just as we suspected."

"But look," I said, "maybe we can make a virtue of necessity. There's no denying that Jack and Amanda were . . . involved. But that gives us an opening, Jane. We can use their affair to explain the worst evidence in the case—Jack's DNA and prints on Amanda's neck and clothing. It was there because of sex, not murder."

Jane was skeptical. "Jack will still need to take the stand to put in that defense. And you say he's still reluctant to let it all hang out."

"He'll come around, I'm sure. But even if he doesn't, the government's pathologist is bound to put the paternity into evidence during the prosecution's case in chief. We can then just argue to the jury that the affair explains the prints and the DNA. We'd still have the option not to call Jack in the unlikely event that he's still putting up a fight."

"I don't agree, Rob. The pregnancy proves only that Jack and Amanda were intimate about six weeks before she was killed. Why would the client's prints and DNA still be on her body six weeks later when she was killed? The jury won't buy the affair defense unless we establish that the two of them had sex within hours of her death. And to prove that . . ."

"Jack would have to testify to every last detail," I finished the thought. "You're right. But I'm convinced we'll get Jack there."

Jane's eyes narrowed. "Remember, Rob. The client denied the affair outright to the police when he was interviewed."

"We can get past that," I offered, perhaps too optimistically. "It's in his best interest. You'd think he would see that. It's obviously the rope burns. The kink. Now an out-of-wedlock pregnancy. Jack's thinking about the history books and not a jail cell."

"I'm sure you're right," Jane answered. "But even if we can sell our scoundrel of a client on telling the unvarnished truth, that still leaves the knife without an explanation, right? Even if Mr. Cutler had some unconventional sex with Amanda right before she was killed, that explains only the pregnancy and the DNA and fingerprints on her clothes and body. How do we account for the knife? And why was the knife wedged into the lining of the briefcase?"

"Maybe Jack gave the knife to Amanda as a gift," I suggested. "And maybe Amanda herself used it before she was killed. Who knows—

maybe the briefcase was jammed in some way, and Amanda used the knife to pry it open. Or maybe she used it to fend off her attacker."

Jane was not impressed. "If Amanda used the knife to jimmy her own briefcase or defend herself, why didn't her prints show up on it?"

I'd read up on this issue. "We can cover that problem with an expert, Jane. People don't always leave fingerprints on the objects they touch, even when they're not wearing gloves. If we call an expert to make that point, we can defuse the issue, I think. There's lots of literature on this. On DNA, too. I'm sure we can get some PhD to address all of that."

Jane looked doubtful. "Experts are not really in vogue these days, Rob."

Jane was right, unfortunately. In the last year or so, some judges had been marginalizing the role of trial experts. Actual expertise offended the New Nationalist credo that your average juror is just as smart as someone with scientific training. But I doubted Judge Edgerton would buy that nonsense.

I told Jane that we could easily find a fingerprint expert good enough to raise a reasonable doubt.

"Maybe so, Rob. But I also think we need to give the jury another suspect to blame. Even if it's just a straw to grasp at, so they don't grasp at Jack. Any thoughts on who else might have killed Amanda?"

"Well, the cops found her body in a pretty public place. In theory, any-one in the park could be the killer. We could acknowledge that Jack had an affair with Amanda—hence the pregnancy, DNA, and fingerprints— but then blame someone else, maybe some random drug dealer, for the actual crime."

Jane hesitated, then said, "Rob, we aren't talking about the proverbial elephant in the room."

I knew where she was going.

Jane lowered her voice and continued. "I know that Jess Cutler is also an old friend of yours. I know that you're fond of her. But we have to at least consider the possibility that she was the killer. The jealous wife—it's a classic."

Oh, Jesus. "Jane, there's just no way. There's just no way Jess could kill anyone. And then finger Jack for the crime? She told me she didn't know Amanda, and I believe her."

"Rob, you're not seeing this clearly. You have only your old friend's word for what she knew and what she did."

True enough. I thought back to the Caroline Morgan meeting at my office. What did Jess mean by the "legal eagle" comment the night Ms. Morgan was working on Jack?

Jane pressed the point. "Look, Mrs. Cutler might well have suspected that her husband was having an affair with Amanda. Maybe she even saw them in some compromising position together. We don't know. You've told me how angry Jess is these days. You've also told me how dependent she's been on Jack most of her adult life."

"I just don't see it, Jane."

"Rob, you don't *want* to see it. Neither of us knows the truth here, and we have to be willing to play any card in the deck."

Jane was right. It would be Jack's call in the end, and even at his most assholic, Jack was not likely to go for a "blame Jess" defense. But we couldn't rule out the option, not yet.

"Let's leave the question open," I said finally. "We owe Jack a visit. He needs to hear about the paternity results. And he finally needs to come clean."

XXI

E n route to Jack's place a week later, Jane and I decided that she'd be bad cop. I'd probably overstayed my welcome in that role. Jane, on the other hand—well, everyone listens to Jane. Plus, this would be her first meeting with the client. Jack might take the session more seriously.

We met Jack in his study. The client began, as he always did when a woman was in the room, by mounting a charm offensive. Jane was having none of it. She put on her glasses, perched them on the bridge of her nose, reviewed some notes on the legal pad sitting in her lap, and greeted Jack formally.

"Mr. President," she began, but Jack cut her off.

"You'll have to start calling me Jack. I can't have my lawyers going into battle with me if we're not all on a first-name basis."

"I'll do my best . . . Jack. First, the bad news." Jack leaned forward in the rocker. "The government has the results of the paternity test on Amanda's baby. You're the father."

"Oh, jeez," Jack mumbled. "They can tell that with a six-week-old fetus?"

"New technology," Jane explained. "It used to take longer to get something definitive. About eighteen months ago, perinatologists at Mass General made some breakthroughs. We can hire our own expert, but the government's paternity test looks pretty righteous."

Jack sat silently for a moment, then looked up at me. "Robbie, what does that mean for the trial?"

Jane answered—it was still time for the bad cop. "It means, Mr. President—Jack—that you've got to acknowledge the affair with Amanda. The sooner you make your peace with that, the easier it will be to prepare your defense."

Jack looked pained. "The ropes? The kink? In open court, with my family sitting there?"

Jane was equally firm. "As the saying goes, Jack, you need the serenity to accept the things you cannot change. Plus, there's a strategic upside to admitting the truth."

"Oh, really? What's that?" Jack asked.

Jane assumed her best professorial look.

"Sometimes the best defense is to admit as much of the government's case as possible, but then offer an innocent explanation for all the evidence. Take that little forgery case Rob tried in June before the same judge we've got here. The prosecutors had eyewitnesses who placed Mr. Karinsky near the mailbox from which the checks were stolen. Rob didn't try to dispute that. He just gave the jury an innocent explanation for the client's whereabouts in that part of town. The government called the pawnshop manager to make a photo identification. Again, Rob didn't try to shake the manager's ID. He just showed the jury that many thousands of other people go into the same shop every week, and that there were perfectly innocent reasons for the client's presence on the days the checks were cashed.

"That's an option we'd like you to consider here," Jane continued. "You really have no choice but to acknowledge the affair. But here's the good news, Jack: If you admit the affair, then we'll have an innocent explanation for most of the government's evidence. Why's your DNA on the victim? Why are your fingerprints on her clothing? Why were a few strands of your hair found on her clothing and on her body? The answer is that the two of you were intimate, up to a day or two before Ms. Harper was killed. Embarrassing? An awkward entry in Wikipedia? Maybe. But all totally legal, and that's what counts."

Jack sat silently for a moment. "Let's say I was willing to say all that. How does that help with the knife?" A fair question, but Jane was prepared.

"Look, Jack, I don't know the truth here. Only you and Amanda Harper do, and she won't be talking. So suppose—just suppose—that you gave Amanda the knife as a keepsake. Yeah, maybe you shouldn't have done so, maybe giving her a piece of White House silver violates federal law. But you'd get only a slap on the wrist for breaking those rules. Murder charges, I don't need to tell you, are for keeps."

Jack looked over at me. He knew I agreed with Jane.

"It's pretty simple, Jack," I said. "You and Amanda had an affair, period. You were still having one at the time of her death. Admit it. Just admit it. That will allow us to neutralize most of the government's evidence. And we have fingerprint and DNA experts already lined up to back up our defense at trial. I've read some of their academic papers—they'll do a great job for you."

Jack considered the option for a few more moments. "Look," he said finally, "I don't mind testifying. I'd be good at it. But the kinkiness. That's the part I find so hard to admit out loud. Any chance we can just leave all the rope shit out??"

"No, Jack, we can't," I said. "There's no such thing as testifying halfway. If you take the stand at trial, then as the oath famously declares, you have to tell the *whole* truth and nothing but the truth."

"It's so sordid."

I broke in again. "Jack, you've got to get over yourself here. There's nothing illegal about a little consensual sex play. Do you think you're the only guy who enjoys . . . dominating in bed? And it's not like you're running for anything. You got no more mountains to climb. Just admit what needs to be admitted, and let's go win this thing."

Jack wasn't ready to say uncle. "Is there any other option?"

"There is, but you won't like it any better." Jane proceeded to describe an alternative hypothesis—that Jess had killed Amanda and planted the evidence incriminating Jack.

Jack thought for what seemed like forever, then looked over at me. "Really, Robbie? You're really prepared to point the finger at Jess? You really have the stomach for that? I don't. Thirty years she and I have been married, and I just won't drag Jess into this. She's already suffered enough because of me."

I pushed back a little. "We don't have to come right out and accuse her of murder, Jack. We just have to show the jury that there are alternative ways Amanda *could* have been killed, and that the cops never considered any of them. And if you okay it, we could even alert Jess about this plan ahead of time so she can get comfortable with it."

"This is my *wife* we're talking about, Robert. The mother of my two children. *Your former girlfriend*, in case Jane was unaware. Yet here you are analyzing this option like it's some mixture problem in Mr. Nadler's freshman algebra class. What the hell's the matter with you?" Jack was boiling mad at this point.

"Jack," I said softly, "Jane and I are just trying to help you. We won't do anything you're unwilling to authorize. You're the client."

"I can't see it, Robbie. I'd still have to take the stand and admit that there was something going on between Amanda and me—that Jess had gotten wind of it, killed Amanda, and framed me for the murder. How does blaming Jess help me avoid talking about my sex life in front of the entire Western fucking world? The internet will feast on this shit forever. It'll be the opening paragraph of my fucking obituary. Even if I was *willing* to blame Jess—*which I'm not, Counselor*—your strategy wouldn't spare me the humiliation of getting on the stand and admitting all this . . . all this rope and choking stuff. The shit I'm into."

"Look, Jack," I answered, "if you can't or won't get on the stand and tell the whole truth, ropes and all, we might still be able to insinuate that Jess *thought* you were involved with Amanda and decided to get even with both of you."

Jack remained adamant. "No, this is a nonstarter for me. We're not making Jess the villain here. I'll plead the case out before I do that."

We sat in silence for a few moments. "You're not giving us much to work with, Jack," I said finally.

Jack was exhausted. "Let me think about all of this, and I'll let you know."

"Don't wait too long," Jane said forcefully. "We pick a jury in a little over a month."

———

When Jane and I got back to the office, Hummer greeted us with a shit-eating grin.

"Tell me you've got something," I said.

"Maybe more than you bargained for," said Hummer. The three of us headed back to Jane's office.

"So here's what I did," Hummer began. "A couple of the boys and I staked out the Overdon Pharmacy last week. The place is open Monday through Saturday, nine a.m. to seven p.m., closed on Sundays. During working hours, people go in and out of the pharmacy, nothing unusual. One of the guys went inside a few times just to look around. Didn't see anything suspicious.

"But here's the thing: Right at two p.m. on Sunday, when the place is supposedly closed, some old lady stops by and opens the padlock from the outside, then lifts the metal gating. She leaves the sign on the front door saying CLOSED, but goes inside the pharmacy and remains there for the next three hours.

"Between two p.m. and five p.m., a few customers walk in. No one slows down just because there's a CLOSED sign on the door, they just go right in. They're usually inside for twenty, thirty minutes. When these folks come out, they're always carrying a plastic bag, the same kind of bag that regular shoppers carry after picking up medications, buying toilet paper, whatever.

"This goes on for three hours. At exactly five p.m., the same woman comes back outside, replaces the gating, locks the shop, and leaves."

At this, Jane scooped up Amanda's banking records from her desk, re-checking them against the calendar on her iPhone. Sure enough, Amanda had made all her Overdon purchases on Sundays. Only on Sundays.

"Bingo," Hummer announced. "Your vic was part of the Overdon after-hours crowd. But just to make sure this wasn't just business as usual, one of the guys and I went inside the place this past Sunday afternoon. We browsed the shaving aisle, then made our way back to the pharmacy counter. We saw a line of a half-dozen or so customers waiting to go into a small room, back behind the counter. One by one they went into the back room, then came out with a small bag with the Overdon logo. Each of them then bought some extra shit—toothpaste, aspirin, whatever. Seemed like these folks were basically pulling shit off the shelf. Let me tell you: whatever these shoppers are doing at Overdon on Sundays, it's not because they've run out of dental floss."

Jane and I gave each other a look. Amanda was almost surely a drug abuser. If nothing else, we had a pretty decent red herring we could offer the jury. We could blame the victim.

Fuck.

XXII

The last time I visited the Cutler White House was just after New Year's, about a year before the trial began. To almost no one's surprise, Jack had lost his bid for reelection and was packing up to leave.

His defeat was mostly just the swing of the pendulum. Jack had beaten Smith four years earlier, but the New Nationalism came roaring back from hibernation, swamping Jack and dozens of down-ballot Democrats. Smith's former secretary of state, the loathsome Aaron Melvin, had promised what an electoral college majority evidently wanted—government subsidies for religious schools (despite their constitutional difficulties); stricter immigration quotas for third-world countries; and a novel wealth tax, indexed to average years of schooling, designed to shift money from blue states to red states.

There was also the fact that Jack got Willie Horton–ized. You may remember the 1988 presidential campaign. I know I do—it was the first election I got to vote in. In the run-up to that election, the Republicans attacked the Democratic candidate, Michael Dukakis, for supporting weekend prison furloughs for a convicted African American murderer named Willie Horton. On one such furlough, Horton had kidnapped and raped a woman, and the Republican ad machine went after Dukakis hammer and tongs.

Much the same thing had happened to Jack. During the Christmas season preceding his final year in office, Jack had pardoned a young man for a petty drug conviction. Two months later the man murdered his common-law wife and their two small children. That alone would have been devastating enough to Jack's political fortunes, but there was one additional detail: the killer was an undocumented alien. So the New Nationalists had a field day tying Jack's "open borders" policy (an utter canard, by the way) to this horrifying crime. By the time the Republicans unveiled their fifth or sixth attack ad, Jack's polls had plummeted by nearly twenty points. His eventual defeat surprised no one.

To lighten his mood after election day, I suppose, Jack started calling old friends for company. He invited me to dinner, just the two of us.

If you've never seen the first family's private quarters, they are something to behold. Some 30,000 square feet in all, they include some of the most iconic rooms in the world—the Lincoln Bedroom, the Lincoln Sitting Room, and the President's Dining Room, which is where Jack and I would be having dinner that evening. I passed Jess and the kids as I arrived, all of them looking glum, no doubt contemplating life after the White House. Jess seemed especially distant, offering just a brief hello as I went to join Jack.

I met my friend in the Cosmetology Room, where he was getting a trim from the White House barber while barking orders on his cell to some subordinate. Right next door, the dining room was already set for two. This small, surprisingly intimate chamber was once known as the Prince of Wales Room, in honor of one of its temporary occupants. Back when it was still a bedroom, it had seen its share of history. Willie Lincoln died in this room. His father was embalmed there. But in 1961, finding the formal dining room immediately downstairs too stuffy, Jacqueline Kennedy converted the room to more intimate dining quarters for her family.

I'd been here with Jack several times before, but the room still gave me a thrill. It's lit by a massive chandelier. The walls are covered in a soft yellow damask. Everything dazzles. Jack took special pride in the flatware. Pearl-handled and silver-gilt, the set had been purchased by President Monroe when he rebuilt the White House after the British burned it in 1814.

Jack was unusually agitated that evening. He spent much of our dinner grousing that he'd never gotten enough credit for his accomplishments. Jack complained—justifiably, I thought—that he'd tackled the most challenging environmental and healthcare issues of our times, and that he'd taken steps no other president had attempted. Even when the Cutler administration fell short, it had laid the groundwork for future presidents.

"No one has taken the fucking risks I've taken," Jack declaimed. "No one has ever been willing to piss off every K Street shitkicker from the petroleum lobby. No one has been willing to look the Chamber of fucking Commerce in the eye and tell them that they don't have a lien on the Oval Office."

It was all true, and I gave Jack some of the consolation he was seeking. But Jack wasn't finished.

"No other president has been willing to give up ten points in the Conway Poll, then fifteen, then twenty, just to do the right thing. Sure, presidents love, they *love*, to talk about all the hard fucking choices they've made. But there's always some pollster sitting in their jacket pocket holding up his finger to the wind."

I assured Jack that when the history books got written, he'd find himself on the right side.

"You're goddamn right," Jack fulminated. "And let me tell you—even when I couldn't get the deals done, even when I couldn't twist enough fucking arms or give up enough in approval numbers, I laid the groundwork for the next decade. I built the foundation. I planted the seeds and got the leads."

And that's when I knew.

We finished dinner and exchanged a few final pleasantries. After excusing myself to use the adjoining bathroom, I rejoined Jack, who was back on his cellphone, berating someone and deeply immersed. When he concluded the call several minutes later, Jack walked me out to the front lawn. We said our goodbyes, and I left Jack to his mementos and his disappointment.

The next day, for the first time in nearly forty years, I got a call from my brother, Evan.

XXIII

At first I don't recognize his voice. It has coarsened, maybe from cigarettes, maybe from age. The call comes into my office late at night, as I am putting the finishing touches on an appellate brief.

"Liddle Man," he says. Only one person ever called me that.

I hang up. No, I'm not being a prick. How many times had I tried to reach Evan over the years? I'd googled him like a stalker, for chrissake, hours at a sitting. I even hired a PI, who found me a cell number (which went straight to automated voice mail) and uncovered a gmail address (which bounced back every time).

Not a word from my brother for four fucking decades, and now he calls with cheerio in his voice?

The office line rings twice more; I answer on his fourth try.

"Evan," I say, trying to keep my voice calm.

"None other, Robert. How's tricks, bro?"

Let him wait, I tell myself. Get his own taste of it. Finally: "Where are you?" Keep the tone even.

"In town for the night, Robbie. Care to meet for a nightcap? Or have you quit drinking these days?"

Sure, Evan, let's have a fucking drink, like it's Raintree's on Flatbush, it's late '87, and the Yankees have just taken a twi-nighter. I've gotten nothing else going on, you dumb fuck.

Good god, how I've missed my brother.

We meet at the bar off the Mayflower Hotel lobby and settle into a teakwood booth against the brick wall. I order two scotches.

As we face each other, I'm sure Evan can register how hurt I still am.

"Come on, Liddle Man, I don't look that different, do I?"

"I barely remember your face," I lie. "I stopped telling people I even have a brother. I stopped telling *myself* at least twenty years ago." My voice is rising—a couple of people shoot us a look from adjoining tables. Fuck them.

"Rob, you're pissed, and I deserve it. Humor me for one drink, can you do that?"

"One drink. Make this good."

We sit in silence until the server brings our order, and I slide one of the glasses over to Evan. The least I can do is muster some civility.

"So where have you been most of my life, Evan?"

That got a half-smile.

"Here and there," he says. "Mostly in California. For years, all I wanted was to be as far from Borough Park as possible."

"I wanted out, too, Evan. I didn't like it any better, but at least I had you. Until you went AWOL."

I search my brother's eyes for some sign of remorse. If there is something there, I can't see it. Just a faraway look, the kind I sometimes get from Josh.

"Rob, I don't have an excuse. I needed to get away. That's what I did. And so did you a year later, when you left for college."

Oh, for chrissake. "Did you own a phone, asshole? Or a laptop? Any idea how many times I tried to reach you? Did you get any of my messages? What did you expect me to think?"

Evan looks stricken. So at least there's that.

"I'm sorry, Robbie. I really have no excuse."

"I thought we might at least see you at Mom's shiva. You didn't show for Dad's, that I get, but at least for Mom. You're named after her, for fuck's sake."

"No go, Liddle Man. If she 'had no older son,' as Evie used to tell me, then I was probably unfit to say Kaddish for her."

"Mom asked for you at the end." Another lie, and Evan isn't buying.

"Nice try, Robert. Let me know when you're done eating my heart out."

"Don't make this my fault. I've been reachable on LinkedIn for many years, and there's good cell coverage in Washington."

"I'm not making this your fault. Or mine. Or anyone's. We were both in that house together. Remember?"

Of course I remember. Most of it, anyway. We finish the first round of drinks, and I signal the server for seconds.

My tics get louder, but I otherwise sit in silence until the server returns with the refills.

"But enough about me," Evan says finally. "Can we change the subject? How's your buddy Jack taking the loss? Personally, I was happy to see the bastard go down to defeat."

"Forget Jack, Evan. Give me at least the broad picture—jobs, wife, kids?"

"Yes, no, and none that I know of. Let's cover my story some other time. Come on. Tell me about the prez."

"It's been pretty tough on him. He's a proud guy, but anyone would take it hard, right?"

A few more gawkers glance in our direction. I'd been photographed with the president over the years, so it's not unusual for a few looks to come my way.

"If I were you, Robbie, I would have gotten off the Cutler Train years ago. That dirtbag never deserved your help."

"He's my friend, Evan. For all his faults, he's been my friend for a very long time." *Longer than* you *at this point,* I find myself thinking. Again.

"Some fucking friend, Liddle Man. I still remember the day you came home bellyaching about the school photographer he sicced on you. Or have you blocked out all the shit your 'friend' pulled on you back in the day?"

"That was just a practical joke in high school, Evan," I say softly.

"Some practical joke, Robbie. You and Jess were mortified. You were bawling your eyes out when you got home that day. Remember?"

"Not really. But look, people grow up, or haven't you heard?"

"Yeah, I've heard. But from where I sit, people mostly become decrepit versions of the same evil fucks they always were. I still think I should have flattened that asshole when I had the chance. No more letting you be the butt of Jack's 'practical jokes.'"

Once my protector, always my protector.

"You certainly put the fear of God into him that day, Evan," I lie. I have only the haziest memories of that event. "I still remember how good it felt to have you in my corner."

"I'm still in your corner. Hard as that may be to believe."

My eyes start to fill. "I've missed you, Evan. I've tried so hard to find you. Did you even know?"

Evan looks away. "I wasn't trying to be found," he says at last.

"Well, you succeeded."

"I'm here now, Robert, and I'm listening. How are Nan and Josh?"

I give him the headlines: how it ended with Nan, how it started with Amanda. How I'm still hoping against hope to work things out with Amanda.

"Rob, that sounds like a lost cause. At some point, you've got to admit defeat and move on."

I am not about to do that, I explain to my brother. "I'm not the moving-on type, Evan." Unlike some people I could name.

"And how about President Jack? Has he mellowed from the arrogant prick he was in the old days?"

Where to begin? I think. "Politics is not for the faint of heart, I suppose. I had a bird's-eye view as Jack rose through the ranks. I headed his fundraising when he was on the way up."

"Sounds like grunt work to me."

Evan has a point. "It wasn't always glamorous, that's for sure. I remember one of those fundraisers. It was a June evening at the Water Club overlooking the East River. Open-air terrace, views uptown to the 59th Street Bridge, a crowd of bankers in blazers. Toward the end of the evening, Jack asked me to fetch him the name of one of the female servers. Like I was his procurer. Jeez, the things we do for love."

Evan's voice drops to a whisper. "For chrissake, Robbie, you're still eating this guy's shit. When does it stop?"

"As they say, Evan, it's complicated. I get things out of the friendship, too."

"Like what, Liddle Man? Like what? He walks all over you, he married your high school squeeze, and from what I hear, he treats Jess like shit. You make your peace with that?"

"Years ago, Evan. Decades ago. We've all moved on, except maybe for you."

"Moving on's one thing. Forgetting the past is something else."

"Jesus, for someone who bailed on us so many years ago, you're the one who's stuck in the past. Let's focus on now."

"Fine, Rob. Let's focus on now. It's obvious you're gonna need some brotherly love to keep you grounded now that your White House buddy is on his way out. Your knuckles look even nastier than I remember them. Too much pressure, Robert?"

"Something like that," I admit. "It's stressful, the work I do."

"Well, I'm at your service, Liddle Man."

I'm such a soft touch, it's pathetic. "Can you hang around for a while, Evan? I'm plenty busy these days, but I'd really love to catch up. Do you have a place to stay while you're in town?"

"I'm at the Willard. Insurance brokers' convention, if you can believe that. And I have a few clients to visit, so I may be back in town over the next month or so. But let's plan to get some quality time, maybe if you take a weekend off now and then. We can toast to Nathan's belt buckle and Evie's high heels."

"I'd like that. Thanks."

XXIV

A bout a month before trial, it happened. The government moved to disqualify me from the case. It was just as Jane had predicted back at the farmhouse—the prosecutors had gotten wind of my affair with Amanda.

I didn't expect to lose the motion, not this close to jury selection, but that wasn't the point. The government was looking to jam me up with Edgerton. His Honor was bound to be pissed that I hadn't raised the issue myself at the arraignment. Now that we were on the eve of trial, finding new counsel for the president would be a logistical nightmare. I was going to get Edgerton's Full Eyebrow, that's for damn sure.

I was pretty pissed, too, I'll admit it. The motion was a cheap shot, especially only weeks before trial, and I called Katherine Hannigan to complain. To her credit, Katherine stood firm. "We had no choice, Rob, and you know it. If I don't take this to the judge and get his blessing for you to remain as defense counsel, I'll be litigating this case for years to come, long after your client has been convicted. Mr. Cutler will ask for a new trial based on your conflict, and my bosses will ask me how the hell I could have let this happen."

Katherine was right, I thought glumly. Once she learned about Amanda and me, she had to bring it to the Court's attention. "May I at least ask how you heard about my . . . history?"

"Come on, Rob, you can't expect me to reveal sources. Let's just say that my informant sounded pretty reliable. He provided chapter and verse about you and the victim."

Chapter and verse? Who had access to that kind of information? Maybe Amanda and I were not as discreet as I had imagined.

Jack and I would both have to testify at the disqualification hearing, so Jane would be in charge for our side. Concerned about adverse publicity, Judge Edgerton conducted the inquiry in chambers, not in open court. He was doing Jack and me a huge favor.

It was unpleasant all the same.

We were seated across from the judge at a long conference table, surrounded by bookshelves, a couple of diplomas, and a large autographed photo of Cellino & Barnes, the famous personal injury lawyers, who must have been among the judge's opposing counsel during his insurance defense days. From the scowl creasing the judge's face, I feared he'd be adding my skull to the wall mountings by day's end.

"We're here on Criminal No. 41-205, *People of the District of Columbia v. John Sherman Cutler,*" Judge Edgerton began, shooting me a quick flash of annoyance. "I will be examining the defendant and defense counsel to determine whether the defendant understands his lawyer's potential conflict and whether we need to find new defense counsel, God help us. Mr. Cutler, please rise and be sworn."

Jack took the oath and faced the judge.

"Mr. Cutler, do you understand that this is a proceeding to determine whether Mr. Jacobson can provide zealous, unbiased counsel in this case?"

"I do," said Jack.

"When did Mr. Jacobson first inform you of his relationship with the victim?"

"I can't pinpoint the date, Your Honor, but it was well before Amanda Harper came to work at the White House."

"Are you saying that you learned of their relationship during the time the two of them were involved?"

"That's correct, Your Honor."

"What was your understanding of the nature of their affair?"

"I knew that Robbie—Mr. Jacobson—was head over heels. I can't say what Amanda was feeling, but I assumed the feeling was mutual."

"So when you decided to engage Mr. Jacobson as your attorney, you were aware of his history with the victim?"

"Completely."

"Did Mr. Jacobson advise you that his ability to represent you in a matter like this might reasonably be questioned, given the nature of the charges against you?"

"He did, Your Honor, in our very first meeting after I was charged. He told me that his relationship with Ms. Harper could compromise his ability to do the job. In fact, he refused to take my case at first. I didn't accept that answer."

"May I ask why, Mr. Cutler?"

"Because Rob Jacobson is the best lawyer I know. Because he is my oldest friend. Because I would trust him with my life." Jack choked up as he said it. So did I, and I wasn't even the one testifying—yet.

"And you knowingly and voluntarily agreed to engage Mr. Jacobson, notwithstanding his romantic past with the victim?"

"Without a doubt, Your Honor."

"You realize that you could engage counsel who has no history with the victim?"

"I do."

"And that if for some reason you could not afford new counsel, the Court would appoint one for you?"

"I know that, but I'd like to stick with Mr. Jacobson."

The judge leaned across the table and looked Jack dead in the eye.

"Do you understand that you will not have another bite at this apple, Mr. Cutler? If you accept Mr. Jacobson as your lawyer, neither this court, nor any appellate court in my opinion, is going to look kindly on a claim that your lawyer had a conflict. Do you understand what I'm saying?"

"I do, Your Honor."

"And you're comfortable going forward with Mr. Jacobson nonetheless."

"I am."

"Any other questions for the president, Ms. Hannigan?"

"No, I think Your Honor has covered it," Katherine replied.

The judge glared at me. "Your turn, Counselor. Stand up and be sworn."

I'll let you in on a secret—lawyers are usually terrible witnesses. They love to talk. They never like to admit that there's something they don't know. They answer questions they shouldn't. Although I'd had some testifying experience in my career, I much prefer to be the one asking the questions.

So I was nervous.

"Mr. Jacobson, let's start with the basics," Judge Edgerton began. "Is it true that you had a romantic involvement with the decedent?"

"That's true, Your Honor."

"When did it begin?"

"About eighteen months before she left our law firm to join the White House Counsel's Office."

"And when did it end?"

"A few months after she joined the White House Counsel's Office."

"Who ended the relationship?"

"Amanda did."

"How did you feel when she broke things off, Mr. Jacobson?"

I paused on that one. *Take a breath.* "I was distraught, Your Honor."

"When did you see her last?"

"In mid-January of this year. So about eleven months ago."

Judge Edgerton stared at me. "How long before she was killed?"

"I can't say for sure. Assuming the police reports are correct, and Amanda was killed in late January, then a little less than a week before."

"Where did you meet her?"

"At her apartment."

"Tell me what happened that day."

"I spent about fifteen minutes there. Just talking. I told her I thought we should keep working on the relationship. I thought we still had a future."

"What did she say to you?"

"She basically explained that it wasn't going to work between us. But it was just a brief moment. As I say, I left after about fifteen, twenty minutes and drove home."

"And you never saw her again?"

"Never."

"Or talked to her?"

"Never."

"Mr. Cutler says that you apprised him of your history with the victim before he engaged you. Is that true?"

"Completely. As he said, the president is a childhood friend of mine. I shared the basics with him during the time Amanda and I were seeing each other."

"What did you tell him back then, Counselor?"

"I told him that I was crazy in love. I'm sure he could tell I meant it."

"And once the president was charged with the crime, did you advise him that he could hire a lawyer who has no such romantic relationship to the decedent?"

"I did."

"Are you satisfied that Mr. Cutler fully understands that you may have divided loyalties in this case?"

"Forgive me, Your Honor, but I reject the premise. I have only a single loyalty, and that's to Jack. Full stop. But yes, I've told him all the pros and cons, and he says he wants me. I'm satisfied that I can do the job."

Judge Edgerton looked over at the government table. "Ms. Hannigan, do you have any questions of Mr. Jacobson before I rule?"

"Just a few, Your Honor."

I gritted my teeth, and Jane leaned forward at the table.

"Mr. Jacobson, you never mentioned your relationship with Ms. Harper during any of our meetings or phone calls. Why is that?"

"Because it was none of your business, Ms. Hannigan."

"I beg to differ, Counselor. If the president wakes up a month after his conviction with buyer's remorse, it's my office that will have to defend the judgment, not you. So it's very much my business, sir."

"Is it really, Ms. Hannigan? So long as I made the requisite disclosure to my client—which I have—my relationship with Ms. Harper is between me and her."

"You say that you made the requisite disclosure to Mr. Cutler—what exactly did you tell him, and what did he say to you?"

Jane objected. "Those are privileged communications, Your Honor. You've already elicited from Mr. Jacobson that he disclosed to Mr. Cutler exactly what the law required him to disclose. Anything beyond that is, as Mr. Jacobson said, none of the government's business."

"I agree, Ms. Cashman. Anything more, Ms. Hannigan?"

"Just one question more, Your Honor. Mr. Jacobson, how much does it pain you to represent the man who, at least in my opinion, killed the woman you loved?"

"It's an honor to represent President Cutler. And it's bottomlessly painful to have lost Amanda."

All true. It was pure *choshek* at the time. And it never abated, not even after I heard the news on the radio that frigid day in February. As the Indigo Girls once sang, "Darkness has a hunger that's insatiable."

"Nothing further, Your Honor."

As I expected, the judge denied the motion. Although the government had taken me down a peg with His Honor, I was relieved.

After all, no one had asked about my history with Jessica Cutler.

XXV

The trial is coming up, right?

Two weeks.

Have you been able to follow the evidence during prep? Helping your lawyers get ready?

I'm doing fine, just fine. So what are you going to tell the judge about me?

Still working on my findings. Let me ask a basic question: Do you understand how you got here?

Robbie tells me that the cops found a piece of tape with a couple of prints. That's all I know for sure.

They matched one of those prints with . . .

Oh, please, I know what matched. Never mind. Just tell me what you and Robbie want from me.

I'm going to show you a few inkblots. It's what we psychiatrists call a Rorschach test. All you need to do is tell me what you see in each picture as I show it to you.

Fire away.

Part II

TRIALS

XXVI

On the weekend before jury selection, Jess invited me over for dinner. The last week of January was unusually cold in the Maryland suburbs. I parked around the corner from the house, and by the time I reached the front door, my glasses were misted and my ears a deepening shade of red.

The table was set for five—Jess, the kids, and Jack, to my surprise. He rose to greet me, flashing just the briefest look of anxiety.

"How's the opening coming?" Jack asked.

"It's coming," I lied. "Working out the last few details."

"When can I see a draft? I may have some ideas for you."

I promised Jack I'd send him something soon. He was the client, after all. And it's not like he would have much time to redo my handiwork.

The trial was starting Monday.

Jess and the kids gathered around me as I shook off the last flakes of snow. Gretchen, now eighteen, looked like herself again. Her dark, curly hair, inherited from her mother, had grown back after the chemo, and she was animated with what I assumed to be nervous energy. How could she not be nervous—I was. "How long will it take to pick the jury?" she asked when we sat down for dinner.

"Not more than a day or two, I think. It usually goes pretty quickly, although there can be delays in cases like this. Then again, there's never really been a case like this."

"I don't get how twelve regular people get to decide Dad's fate. It's not like they're experts or anything," Gretchen said.

"They're not experts, you're right. But you need to have faith that they'll get it right. And Jane and I will be there to make sure they do."

"Can you keep all the Republicans off the jury?" Harlan, just turned sixteen, asked me. "They never liked Dad much. Isn't he entitled to a jury of his peers? What are peers, anyway? Other presidents? Other politicians? No way is a Republican Dad's peer."

"It's a good question, Harlan, but I'm not sure we can ask potential jurors how they voted. And if we go down that road, the government will retaliate and start striking Democrats. I think there are better ways to deal with this issue. For example, the judge will ask the jurors whether they're able to judge your dad's case fairly. If a juror is biased, he may admit it, and we can strike him."

"Or he could lie about it," Jess interjected. "Maybe the jurors who don't like Jack will keep it to themselves so they can stick it to him."

This was obviously a possibility, but I chose to deflect the concern. "I'm not worried, Jess," I said with some overstatement. "The jurors will all be from D.C., where nearly everyone voted for Jack. Anyway, we'll be on the lookout for partisanship, believe me."

As Jess refilled our glasses, Jack sat morosely at the other side of the table, in a way that reminded me of that dinner in Park Slope, years ago, when I'd first met his father. The conversation turned from jury selection to the likely witnesses, and then to whether I had any tricks up my sleeve.

"How about surprise witnesses, Robbie?" Harlan asked. "That always works on TV."

Jack, now three cocktails in, struck out. "This is not fucking TV, Harlan. This is actually happening. To me."

Harlan looked down. Jess placed her hand atop her son's. "Jack," she said softly, "Harlan's trying to help. And this trial is happening to him, too. It's happening to all of us."

Jack pretended not to hear. "Harlan," I interjected, "in real-life trials it's hard to have surprise witnesses. The prosecutors and the defense lawyers are supposed to notify each other of the witnesses they expect to call. Sometimes there can be surprises, but not often."

"What can you tell us about the prosecutors?" Gretchen asked. "Do you expect them to take cheap shots at Dad?"

"The lead prosecutor is Katherine Hannigan. She's capable. Not fancy, I'm told, but solid, well prepared. She'll do a good job at telling her side of the story."

"But you're better than her, right?" Harlan asked, though more as a statement than a question.

"Way better," I said.

"How about the judge?" Jess asked. "What's he like?"

I gave them a primer on Judge Edgerton. A good draw for us, I said. "The hardest thing for all of you will be sitting through the government's case. You need to look attentive but unconcerned. And that will be hard—the government's witnesses go first, so several days will pass before it's time for us to present our case. It will take a lot of courage from each of you."

"Gretchen and Harlan are profiles in courage," Jess offered. "They've been through hardship before and come out the other side."

I looked over at Gretchen, who certainly knew courage firsthand. The years of chemo. Losing her hair as a middle schooler. Days in hospital isolation. But look at her now, the picture of teenage health. The spitting image of her mom.

"No doubt about it," I agreed. "And having you guys in court will be a huge plus for your dad and me. It will be harder for the prosecutors to take cheap shots with the three of you sitting there. Though there will be some rough days ahead."

"Do you think you can get someone else to confess to the crime on the witness stand?" asked Harlan. "Get the jury to see who the real killer was?"

Jack gave his son a withering look. "Harlan, for chrissake, this is not fucking *Law & Order*. The case doesn't get solved in forty-two minutes plus commercials," he said at his whinging worst.

"I know that, Dad," Harlan shot back. "But it would still be nice to be able to show people that someone else killed this woman. You think it's been easy for Gretchen and me, Dad? Is that what you think? You think we enjoy hearing our friends make jokes about your gal pals? You think we get a kick out of seeing your picture Photoshopped with ropes and sex toys? Or choking memes? You think we don't see the same shit you see every day?"

"Oh, I'm so sorry about your tough fucking life, Harlan," Jack snarled. "What a letdown it must be from ordering cheeseburgers at any hour from the White House mess. Are you worried you're not gonna get into Dartmouth like your worthless piece-of-shit grandfather? Is life letting you down? Is it letting you down, Jess? How about it, Gretchen? Want to kick your old man to the curb?"

I looked over at Jess. Her eyes were wet. "Buddy," I said to Harlan, "this is brutal for all of us. Your dad knows that, even if he is too tired and scared to show it. He's counting on you and Gretchen and your mom to be there in court for him, no matter how nasty it gets. But I promise you, we've got a lot of cards to play. Just watch what we do to the government at trial. You'll feel proud to be your dad's son. You have my word."

Gretchen got up from the table to give me a hug. "We've always looked up to you, Robbie. You've always been there for me and my brother. And for Mom."

I glanced over at Jack, who was taking this moment to closely scrutinize the minute hand on his watch. He did not look happy.

XXVII

D^{ays 1–2}
Bright and early on Monday, January 26, the trial began.

Jane and I had arranged to meet Jack at the courthouse about an hour before jury selection. I'm not sure I can quite convey the scene that greeted us that first day. The crowd hoping to get seats in the courtroom rivaled the masses that surely gather in Heaven for the reunion tour of Jimi Hendrix, Janice Joplin, and John Lennon. By the third day of trial, I'm told, spectators were using cash apps to buy and sell premium spots in line, while "Jack Squatters," as they were called, got paid to reserve closest entry to the courthouse for the well-heeled. There were protesters, of course, mostly arrayed against us. Some of them had repurposed the LOCK HER UP signs of yesteryear. A few of these geniuses had even neglected to update the pronoun.

Amidst the swarm of reporters and photographers, I spotted a couple of producers for *The MacGregor Solution* whom I'd met back in September. I could only imagine the meal MacGregor would make of this trial. Sure enough, a few paces from his producers was the man himself, holding court with some of the demonstrators. As Jane and I forced our way through the crowd, MacGregor tried, without success, to catch my eye.

I chose to ignore him. Although the interview last September had gone as well as I had hoped, it didn't materially improve Jack's favorability ratings. In retrospect, it's easy to see why. MacGregor's viewers don't watch him to be informed, updated, or persuaded. They come to have their prejudices validated. If they believe that Hillary Clinton sacrificed young children and harvested their blood, someone is bound to come on MacGregor's show and claim that her victims' remains are stashed in the back room of a D.C. pizza parlor. If viewers believe that Jack Cutler stole the election from President Smith, some goofball with a JD will tell MacGregor that electronic voting machines turned red votes blue. I should have realized going in that talking to MacGregor would have no upside.

Jane and I passed through the phalanx of identity scanners specially installed at the courthouse entry. You press your thumb to an optical strip, and it registers your name, date of birth, and citizenship status. If it matches the log maintained by the federal marshals, you're waved through to the elevators.

We headed to Judge Edgerton's courtroom on the fifth floor. On either side of the adjoining hallway, court officers had reserved one room for the prosecutors and their witnesses, another for us and ours. A few mismatched faux-leather-backed chairs surrounded a conference table bearing the signatures of previous defendants. Twenty-five banker boxes, containing evidence, legal briefs, and other materials, were already stacked against the walls, carted in earlier that morning by L&H support staff.

Jane and I had each brought our lucky charms to trial. For me, it was several boxes of peppermint Life Savers to keep me alert during trial (and to quell my knuckle-biting habit). For Jane, it was a collection of multicolored highlighters to mark arguments in order of their importance.

After keeping us waiting for twenty minutes, Jack swept into the conference room as if "Hail to the Chief" were being piped through the radiator ducts. I motioned him to take a seat at the table and got down to business.

"We start by trying to pick the best jury we can. If we get a good defense jury, that's a huge lift for Team Cutler."

"What does a *good defense jury* mean in a case like this?" Jack asked.

Jane and I had been grappling with that question for days. I was partial to using the G-DaMN database, but Jane was dead set against it. It was our first tactical disagreement in years.

"Talk about Big Brother, Rob," Jane had said when we first discussed the issue. "You really want to encourage such intrusions on private lives? What's next—a camera in every bathroom?"

"Oh, come on, Jane. We're not Peeping Toms. We're just using information people have voluntarily made public."

"I doubt any of them expected the government to be scooping up that data, then using it to appeal to their every appetite."

"Seriously, Jane? Data mining goes on all the time. How does your laptop know to send you eyeglass ads two minutes after you've surfed for new frames? How does the travel bureau in Bora Bora know to offer you overwater bungalows an hour after you've scrolled through Travelocity? It's all the same."

"I guess I take the justice system more seriously than deciding where I should go to sip umbrella drinks on vacation," Jane said a bit derisively.

"Agreed, Jane. But we can't afford to bring a knife to a gunfight. You can be sure the prosecutors will make full use of this technology."

"I don't doubt it. Let them try. This 'technology,' as you call it, depends on the worst sort of stereotyping. Does someone shop at Mirage Garage? Well, I do. Does someone listen to country music and not Bach? Guilty as charged again. Does that mean you'll challenge all the Blacks on the jury?"

"Come on, Jane. You're not like most Black jurors."

"Bingo," Jane announced. "There's your liberal sensibility. What are most Black jurors *like*, Rob? The ones I know best go to church every Sunday, get squeamish about abortion, and, when it comes to first-degree murderers, would happily pull the switch personally. What are your Black friends like?"

I realized that Jane was my only African American friend. "Let's do this," I proposed at last. "I'll look at the G-DaMN data alone. I'll run a few algorithms, circle the candidates that interest me, and we can present the results to Jack. He'll decide."

Now it was decision time, and I told Jack what I'd found. "At least a dozen of the potential jurors bought the 20th Anniversary *West Wing* box set. In my opinion, we want all of them. Several more listed *The Trial of the Chicago 7* as their all-time favorite movie. We want all of them. I would have liked some recent immigrants as well, folks you always polled favorably with, but the English as a First Language Act, which President Melvin rammed through Congress last month, probably makes that impossible."

It was Jane's turn, and as expected, she teed off on G-DaMN data.

"Rob's the best criminal lawyer I know, Jack, but I think he has this data mining stuff wrong. People are *individuals*. Remember the refrigerator test? When *The New York Times* juxtaposed the inside of several people's refrigerators and asked readers to guess whether the owner was a Democrat or Republican? I don't know about you, but I guessed wrong roughly half the time. And that made me happy. It told me that you can no more judge a person by his buying habits than you can choose a book by its cover.

"I've picked hundreds of juries, Jack, and in my humble opinion there's no secret sauce. For a defense jury," she said, "I want jurors who are independent minded. Leaders, not followers. People who are comfortable disagreeing with authority figures like the prosecutors. So I want professionals on the jury. I want people who have started businesses or who run them now. I want dissenters, folks who have chosen to follow a different drummer. I want smart jurors, since they'll appreciate lawyers like Rob and me. And I want *disagreeable* jurors. A jury that gets along too well is more likely to reach a unanimous verdict."

"Don't we need a unanimous verdict to get an acquittal?" Jack asked.

"That's true," said Jane. "That's the goal. But I'll happily take a hung jury over a conviction. And if the jury is divided in your favor—say, ten for acquittal and only two for conviction—you can sometimes persuade the prosecutors to drop the case, rather than try it again."

"The prosecutors will never give up on this case," Jack said.

I suspected he was right.

"How about trying to get as many women on my jury as possible?" Jack asked. He'd been pushing that idea for days.

Jane shook her head. "Experience has taught me that generalizations about gender are usually misleading. I realize that you used to poll well with women, Jack, but those days are over."

Plus, I thought to myself, women might react badly if, despite our client's objections, Jane and I had to throw some shade at Amanda or Jess.

"How about minorities?" Jack offered. "They're usually pretty loyal Democrats. Present company excluded, of course."

Jane gave Jack a wry smile. She'd heard this kind of thing a million times. "Black folks are not a monolith, Mr. President. Neither are Hispanics, Asians, or anyone else. None of us checks with our tribal leaders before making up our minds."

A little fierce, I thought. But vintage Jane.

At 9:30 a.m. sharp, a court officer unlocked the double doors to Judge Edgerton's courtroom, and the three of us sat down at the defense table. A pool of about 150 potential jurors parked themselves in the ten rows directly behind the counsel tables. A minute or two after ten, Judge Edgerton entered the courtroom, greeted the jury pool, and briefly described the nature of the case. The jurors hardly needed the introduction, as the airwaves had been reprising All Things Jack for the past month. The paternity test results made for especially unpleasant watching.

Jury selection lasted until the late afternoon of the second day. We used our peremptory strikes to get the least deferential jurors we could find, so we dismissed every "assistant to the whoever" and "junior vice president of whatever" that we could. In a compromise with Jane, we also struck any juror who listed Smith TV as a principal news source or streamed NCIS reruns. Conversely, we tried to seat anyone whose online purchases at Urban Outfitters or Forever 21 exceeded the median, since both outlets catered to young urban hipsters, my kind of juror.

For their part, the prosecutors tried to seat jurors who would play well together in the sandbox, so they used their challenges to ensure that every juror had at least one "friend." If there was one woman, there had to be at least two. If there was one Hispanic male, there had to be at least two. The government also struck every lawyer in the pool, to eliminate anyone who might dominate the deliberations. We, of course, tried to do the opposite.

By around 4:15 p.m. on the second day, we had a jury of six men and six women, with two alternates in case one of the first twelve had to be excused during trial. As usual, neither side got everything it wanted. We were able to seat a couple of entrepreneurs, four jurors with graduate degrees, and two jurors who had bought Tana French novels online (and who might therefore try to outfox the government's police witnesses). Jane and I were especially pleased that we had seated our number one pick, Shirlene Mills, juror 5, a secretary in the public defender's office. On the other hand, I wasn't crazy about jurors 3 and 9, each of whom held a security clearance, had several relatives in federal law enforcement, and regularly ordered from Mirage Garage.

Judge Edgerton swore in the jury and gave them an initial instruction:

"From this moment on, you are the ones who decide what the facts are in this case. That is a solemn responsibility, and I know that each of you will take it very seriously.

"As I'm sure I don't need to tell you, this case will be the subject of considerable media attention. You've already seen the cameras and reporters outside the courtroom. Some reporters may try to contact you, either here or at home. I instruct you, in the strongest possible terms, that you must not talk to anyone, whether press, family, or others, about this case. Do not go online to read about the case. Do not look at newspapers, do not listen to television accounts, and do not keep up with social media. I will repeat this instruction at the end of each court day, and I will insist that you follow that instruction to the letter. Your oath as jurors commits you to serve fairly and impartially, and to base your verdict only on the evidence you receive in this courtroom."

Judge Edgerton closed by explaining the difference between civil and criminal cases, the meaning of "beyond a reasonable doubt," and the presumption of innocence. He then dismissed the jurors after repeating his admonition that they not discuss the case—with one another or with anyone else.

The trial of our lives would begin tomorrow, at 9:30 a.m. sharp.

XXVIII

D ay 3, morning session
    I try to get to courtrooms early. It gives me a sense, maybe a false sense, of control. There are so many parts of a trial you can't control, at least you can manage to show up ahead of the crowd.

Not today. Despite wrath-of-god winter weather, a restless crowd had queued up before dawn to compete for the few seats open to the public. By the time I arrived around eight-thirty, my eyes watering from the slashing winds, the line was three blocks long.

The marshals had set up a side entrance for lawyers and family members, but you had to pass the press portal to get there. Abbie Leonard, who hosted Smith TV's graveyard shift, jammed a mic in my direction.

"Counselor," he called out, "any comment on reports that President Cutler killed Amanda because she was about to reveal their affair? How about your client's love child? Come on, Robbie, speak up. Your fan club is waiting."

They'd have to keep waiting.

Jane joined me in the lobby about ten minutes later, and we hurried upstairs to meet Jack, who showed just before curtain time. At 9:30 on the dot, Judge Edgerton entered the courtroom, gaveled for quiet, then reiterated a few basic instructions. You could see the jurors checking one another out, first-date style, and stealing awkward glances at the former commander in chief as he doodled on a yellow legal pad. A couple of the jurors were already taking notes in small ringed notebooks provided by the court officers. I quickly scanned the courtroom. Jess, Gretchen, and Harlan were huddled together in the public section right behind us.

Katherine Hannigan opened for the government. As I'd told Gretchen at dinner, Katherine was not flashy. But I found her presentation quietly authoritative. She ticked off all the physical evidence, paternity results and all; advised the jury, without lecturing them, that circumstantial evidence is as good as any other; and explained that the jury's basic task is to apply common sense to the evidence it receives. If the jury did that, Katherine said as she wrapped up, it should have no trouble reaching a unanimous guilty verdict.

By the time she sat down, I was sure that Katherine had earned major credibility points with the jury. It was like listening to your longtime family doctor, someone who patiently but firmly tells you nothing but the truth as she knows it.

It was my turn. Defense lawyers always have a delicate decision to make when they open to the jury. How much of your defense do you telegraph in the opening? The more of your case you reveal, the more the prosecutors can prepare for it. On the other hand, the less you reveal, the less the jury will be prepped to greet the government's proof with skepticism. With that issue in mind, I approached the jury rail, looked at each juror, one by one, and began to speak in my usual conversational style.

"Ladies and gentlemen of the jury, good morning." A few *good mornings* back—always a good sign. "Together with my colleague Jane Cashman, it's my honor to represent Jack Cutler, former president of the United States.

"You've just heard a compelling opening by Ms. Hannigan. She told you about the brutal strangulation of a young woman with a storybook future. All of us must surely be appalled by so atrocious a crime. Our hearts go out to Ms. Harper's family and the many friends who mourn her loss.

"But as Judge Edgerton told you when you were selected as jurors, this case cannot be about emotion. No one in this courtroom, least of all Jack Cutler, denies for a second that this was a horrifying crime. No one disputes that the real perpetrator of this crime deserves the most severe punishment the law permits.

"And while we're talking about things this case is *not* about, let me add another: This case is *not* about politics. Some of you may have voted for President Cutler. Some of you may have voted for his opponent. Some of you may have made some other choice or made no choice at all.

"But all of you took an oath to leave politics outside the courtroom and to judge Jack Cutler on the evidence alone. I'm confident that you will honor that oath.

"Now as I listened to Ms. Hannigan itemize some of the evidence, I was struck by one thing Ms. Hannigan told you, and several things she did *not* tell you.

"The one thing she *told* you is that her case against Jack Cutler is purely circumstantial. *Circumstantial* is just a lawyer's term for indirect evidence. *Direct* evidence would be an eyewitness. Or a confession. Or a video showing the actual crime. But the prosecutors have none of that. You might have noticed how defensive Ms. Hannigan sounded when she told you that circumstantial evidence is as good as direct evidence. Believe me, if the prosecutors had even a shred of direct evidence, they

would have paraded that evidence in their opening statement this morning. But they don't, so they didn't.

"Now for the things Ms. Hannigan did *not* tell you. She did *not* tell
you about the government's burden of proof. But Judge Edgerton already
has and will do so again at the close of the case. You heard the Court say
that Mr. Cutler is *presumed innocent*. That means he stands before you as
an innocent man and remains an innocent man unless and until each and
every one of you is convinced beyond a reasonable doubt that he committed this horrible crime.

"*Beyond a reasonable doubt*. We hear those words all the time, and the
judge has already told you what they mean. In the simplest terms, a reasonable doubt is the kind of doubt that would make you hesitate before
doing something very important in your life.

"Would you buy a home with circumstantial evidence? What if someone simply *described* what the house looked like, but you had never laid
eyes on it for yourself? Would you hesitate before signing the deed?

"Would you commit to a marriage on the basis of purely circumstantial evidence, or would you demand more proof, better proof, different
proof? Would you select a spouse from a catalogue or based only on a
friend's impressions? Or would you insist on actually meeting your future mate and getting to know him or her directly?

"I suggest that you would and should hesitate before convicting Jack
Cutler on the kind of secondhand evidence the government intends to
offer. Here are some questions you should ask yourselves as you hear the
government's totally circumstantial case:

"Is there a single eyewitness to this horrible crime?

"Is there a single person in this highly traveled part of Rock Creek
Park who saw Jack Cutler anywhere in the vicinity of Ms. Harper's body?
Is there a single person who observed Jack Cutler—one of the most rec-
ognizable people on earth—in this very public location?

"Is there a single person who can explain why the silver knife was placed in the lining of Ms. Harper's briefcase? Or a witness who can explain why Jack Cutler would have the slightest interest in the contents of Ms. Harper's briefcase?

"Is there any evidence that the gray hair found on Ms. Harper's body actually belongs to the president? Did the government conduct any tests that match those hairs to Mr. Cutler? Has the government even attempted to distinguish those hairs from the gray hair sitting on the heads of tens of millions of Americans?

"Did Ms. Harper ever express any fear that Jack Cutler might hurt her? Is there a friend or a relative who will come into this courtroom and tell you that Amanda Harper was afraid of Jack Cutler?

"Did the government ever investigate other ways, completely innocent ways, that Mr. Cutler's fingerprints and DNA might have ended up on Ms. Harper's body and clothing? Did they even *ask* themselves that question before concluding that the former president must be guilty of this heinous crime?

"Has the government investigated anyone else for this crime? Did the cops investigate aspects of Ms. Harper's past or analyze the motives of others who may have wished Ms. Harper harm?

"And speaking of motive, do the prosecutors have any explanation as to why the former president of the United States would kill a young lawyer who simply wanted to serve her country by working in his administration?

"Ladies and gentlemen, I submit to you that there is and must be reasonable doubt if the answer to even *one* of these questions is no.

"As you will learn, the answer to *all* of them is no.

"And remember. There are two sides to every story. The prosecutors will have their side, and we'll have ours. Please be patient. The evidence doesn't all come in at once, and it may be a while before it's our turn."

I concluded with an old defense lawyer's gambit. I raised my right hand and, with my palm facing the jurors, said, "So let me ask you, ladies and gentlemen. Can you all see my hand?"

Most jurors nodded. I then turned my hand around so that the back was facing the jury.

"Remember. You have not seen my hand—until you've seen the other side."

At that, the Court signaled that it was time for our lunch break.

XXIX

Day 3, afternoon session

The government's first witness, Pete DeLuca, was a highly decorated twenty-eight-year veteran of the D.C. Metropolitan Police Department, now known as the State Police Department since D.C.'s admission as a state. He stood about six-four (which made him a half foot taller than I am) and sported a full head of neatly coiffed graying hair (which made him almost a full head hairier than I am). He also radiated command, all uniform and medals.

This was a smart opening move by the government: put your best foot forward with a witness the defense can't easily impeach. Katherine handled the direct.

"Sergeant DeLuca, please tell the jury how you first came upon Ms. Harper's body."

DeLuca sat forward in the witness box and faced the jury. This obviously wasn't his first time testifying in a courtroom.

"On February 2 of last year, our precinct received a call from a stable hand at the Horse Center. In the course of his morning chores, cleaning and feeding the horses, he had discovered Ms. Harper's body."

"For the jury's benefit, Sergeant, what and where is the Horse Center?"

"So Rock Creek Park is in the northwest quadrant of D.C.," DeLuca explained, "and the Horse Center is in the middle of the park. It's often used by the Rock Creek Riders, which is a therapeutic riding program for adults and kids with special needs. I knew the place well, since my son is autistic and we've used the riding program."

DeLuca snuck in that personal item before we could object. Doing so now would only focus the jury more intently on that sympathetic detail.

"What did you do when you arrived at the Horse Center?" Katherine continued.

"Two officers and I got there first and interviewed the stable hand. We wanted to be sure that he had not tampered with the body or the crime scene. Once we got that assurance, a forensics team joined us, a few minutes later. We cordoned off Ms. Harper's body, which lay behind some haystacks in one of the stalls in the horse barn. The pathway to the barn was partly obscured by the massive snowfall that hit us late last January."

"Do you know whether Ms. Harper was actually killed in the barn?"

"From markings both in her apartment and at the Horse Center, we concluded that the victim was killed in her apartment and moved to the barn."

"How did you determine that, Sergeant?"

"The victim discharged some bodily fluid at her apartment that indicated a precipitous loss of oxygen. There were also tire markings and some tracking between snowdrifts, suggesting that the body had been moved to the Horse Center."

"Why didn't the killer just leave Ms. Harper's body in the apartment? Why take the body to the park?"

Jane rose to object. "Unless the sergeant is clairvoyant, I should think this would be utter speculation, Your Honor."

"I'll allow it," Judge Edgerton ruled. "The detective can offer an opinion, if he has one, based on his experience."

DeLuca smiled faintly and turned to the jury again. "There are some obvious advantages to dumping the body in the park. For one thing, the park is a very public venue. There are lots of potential perpetrators in a public place like Rock Creek Park, so leaving the body there could distract investigators from the real killer. Also, because Ms. Harper was left out in the cold, exposed to all the elements, there was a chance that forensic evidence, such as fingerprints and DNA left by the perp, would get compromised. That would make any criminal's day."

"I take it that didn't happen here."

"No, we were lucky. The evidence was preserved."

"Did you discover any other forensic evidence at the victim's apartment?"

"We recovered the victim's iPhone, which was left behind when the body was moved. I turned the phone over to our IT people for examination."

"When you first saw Ms. Harper's body in the park, could you determine anything about the cause of death?" Katherine asked.

"Yes," said DeLuca. "We noticed severe bruising on Ms. Harper's neck, along with what appeared to be fingernail impressions just above her collarbone. Her right eye was bloodshot and there was some red spotting, or *petechiae,* as it is called technically, in her left eyeball. Her lower lip was swollen. It appeared to us that she'd been the victim of manual strangulation."

"I show you, Sergeant DeLuca, what I've marked as government exhibit 1. Do you recognize these photographs?"

"Yes. These are pictures that our forensics team took of Ms. Harper within the first ten minutes of our arrival at the barn."

"Do they fairly and accurately depict how Ms. Harper appeared when you first found her body?"

"They do."

"Your Honor," said Katherine, "I ask permission to circulate these photographs to the jury."

Again, there was no point in objecting. The photographs would almost certainly get admitted, and making a fruitless objection is almost always a mistake. Plus, if we objected and lost, which I figured we would, the jurors would look extra hard at the photos as they passed them around.

"Sergeant, I've placed on the screen a blowup of one of the photos taken at the Horse Center. I'm also handing you an infrared pointer so that you can isolate a few details for the jury. First, you mentioned that Ms. Harper suffered some red spotting in her left eye. May I ask you to pinpoint the spotting for the jury?"

"Sure. You can see a series of red dots, here, here, and also here," De-Luca said as he moved the infrared pointer from one spot to another.

"You also testified that you saw some fingernail impressions above Ms. Harper's collarbone. Can you point those out, please?"

"They're hard to detect on the photo, but this is the spot where we saw them."

"Were you able to determine whose fingernails left the marks?"

"No, we couldn't extract any forensic evidence from the impressions as such. But we did find the president's fingerprints on the victim's clothing close to her neckline."

Jane started to object, but Katherine moved quickly ahead.

"We'll get to that in a moment, Sergeant. Let me first call your attention to what appear to be abrasions on the victim's wrists and above her ankles. Can you show those with the pointer, please?"

DeLuca complied. "You can see the cut marks in each of these places."

"What can you tell the jury about those markings?"

"We noticed these perforations in Ms. Harper's skin when we first examined the body. Further analysis of the markings revealed a pattern consistent with the application of some kind of rope restraints. As if the victim had been tied at the end of each limb to some other structure."

"Like the corners of a four-poster bed?"

Judge Edgerton sustained Jane's objection to this obvious call for guesswork. But Katherine made a nice pivot.

"Sergeant, without speculating, can you tell the jury whether you had an opportunity to examine the furniture in the victim's apartment?"

"I did."

"Was there a bed in her apartment?"

"There was a four-poster bed."

"Did you examine the corner posts, and if so, what did you see?"

"There were markings consistent with the use of rope restraints on each of the four posts."

"Did you recover any such rope restraints at the crime scene or in Ms. Harper's apartment?"

"We did not."

"Sergeant DeLuca, did the D.C. forensics team perform any subsequent examination of the body?"

"Yes. They followed the standard protocol—fingerprint and DNA analysis and an autopsy."

"Tell the jury what you learned."

"As we had initially surmised, Amanda Harper was strangled. The medical examiner certified asphyxiation as the cause of death."

"Knowing the cause of death, Sergeant DeLuca, did you and your forensics team look for particular pieces of physical evidence?"

"We did," said DeLuca. "We first looked for DNA in the vicinity of the victim's neck and the clothing areas closest to her neck. We were lucky: there was recoverable DNA on the victim's neck, as well as on her shirt collar and other parts of her upper clothing."

Several of the jurors looked over at Jack at the mention of DNA. Not a good sign.

"Were you able to trace that DNA to a particular individual?" asked Katherine.

"We were," DeLuca replied. "It matched the defendant, Jack Cutler."

More juror eyes on Jack. And the judge didn't help matters by glancing our way as well.

"How did you happen to have a sample of President Cutler's DNA to compare, Sergeant?"

"The FBI keeps a national DNA database and assists local law enforcement, such as the D.C. State Police Department, by making that database available for use in investigations," DeLuca explained. "As it turned out, the database included DNA from President Cutler. So when we screened the DNA found at the crime scene, we got a hit on President Cutler."

"Can you briefly explain to the jury, Sergeant, why President Cutler's DNA was already contained in the FBI database?"

"Sure," DeLuca answered, turning again to the jury. "Some of you may remember the controversy over what's been called the Davos Collection. Along with other world leaders, President Cutler attended the World Economic Forum in Davos, Switzerland. Some outfit, probably working for Russia, extracted the DNA of several world leaders from discarded napkins and paper coffee cups. President Cutler's DNA was among the material extracted. U.S. intelligence operatives managed to obtain copies, and they uploaded the president's DNA to the FBI database."

"After you got the initial DNA hit from the Davos Collection, Sergeant DeLuca, did you perform any further tests to verify those results?"

"We did," said DeLuca. "When we were ready to surface our investigation, we took a DNA swab from the president, and it once again matched the DNA found at the crime scene."

"You used the phrase *surface our investigation*. What did you mean?"

"It's important to keep an investigation confidential," DeLuca explained, "especially one as sensitive as this one, until you're ready to go public. You don't want to alert a potential suspect that he is under investigation."

At this point, Katherine moved into evidence some blowups of Jack's DNA and the DNA recovered from Amanda's neck and clothing. There was no point in denying that they were a match.

"Sergeant DeLuca, you mentioned an autopsy earlier. When was the autopsy completed?"

"In late November, about ten months after we discovered the body."

"Without going into details, Sergeant, can you briefly tell the jury why it took so long to get results?"

"There were some complications. I'd prefer to leave it to Medical Examiner Zaid to explain."

"Very well. Did you find any other evidence at the horse barn?"

"We did. We recovered a briefcase on the ground about a foot from the victim, a knife that had been partly inserted into the briefcase, and a partial thumbprint on the victim's shirt collar, which also matched the president's prints."

"How did you happen to have a set of President Cutler's fingerprints to compare to the prints found on Ms. Harper's clothing?"

"Again, we used the FBI database, this time the fingerprint database. Fingerprints of all presidents are routinely collected during their time in office, if not before. So we had President Cutler's prints on file."

Katherine showed DeLuca blowups of the crime-scene fingerprints and the ones taken from Jack. Katherine presented those to the jury as well.

"Could you tell the ladies and gentlemen of the jury about the knife?" the prosecutor asked next.

The question allowed DeLuca to play amateur historian to a rapt audience. It was painful to watch.

"The knife is part of the White House silver collection, originally purchased in the early nineteenth century by President James Monroe. It was regularly used at dinners during the Cutler administration."

"Sergeant DeLuca, can you identify what I've marked as government exhibit 2?"

"Yes. That's the knife we recovered at the crime scene."

"How about government exhibit 3?"

"That's Ms. Harper's briefcase, also recovered at the crime scene."

"And when you say that the knife was wedged into the briefcase, Sergeant, can you demonstrate to the jury what you mean?"

DeLuca held up the briefcase and fitted the knife into the narrow opening at the top. "It appeared," said the witness, "as if someone had forcibly inserted the knife into the case, perhaps trying to break it open. The briefcase was still locked when we recovered it."

"Did you subsequently manage to open the briefcase, Sergeant?"

"We did."

"And what, if anything, did you find inside?" Katherine asked.

"From a separately closed compartment, we recovered a series of memos apparently prepared by Ms. Harper during her tenure in the White House Counsel's Office."

"I show you government exhibits 4 through 41. Are these the memos you recovered from the crime scene?"

"They are," said DeLuca.

"What else, if anything, did you recover from the Horse Center?"

"We located some hair strands both on Ms. Harper's clothing and in her underwear."

"Tell us about the hair, Sergeant."

"The hair strands were curly, gray, with a rough texture. We sent the recovered hair strands to the FBI forensics lab at Quantico for analysis."

"One last line of questions, Sergeant. You mentioned that at some point your investigation surfaced and focused on President Cutler as a suspect. Correct?"

"Yes," DeLuca answered.

"What steps, if any, did you take once you decided to go public with your investigation of the former president?"

"After we got the DNA and fingerprint results, we decided to try to interview the president as a suspect in the murder. One of my colleagues and I went to the president's home to speak with him. He came out to the front porch to meet us and said that he would prefer to conduct the interview at our office."

"What happened next?"

"At about two p.m. on April 12 of last year, the president came to our office and met with me and two of my colleagues from the state police."

"Did the president have a lawyer present?"

"No. We told him that he was free to have counsel with him, but he insisted that he had no reason to hire a lawyer."

"How long was the interview?"

"About ninety minutes."

"Did you make and keep notes of that interview?"

"I did," said DeLuca.

"Would you tell the members of the jury what the president said during the interview?"

On cue, DeLuca turned to the jury again and recounted Jack's false answers. With gusto.

"He told us that he'd barely even spoken with Ms. Harper, had never been alone with her in the Oval Office, and had never touched her, except perhaps when the two of them posed for a photograph soon after she joined the Counsel's Office. And the president denied having anything to do with Ms. Harper's death."

"Did you confront Mr. Cutler, Sergeant, with any of the evidence you recovered—the DNA, the fingerprints, the gray hair, the iPhone data, and the James Monroe knife?"

"We did."

"And what did Mr. Cutler say about the physical evidence you'd found at the Horse Center?"

"The president told us that he could not account for any of that evidence," DeLuca declared.

Katherine was finished with the witness, just in time for the mid-afternoon break.

Jane and I met with the client in the witness room to take stock of De-Luca's testimony. Jack looked shell-shocked. "I really did fuck up sitting for that interview."

Exactly, I thought. But in the months since Jack and I had our row about this, I'd amortized most of my anger. "We've got this, Jack," I assured him. "DeLuca is their best witness—he testifies for a living. You've got to figure he'll do a good job. But you're about to see the best lawyer I know in action. Watch Jane take this guy down a few pegs."

I drew Jane aside for a moment. "DeLuca is formidable," I whispered. "Maybe keep the cross short and get him off the stand."

Now it was Jane's turn to assure me. "Ye of little faith, Robert."

We went back into the courtroom, and Jane began her cross.

"Sergeant DeLuca. You've been on the police force for nearly thirty years, correct?"

"That's right."

"And you've probably investigated hundreds of violent crimes, am I right?"

"I have."

"You've seen or heard of cases, am I right, in which someone's fingerprints were found at the scene of a crime, and yet the person had nothing to do with the offense, correct?"

We were confident DeLuca would have to acknowledge the point—such cases are legion.

"That happens, sure," DeLuca agreed.

"And you've also seen many cases in which you might have *expected* to find someone's fingerprints on an object, say a knife like exhibit 2, and yet no such fingerprints were found?"

"That's also true," said DeLuca.

"So the mere fact that you didn't find Ms. Harper's prints on the silver knife doesn't mean she never handled it, correct?"

"Correct, Ms. Cashman."

"Let's talk about DNA now. A person's DNA can end up at a crime scene for reasons having nothing to do with the crime itself. Right, Sergeant?"

"That happens less frequently, but it does happen."

"In fact, Sergeant, you've heard or read about cases in which someone has *planted* another person's fingerprints and DNA at a crime scene."

"As I said, it happens, though rarely." Grudging, but good enough.

"You've certainly seen weapons planted numerous times, have you not?"

"That does happen from time to time."

"And you know, do you not, that persons other than the president had access to the Monroe silverware during the Cutler administration."

"Certainly."

"Such as Mrs. Cutler."

"I assume so."

"And Amanda Harper herself."

"Quite possibly."

Jane looked over at the jury for just a moment. "So I imagine you spent some time investigating both Jessica Cutler and Amanda Harper as persons who might have placed the Monroe knife at the crime scene.

DeLuca paused. A long pause, I thought. "We did not," he said at last.

"Well, at least you asked someone on your staff to check White House logs to see how often Jessica Cutler or Amanda Harper were present when the Monroe cutlery was used, right?"

"No, Ms. Cashman, I didn't." DeLuca was starting to tighten up. Did the jury notice?

"And the reason you didn't take any of these basic steps, Sergeant, is that you'd already made up your mind that Mr. Cutler was guilty."

"Not true."

"And once you'd made up your own mind, why bother to give the jury any other choices, right?"

"We charged the person we thought was guilty, Counselor."

"Is that right, Sergeant? Let's talk about the gray hair. I notice you yourself have curly gray hair. Do you suppose that curly gray hair is common among men and women our age?"

"I expect so."

"I myself have a head full of it, don't I, Sergeant?"

"So it appears, Counselor."

"What percentage of the country has curly gray hair?"

"I have no idea, Ms. Cashman."

"Again, you took no steps to determine that, correct?"

"There was no need to do so."

"Again, that's because you stopped looking when you settled on President Cutler, right?"

"Not true. We didn't consider other persons with gray hair, because none of them fit the remaining evidence we'd uncovered by then."

"But I'm correct, am I not, Sergeant, that you were not able to run a DNA test on the hair strands?"

"That's true. The FBI lab informed us that, without the hair follicles, DNA testing could not be performed."

"So, for example, you don't know whether the gray hair comes from a man or a woman?"

"We did not perform any tests to determine that."

"Do you even know whether such tests exist, Sergeant?"

"I don't, but I assume the FBI performed whatever tests they thought appropriate."

"And as far as you know, none of those tests showed the gender of the person whose hair was found at the scene."

"Correct."

"Sergeant DeLuca, you say that the knife was wedged into the briefcase. I take it that the knife did not actually force open the briefcase?"

"That's correct," DeLuca answered. "The briefcase was locked when we recovered it."

"Did you determine whether the knife *could* have opened the briefcase, had a perpetrator wanted to open it?"

"I suppose it could have."

"So it's a fair inference, Sergeant, that whoever wedged the knife into the case didn't try especially hard to force the briefcase open, is that correct?"

"I can't really speculate."

"In any event, Sergeant, there was no indication that the perpetrator touched any of the memoranda inside the briefcase."

"That's true. The briefcase was locked when we arrived, and we found no fingerprints on the memos other than Ms. Harper's."

"So there's no evidence whatsoever that President Cutler ever touched any of the contents of the briefcase."

"Correct," DeLuca conceded.

"Nor is there any evidence that Mr. Cutler ever saw any of the contents of the briefcase."

"Well, he might have seen one or more of the memos when he was still president."

"But you don't actually know, do you?"

"No, I guess not."

"In fact, sir, you've developed no evidence that President Cutler had the slightest interest in the contents of Ms. Harper's briefcase, correct?"

"None that we know of," DeLuca countered. He was pissed now—anyone could see it.

"Let's talk for a minute about how the victim's body was moved. You've told us, Sergeant, that by moving the body to the park, the perpetrator made it look as if any member of the public could have been the killer."

"Correct."

"Do you suppose that President Cutler is a recognizable figure?"

"Sure."

"And do you suppose that hauling a body across the snow in a very public place like Rock Creek Park increases the odds that someone will catch the perpetrator in the act?"

"Probably."

"Did you interview any of the other people who live in Ms. Harper's building?"

"We did."

"Did any of them see President Cutler in the vicinity of Ms. Harper's apartment on the night of the murder?" We knew from pretrial discovery that DeLuca would have to say no, which he did.

"So let's see if I have this down, Sergeant. A man with one of the most recognizable faces on Earth commits a murder with no eyewitnesses, but then moves the body to a highly public spot, where anyone in the park might have seen him. Are you really going with that, Sergeant?"

Katherine objected, but Jane withdrew the question and tried a new one.

"You know, Sergeant, that Mr. Cutler kept a horse at the barn for years, am I right?"

"That's true."

"And you know that he's been to the Horse Center dozens of times to go riding with his family, correct?"

"Correct."

"And you likewise know that Mr. Cutler has been photographed during some of those outings and questioned by the press at some of those outings and seen by hundreds of members of the public on some of those outings. All of that is also true, is it not?"

"It is, Ms. Cashman."

"So to sum up your theory, Sergeant: Mr. Cutler killed Ms. Harper in her apartment, was seen by no one there, then dragged her to one of the most public locations in D.C. and left her in a spot that he and his family were widely known to use regularly."

The judge finally put DeLuca out of his misery. "You've made your point, Ms. Cashman. Please move on."

"Of course, Your Honor. Sergeant, you also told us that you searched Ms. Harper's apartment, is that correct?"

"It is."

"And you performed a thorough search?"

"We did everything we thought appropriate."

"You went through every room in the apartment?"

"We did."

Jane approached the witness and handed him a copy of a police report of the search.

"Sergeant, do you recognize this document?"

"It's what we call an inventory from a search. It lists every item we examined or seized from the victim's apartment."

"The purpose of this inventory, am I correct, is to have a complete record of the search in case someone asks questions later about what the police did or did not do during the search."

"That's certainly one reason we create the inventory, yes."

"And you and your fellow officers are trained to be as complete and accurate as possible when you prepare the inventory, right?"

"We do our best."

"I notice that the inventory is broken down by individual room, so that we can see what you and your team examined or seized in each room. Am I correct?"

"That's true, Counselor."

"Did Ms. Harper have a bathroom in her apartment?"

DeLuca looked down at the inventory, then back up at Jane. "I'm sure she did," he answered softly.

"Can't you be a little more definitive than that, Sergeant? Didn't Ms. Harper's building have indoor plumbing?"

"I'm sure it did."

"And yet, Sergeant, there is no indication in the inventory that you and your team ever looked in the bathroom."

"That's how it appears."

"Did you direct your team to ignore Ms. Harper's bathroom?"

"Not that I recall."

"Did you have a reason to ignore the bathroom?"

"None that I know of."

"And yet, if this inventory is as complete and accurate as you say it is, you and your team did not search Ms. Harper's bathroom, correct?"

"That's how it looks, Ms. Cashman."

"So you would therefore have no way of knowing whether, for example, Ms. Harper kept narcotics or other controlled substances in her medicine cabinet?"

Katherine started to object to the question as argumentative, but Judge Edgerton motioned to her to stay seated.

"As I said, Ms. Cashman, we appear not to have searched the bathroom. I cannot speculate what Ms. Harper did or did not have in her cabinets."

"Sergeant, the inventory indicates that your officers *did* at least search the bedroom, correct?"

"That's correct."

"And that's where they saw the four-poster bed with the rope markings, right?"

"Right."

"And just so we're all clear, you're not aware of any evidence suggesting that the rope restraints had anything to do with Ms. Harper's death."

"That's correct. The victim was manually strangled."

"And while it may not be our cup of tea, Sergeant, there are a great many people in this country who enjoy *unconventional* sex, let's call it."

Katherine stood to object again, but again Jane moved on. The point was made.

"Let's turn, finally, to your interview with the president. Did you advise the president of his rights before you began the interview?"

"The president was never under arrest, so we had no obligation to do so."

Jane decided to brush the witness back a little.

"So, Sergeant, to be clear, the answer to my last question is 'No, I did not read the president his rights before I began to question him.'"

"That's correct."

"And it's also correct, Sergeant, that before you began the interview with the president, you already knew the answers to most of the questions you planned to ask him."

"That's true, but we still wanted his side of the story."

"Perhaps, Sergeant. But what you were really trying to do that day was to catch the president in a lie. You were hoping for a lie, not a truthful answer, isn't that the case?"

"I don't accept that assertion. We were there to hear whatever the president wanted to tell us. It was his choice to lie to us."

"Is it your testimony, Sergeant DeLuca, that you were not trying to elicit a false statement from the president?"

"That was not our intention," DeLuca insisted.

"Let's test that claim, Sergeant. You told us on direct that you took notes during the interview?"

"Yes. Scrupulously."

"And the reason you took notes of the interview was so that you could record precisely what was said and by whom, correct?"

"That's true."

"And the notes would also reflect, would they not, the *order* in which statements were made during the interview?"

"That's also correct. We are careful to write down every significant portion of the interview in the order in which it takes place. We don't shift things around afterwards, if that's what you're asking, Counselor."

"But that's what interests me, Sergeant." Jane now fixed DeLuca in a hard stare. "I see from your notes that you did not tell Mr. Cutler that his DNA and fingerprints were at the crime scene until *after* you'd asked him whether he had had any physical contact with Amanda Harper, correct?"

"Based on my notes, that appears to be true," DeLuca conceded.

"And the reason you proceeded in that order was that you did not want to alert President Cutler to the physical evidence you had obtained until *after* you'd asked him about his contact with the decedent."

"I can't really agree to that." DeLuca was not going to roll over easily.

"Come on, Sergeant. You asked your questions in the order you did precisely to catch the president with a gotcha question."

"I don't agree." DeLuca was now openly glaring at Jane. At least a couple of jurors nodded at Jane's last question. It was the best she could do with such a skilled witness.

"Nothing further, Your Honor," Jane said.

Katherine Hannigan had a few additional questions she'd saved for redirect.

"Very briefly, Sergeant DeLuca. Ms. Cashman asked you on cross whether you've seen cases in which a person's fingerprints were at a crime scene but that person had nothing to do with the crime. And you admitted that that sometimes happens."

DeLuca was back on friendly turf. He relaxed and sat back in the witness chair.

"Correct," he said.

"You also told Ms. Cashman that, on rare occasions, an innocent person's DNA may be planted at a crime scene."

"Also correct."

"So let me ask you, Sergeant: How many times have you seen someone's fingerprints *and* DNA at a crime scene, along with a knife that only that person and a very few others have access to, as well as gray hair strands that look just like the hair on the head of the same person with the fingerprints, the DNA, and the knife?"

"Only once," said DeLuca, nodding.

"And when was that, Sergeant?"

"This case."

It was nearing four-thirty, and the judge decided to let the jury leave for the day, after giving them his usual caution about avoiding media.

One of the jurors must not have been paying attention.

XXX

D ay 4
   Judge Edgerton was already on the bench when the lawyers arrived this morning. He was holding a piece of paper and scowling like the cover model from *Disappointed Judges Monthly*. "I've marked this as court exhibit 1. It's a note from the foreperson of the jury that reads: 'One of the jurors accidentally saw a television program about the case last night. He's really sorry. We thought we should notify the Court.'"

The judge peered at the lawyers. "Frankly," he continued, "in a case of this notoriety, I'm not surprised that a juror has strayed. But 'accidentally'? I doubt it. Anyway, I will call this juror to the bench, find out what he heard on TV, and see if he told any of that to the others. Make sense?"

Both sides agreed, and the court officer went to the jury room to summon the offending juror. When the culprit entered the courtroom, I breathed a sigh of relief—it was juror 3, Reid Harkmann, one of the government's favorites, holder of a top secret security clearance, a starched white shirt, and a pocket protector. According to the data mining, Harkmann was one of two jurors who'd ordered *Braveheart* on Netflix. I wouldn't mind saying goodbye to him.

The judge began the questioning. "Mr. Harkmann, thank you for reporting what you did. Tell me exactly what happened."

His voice shaking, his eyes darting from one person to the next, Harkmann began. "My daughter was watching a show last night. I've stayed away from the tube all week, like you instructed. I would never disobey a judge's orders, believe me. Anyway—"

"What show was your daughter watching?" the judge interrupted.

"*The MacGregor Solution*. On Smith Universal at ten. I only saw about a minute."

The judge seemed to be familiar with Ryan MacGregor's work. "What did Mr. MacGregor say during the minute you were watching?"

Harkmann paused momentarily. "Mr. MacGregor reported . . . well, he said . . . that President Cutler had lots of affairs when he was in the White House. He claimed that Your Honor kept that evidence from the jury, and that if we knew the whole truth, we'd convict the defendant in five minutes."

Judge Edgerton visibly stiffened as the juror recounted MacGregor's commentary. "Is that the full extent of what you heard on the show last night?"

"That's all," Harkmann assured the judge.

"And is that the only media you've heard or seen about this case since you were sworn in as a juror?"

"Absolutely," Harkmann said, brightening to the prospect that he'd be allowed to remain on the jury.

"Have you told any of your fellow jurors what you heard last night?" the judge asked.

"All I told them is that I accidentally saw a show discussing the case. I didn't mention the content, I swear."

Judge Edgerton turned to the lawyers to see if we had follow-up questions. Katherine began. "Mr. Harkmann, I appreciate your candor. Do you think you can set aside what you heard last night and judge the defendant's guilt or innocence based solely on the evidence presented in this courtroom?"

Harkmann was only too happy to say yes. *Of course* he could remain fair and impartial.

Katherine said she was satisfied with the juror's response and saw no need to replace him. I was about to lodge a legally respectable version of "what utter horseshit" when the judge cut me off. "Mr. Harkmann, you are excused from further service on the jury. Please pick up your things and leave the building without speaking further with any of the other jurors. My security officer will assist you in gathering whatever you brought with you this morning and see that you promptly exit the courthouse."

Juror 3, turning a whiter shade of pale, went back to the jury room with his chaperone, and the judge turned to us. "We need to talk to the remaining jurors to see whether Mr. Harkmann did any further damage. If he didn't, then we'll just replace him with the first alternate and continue the trial."

One by one, the other jurors came to the bench to be interviewed. Turned out, Harkmann had shared only what he'd admitted to sharing. The trial would proceed.

But the judge was not finished with the issue. With the jury out of the courtroom, Judge Edgerton stared at the prosecutors. "I closed the courtroom when you argued the prior affairs motion," he began. "I put all the motion papers under seal. I did that precisely so that a day like today wouldn't happen. Goddamn it, it's hard enough avoiding the press all day long without having to worry that confidential materials are being leaked. Ms. Hannigan, do you have any idea how this garbage got to MacGregor?"

"No, Your Honor, I have no idea. It certainly didn't come from the government."

"Maybe not from your office, Ms. Hannigan, but I wasn't born last night. The state police have been known to poison the well against criminal defendants. I've seen it before. A tough, public case like this one? Wouldn't surprise me if some front-office type in the Barry Building sent this material over to the network. Anyway, I'm directing you to get to the bottom of this leak. And make sure it doesn't happen again. In the meantime, I will give an extra emphatic instruction to the jury about staying away from the media. Maybe when they see what happened to Mr. Harkmann, they'll take my directives more seriously."

The government had three witnesses on tap today: Samir Zaid, the D.C. chief medical examiner; Leslie Harrison, an expert in cellphone technology; and Arlen Mathews, Jack's White House Counsel.

Sam Parker conducted Dr. Zaid's direct.

"Please introduce yourself to the jury, sir."

"My name is Samir Zaid. I'm the D.C. state chief medical examiner."

"How long have you held that position?"

"Since the District of Columbia was admitted as the fifty-first state— so for close to a year now."

"Tell the jury about your educational background, please."

I rose from my chair. "Your Honor, the defense is happy to stipulate that Dr. Zaid is qualified to give the testimony he's been called for." It's often better to stipulate, rather than allow a highly credentialed witness to parade his CV in front of the jury.

But Judge Edgerton let him. "Overruled. The witness may give a brief background."

The witness continued. "I received my BS in molecular biology and biophysics from Princeton, and my MD and PhD in biology from Johns Hopkins."

"Prior to your appointment as D.C. medical examiner, did you have a specialty within the field of medicine?"

"I did. I practiced neonatology for about eighteen years, at Brigham and Women's Hospital in Boston and later at Hopkins in Baltimore."

"And for all of our benefits, what is neonatology?"

"It's the care and treatment of newborn babies."

"In the course of your practice, did you become familiar with paternity testing?"

"I did."

"And what is it?"

"There are actually several different tests, but all of them are used to determine the identity of the father of a child, usually based on DNA matching."

"Have you performed paternity tests in the course of your practice?"

"Hundreds of them."

"Can paternity tests be performed on an unborn child?"

"Yes. Until about two years ago, doctors generally had to wait until the fetus was about nine weeks old before it was safe to perform a paternity test. Since then, important advances in the field have allowed us to test for paternity as early as five weeks into a pregnancy."

"How do doctors test for paternity as early as five weeks?"

"We compare DNA taken from fetal cells in the mother's bloodstream to DNA taken from the alleged father. If the DNA matches, paternity is established."

"I take it, Doctor, that you supervised the autopsy of the victim in this case, Amanda Harper?"

"I did, yes."

"Was Ms. Harper pregnant at the time of her death?"

"She was about six weeks along."

"Did you perform a paternity test in this case, Doctor?"

"I did."

"Tell us what you did."

"As part of the autopsy for Amanda Harper, we extracted a blood sample from the victim and performed a DNA test. Because of the condition of the body, the extraction was difficult and delayed. We then compared the results to DNA contained in the federal DNA database."

"Is that the same database about which Sergeant DeLuca testified yesterday afternoon?"

"It is."

"What was the result?"

"We determined that former president John Sherman Cutler is the father of Ms. Harper's unborn child."

"Thank you, Dr. Zaid. I have nothing further, Your Honor."

I had to make my cross as brief as possible—there was no upside to keeping this witness on the stand a minute longer than necessary. Nor did it make sense to ask what aspects of the condition of the body had delayed the paternity test—that would only give the prosecutors another opportunity to display the grisly crime scene photos.

"Dr. Zaid, you say that Ms. Harper was six weeks pregnant at the time of her death?"

"Yes, about six weeks."

"Before you actually commenced the autopsy, did you have any idea that she was pregnant?"

"You mean just by eyeballing the decedent?"

"Yes, Doctor. Before you performed any medical tests on the body, did you have any idea that Ms. Harper was pregnant?"

"No. At six weeks, most women do not show, especially for their first child. In this case, it was only during the autopsy that we realized that Ms. Harper was pregnant."

"Indeed, there is some chance Ms. Harper herself did not know she was pregnant as of late January last year?"

"It's possible. Of course, she may have known as well. I can only speculate."

"In any event, without a test, even an expert like you was unable to tell that Ms. Harper was pregnant at the time of her death."

"That's right."

"So unless Ms. Harper told President Cutler of her pregnancy—assuming she even knew about it herself—he would have had no idea, isn't that right?"

Sam Parker stood up to object, but too late.

"I suppose so," Dr. Zaid answered.

"And you have no idea whether Amanda Harper said anything to President Cutler about her pregnancy."

"That's correct."

"Nor do you know whether she told anyone else."

"Also correct."

I started to return to the defense table and sit down—then did my best Lieutenant Columbo shtick and turned back to the witness.

"One more question, Doctor. You mentioned that you've been the D.C. medical examiner since D.C. became the fifty-first state."

"That's right."

"Do you recall which president signed the legislation admitting D.C. to the Union?"

This time Parker was quicker to his feet. "Objection. Relevance."

"I'll withdraw the question. Thank you, Doctor. Nothing further."

———

Leslie Harrison, from the IT unit at the DCSPD, was the government's next witness. She was about my age, but heavyset and dour.

Sam Parker again handled the direct for the prosecution. After some background questions, Parker approached the witness.

"Ms. Harrison, I show you government exhibit 43. Do you know what it is?"

"This is the iPhone belonging to Amanda Harper we were asked to examine."

"Did your office examine the phone?"

"We did."

"Please tell the jury what steps you took."

"We first examined the incoming and outgoing calls logged in the phone's memory bank."

"What did you find, Ms. Harrison?"

"One of our findings involved what we call a Burner app. Ms. Harper received roughly three dozen calls within a seven-month period, from June to December of her year in the White House, from one or more persons who were using a Burner app on their iPhones."

"For the benefit of those of us who have never used such an app, what does a Burner app do?"

"It enables a user to create temporary disposable phone numbers on his iPhone or other compatible device. Once a particular number has been used for a call, it can be discarded and never used by the subscriber again. People install Burner apps for different reasons, including to make it harder to determine whether they participated in the phone call."

"Now you testified that Ms. Harper received about three dozen such calls from persons using the Burner app?"

"Correct."

Parker leaned into the next question. "Were you able to determine who was using the Burner app to place those phone calls to Ms. Harper?"

"Following the execution of a search warrant, we determined that all but three of Ms. Harper's calls using a Burner app came from President Cutler's iPhone."

"Were you able to ascertain how long the calls between Ms. Harper and Mr. Cutler lasted?"

"They ranged from ten or twenty seconds to about an hour and a half," Ms. Harrison replied.

"Did Ms. Harper's iPhone also have a Burner app at the time of the three dozen calls?"

"No. She just used her assigned cellphone number."

"So for the phone calls with President Cutler, only he, and not Ms. Harper, was using the app."

"That's right."

"One last line of questions," said Parker. "Did Ms. Harper's phone have a tracking device?"

"It did."

"Tell the jury what a tracking device does."

"It automatically registers and stores the geographic location of the iPhone to the nearest five feet."

"So basically, by looking at the stored information, you can determine exactly where the iPhone was located at any given time?"

"That's correct."

"And hence where the owner of the iPhone was located at any given time?"

"Yes, unless the owner gave the iPhone to someone else. All we can say for sure is where the iPhone itself was located."

"Do you have any reason to believe that the victim in this case gave her iPhone to anyone else in the two years before her death?"

"No."

"Did you examine the tracking data in Ms. Harper's phone?"

"We retrieved most of the data. Not all of it could be extracted, but we examined all the data we could recover."

"Did the data permit you to trace Ms. Harper's movements going back at least eighteen months?"

"Yes. The data we extracted covers the eighteen months ending in late January of last year, when Ms. Harper was killed."

"Did the tracking data record Ms. Harper's presence in Rock Creek Park?"

"No. The last recorded location was the victim's apartment, where the police found the iPhone."

"What did you learn from the data on Ms. Harper's phone, Ms. Harrison?"

"We found that Ms. Harper had been in the Oval Office of the White House at least nine times during the final eight months of the Cutler Administration."

"Were you able to tell how long those Oval Office visits lasted?"

"Several were only about ten or fifteen minutes. But three of those visits, on June 25, June 30, and December 24, lasted more than an hour."

"Do you know who else, if anyone, was present besides Ms. Harper during those Oval Office visits?"

"I don't, no." Several jurors looked over at Jack. Well played, Sam.

Parker passed the witness, and Jane took the cross.

"Ms. Harrison, good afternoon. It's fair to say that you have no idea what Ms. Harper discussed with President Cutler when the two of them spoke on cell."

"That's fair."

"But you do know," Jane continued, "that Ms. Harper was one of the president's lawyers and was handling the White House's response to congressional subpoenas?"

Parker started to make a hearsay objection. Too late, again.

"I believe I heard that secondhand," Harrison confirmed before the judge could rule.

"And it wouldn't surprise you to learn that the president had occasion to talk to lawyers handling important White House business."

"I suppose not."

"And it wouldn't surprise you to learn that the president discussed some of those matters in the Oval Office?"

"I guess not."

"And you have no idea whether there were other persons present when Ms. Harper and the president met in the Oval Office."

"That's true."

"Nor do you have any reason to believe that the police even questioned anyone who may have been present in the Oval Office along with Ms. Harper and the president, correct?"

"Correct."

"And you have no idea, do you, whether the White House routinely keeps records concerning who is present in the Oval Office at any given time?"

"I wasn't asked to look into that, no."

Jane paused, glanced over at the jury, then shifted gears.

"You told Mr. Parker on direct that all but three of the calls to Ms. Harper using a Burner app came from President Cutler's iPhone. I take it that means that three of the calls came from someone else's Burner app, is that correct?"

"Yes," answered Harrison.

"Were you able to determine whose Burner phone made the other three calls?"

"We were. The calls came from a business in Southeast Washington, D.C., called Overdon Pharmacy."

Sam Parker kept a poker face but fidgeted slightly in his seat.

"And those three calls, Ms. Harrison, ranged between about thirty seconds and three minutes long, am I correct?"

Harrison checked her notes. "Yes," she said.

"And am I correct that you have not performed any investigation of that pharmacy?"

"No, we were not asked to do so."

"So you have no idea whether that pharmacy is located anywhere near Ms. Harper's apartment, correct?"

"Correct."

"Nor do you know whether the Overdon Pharmacy provides any services other than ordinary pharmacy business."

"Also correct," Harrison said.

"Nothing further, Your Honor."

Sam Parker had one last question on redirect. "Ms. Harrison, defense counsel asked whether you were aware that Amanda Harper had legal business that would require her to talk to President Cutler. Can you think of a reason why Mr. Cutler would use a Burner app to discuss ordinary legal business with one of his lawyers?"

"No, I can't," Harrison answered.

Ouch.

———

Arlen Mathews was central casting for a White House counsel. He was in his early seventies and stood about six-two, with a shock of white hair that he doubtless paid some D.C. hair stylist a small fortune to cultivate.

Katherine Hannigan handled the brief direct.

"Mr. Mathews, you served as President Cutler's White House counsel during his four years in office?"

"That's correct."

"And you knew the decedent, Amanda Harper?"

"I did," said Mathews. "Amanda joined the White House Counsel's Office in the president's final year in office."

"Can you tell the jury a little about Amanda? What kind of colleague was she?"

The former White House counsel knew the drill. He turned and faced the jury. "Amanda was a superstar, really one of the best and the brightest. She had an amazing work ethic, always one of the first to arrive and the last to leave. She was indefatigable. She had boundless energy and enthusiasm for the work of our office. And she was a great lawyer."

"Did she have a particular specialty within your office?" Katherine asked.

"At the beginning," Mathews answered, "she was a generalist, handling whatever the crisis du jour was. After a few months, because of her judgment and tenacity, I asked her to run what we call our subpoena docket, which means she dealt with all the demands for testimony and documents that came into the office. She also advised me on judicial nominations and some of the other high-profile questions we faced."

"And when you say that Ms. Harper advised you on nominations and other matters, did that include both oral and written advice?"

"It did."

"Were lawyers in the Counsel's Office issued government cellphones for work-related calls and texts?"

"They were. We did not want official business conducted over personal devices. Much of our work is classified, even highly classified."

"So if you needed to call the president on official business, you would do so only on your office cellphone, is that correct?"

"That's correct."

"And if the president needed to call you, did he likewise have a government-issued cellphone for such confidential phone calls?"

"He did."

"Did you have occasion to see the president's cell during your time as White House counsel?"

"I did. It was the same make and model as the ones issued to the lawyers in my office. That's the phone he used every time I saw him make a phone call in the White House."

"Did your office keep records of calls between the president and members of the White House Counsel's Office?"

"We did, yes."

"What kind of information was reflected in those records?"

"The phone numbers of all parties to the call, along with the date and duration of each call."

"So, Mr. Mathews, if the president called you on a given day and the two of you spoke for, say, eighteen minutes, what information would appear in your office's record of that call?"

"The records would show the president's cellphone number, my cellphone number, the date of the call, and the fact that it lasted for eighteen minutes."

"Mr. Mathews, in preparation for your testimony today, did my office ask you to review all the records of your own phone calls with President Cutler?"

"Yes. And I did so."

"Were you able to find Mr. Cutler's cellphone number in the records of the calls you and he had?"

"Yes. For each cellphone call the president had with me during the four years, the same specific cellphone number was reflected in the records. In his case, it was the cellphone number officially assigned to the president."

"So for all the calls you had with the president, for all four years, the records show that he used only that specific phone number, and no others?"

"That's right."

"Do you happen to know what a Burner app is, Mr. Mathews?"

"I think I've heard the term, but I'm not an expert on it."

"I take it, however, that neither you nor anyone in your office used such an app for official White House business."

"That's correct, Ms. Hannigan."

"Nor, to your knowledge, did President Cutler."

"Not that I've ever seen, no. As I said, the records of my calls with the president show that he used only his official cell number."

"And if, for some reason, the president used some *other* phone number when he spoke to you, that different number would appear in your records?"

"That's true."

"And no such different numbers appear in your records of calls with President Cutler?"

"Correct."

"Nothing further, Your Honor."

Katherine had scored some points on direct. She showed that Jack had never used a Burner app for any official calls with the White House counsel. That obviously contrasted with his use of Burner numbers with Amanda. I needed to defuse that testimony, then use Arlen Mathews for some affirmative points of my own.

"Good afternoon, Mr. Mathews. Am I correct that you were not asked to review all the cellphone records between your office and the president—just the calls you yourself made."

"Correct."

"So if the president sometimes used a Burner app for certain sensitive phone calls with other persons in your office, you might well not know about it, correct?"

"Correct."

"Let's change subjects for a moment, sir. When you were White House counsel, about how often did you meet with President Cutler?"

"It varied, but I would say that we met regularly. Depends what was going on."

"Did you conduct some of those meetings with the president in the Oval Office?"

"That's where most of them took place, yes."

"Did the lawyers who worked for you in the Counsel's Office also meet with the president from time to time?"

"They did."

"And most of their meetings were likewise in the Oval, right?"

"That's true."

"You mentioned that Ms. Harper handled what you called the subpoena docket. Was that docket pretty active during the time Ms. Harper had that responsibility?"

"It was very active. We were getting bombarded with document and testimony requests, mostly from the Senate."

"And the president took a personal interest in how your office responded to those requests, correct?"

"He did, yes."

"So it would not surprise you to learn that Ms. Harper met with the president in the Oval Office on numerous occasions during that time?"

"I'm sure she did. That's the only way she could have done her job."

"And just to complete the point, Mr. Mathews, you wouldn't be the least bit surprised to learn that the tracking function on Ms. Harper's phone placed her in the Oval Office on numerous occasions, and often for lengthy periods of time."

"On the contrary, I would expect that."

"Last line of questions, sir. You say you worked closely with Ms. Harper during her tenure in the Counsel's Office, is that correct?"

"I did."

"That was a 24/7 assignment, am I right?"

"Most weeks, yes. We worked every day."

"Did you notice that she was pregnant toward the end of the administration?"

"No," said Mathews. "The first I learned of it was in media accounts after Amanda's death."

"And that's true, even though you saw Ms. Harper just about every day of the week, often multiple times a day?"

"That's right. I never noticed, and she never said anything about it."

"And you saw no indication that the president knew anything about it, either, correct?"

"Correct," Mathews agreed.

"You also say that Ms. Harper had a terrific work ethic?"

"She did."

I decided to take a chance, having no inkling as to how Mathews would answer. "Were there times that Ms. Harper would be absent from the office during the workday?"

Mathews hesitated, then dodged the question. "We don't take attendance at the Counsel's Office."

"I appreciate that, Mr. Mathews. Did you ever try to get in touch with Ms. Harper during the workday and find that you were unable to reach her?"

"That did happen a couple of times. Only on weekends, as I recall."

"Mr. Mathews, did Ms. Harper's absences always fall on Sunday afternoons, by any chance?"

I could see that Mathews was as puzzled by this question as the prosecutors.

"I can't recall if it was a Saturday or Sunday. I just recall that there were a few weekends when I tried to reach Amanda and was unable to do so. But she was always back in the office soon after, with more energy than ever."

"Did you ever ask Ms. Harper where she was when you were unable to reach her?"

"I don't recall doing so, no. Amanda always got her work done, and did it well. That's all I cared about."

"Did you ever ask Ms. Harper what accounted for her bursts of energy when she returned to the office from wherever she'd been?"

"No. I didn't think that was any of my business."

"Nothing further, Your Honor."

That evening, as I was at the office preparing for the next day's witnesses, my ex called. Nan rarely called these days, and never this late at night.

The next twenty minutes are still a blur. I know I drove to the emergency room at Georgetown Hospital. I recall searching my pockets for a Klonopin and discovering that I'd used my last one earlier in the week. And I remember meeting Dr. Suen, the attending physician, who directed Nan and me to a small waiting area just off the ER.

"Josh is out of immediate trouble," Dr. Suen began. "He's pretty heavily sedated. Most of the cuts were superficial, but three of them drew blood from just below his left hand."

"*Most of the cuts,*" I quoted back to the doctor. "How many were there?"

"About a dozen," Dr. Suen reported. "A Good Samaritan found Josh in Rock Creek Park. He'd passed out from blood loss. Josh probably owes that guy his life. Any idea what your son was doing in the park tonight?"

Nan answered. "Rob and I sometimes took Josh riding at the Horse Center nearby. Jack . . . President Cutler has a horse there, and Josh sometimes got to ride her. He may have just been looking for a familiar place. Some safe spot. I assume you've seen Josh's chart."

Dr. Suen nodded. "I saw the diagnosis of schizophrenia, yes. I'm so sorry. But I didn't see any history of self-mutilation in the records. Has this happened before?"

"Not to our knowledge," I said. "Can you tell if this was an actual suicide attempt?"

"It's hard to tell," the doctor replied. "As I said, the bleeding was mainly from surface wounds. But without other episodes to compare, I can't be sure what your son was intending. Is there any family history of self-harm?"

Nan glanced at me sideways.

"My mother was bipolar," I answered, "but I'm not aware of any instances of self-injury."

As I said this, I found myself trying to shield the backs of my own hands. Dr. Suen must have noticed. "I hate to pry, Mr. Jacobson, but I see that you have some calluses on your left hand and some redness on your right knuckles. What can you tell me about them?"

"It's just a nervous tic," I told Suen. "Despite how it looks, the calluses aren't painful. Just a little embarrassing."

"Believe me, Mr. Jacobson, I don't mean to embarrass you. I'm just trying to get as much context as I can for Josh's behavior."

I explained that it was a long-standing nervous tic and a common symptom of situational anxiety, now exacerbated by the little matter of defending the former president of the United States on a murder charge. Dr. Suen knew all about that and did not press further.

"We'll need to keep Josh for a few days to see how he responds to the medication. I've contacted his treating psychiatrist. But you can go in and see him for a few minutes."

Dr. Suen directed Nan and me to a small room three doors down on the left. Josh was strapped to an IV and heavily bandaged. He appeared to be asleep when we entered, but opened his eyes halfway a few moments later. His voice was soft and hoarse.

"Mom, I'm so sorry." Josh didn't even look at me.

"Oh, sweetie, we love you," Nan said. "Just rest. Can we get you something to eat or drink?"

"No thanks," Josh said weakly. "I can barely remember what happened. I know I went to the park. To the barn. Where they keep the horses. After that, it's all a blank."

"Maybe you were looking for something familiar," I ventured. "It's a place we've been to several times."

"How would you know?" Josh asked quizzically, turning to me for the first time. "Who are you?"

I was speechless.

"I don't know this guy," Josh said, louder now. "Tell him to leave, Mom. And call Dad and see if he can come see me."

Jesus, I thought. My little boy doesn't even recognize me. He'd stopped taking my calls, sure, but this was beyond imagining. Who does he think I am?

Josh got even more agitated. "Mom, this guy is scary. Tell him to get out. Now."

I stepped outside and let Nan do the talking for a while. About a half hour later, I came back into the room. After a few minutes, Josh looked over at me wearily and gave me a half-smile. "Dad, hi," he said finally.

My eyes welled with tears of relief. "Hey, Josh. Can Mom and I get you anything?"

Josh shook his head slightly. "I think I want to sleep for a while now. Can you come back later?"

"Of course," Nan said. "We'll be back after you've had some time to rest."

I needed to finish prep for court tomorrow. But I also needed company. En route to the office, I called Jane, who was staying at a nearby hotel during the trial.

Jane met me at the office about fifteen minutes later, and I told her about Josh. "Good god, Robbie, I'm so sorry. We should ask Judge Edgerton to recess the trial for a day or two. No need for heroics. He'll understand."

"Thanks, I'll be fine. Josh is stable, and Nan will take a few days off to stay with him, then bring him home when he's ready."

"How is Nan doing?" Jane asked.

"She's a rock. Always has been. She knows I need to be prepping for tomorrow."

Jane took two glasses from the cabinet in the corner conference room and poured us each a scotch, neat. "Did you have any sense this was coming? Had Josh done anything like this before?"

"No. He'd been taking his meds and seemed fine the last time I saw him before the trial started. He hadn't been speaking to me lately, so maybe I've missed something. But no, he's never hurt himself before."

"Any idea why he was in the park tonight?"

"Not really. Nan thinks he was just looking for a familiar place."

Jane paused a beat or two. "Rob, it must have crossed your mind that Josh knew that Amanda's body was found nearby."

"No, Jane, it didn't, and it still doesn't," I lied.

Jane persisted. "Did you and Josh ever talk about Amanda? Either when she was alive or . . . after?"

A painful memory. "Josh met Amanda once, when the three of us went riding at the Horse Center. Really stupid mistake. I should never have introduced them. The day went badly."

"How so?"

I recounted that unpleasant day. "Josh was sullen. He asked whether Amanda realized how much older than her I was. And he asked if Amanda had ever met Nan."

"Is that the only time Josh met Amanda?"

"Just that once, out at the Horse Center. What are you getting at?"

Jane paused. "Rob, I was sworn to secrecy about this, but maybe I need to break a confidence. Amanda came out to Maryland to see me after she'd been in the Counsel's Office for a few months. One topic led to another. As she was getting ready to head home from the farm, Amanda asked after you. I hadn't seen you in a while but said that you were fine, as far as I knew. She told me that she'd gotten a call from Josh."

"From Josh? He called her at the White House? What for?"

"Amanda said he sounded upset. He kept saying, 'You stole my dad.' Has he said anything like that to you?"

"Not in so many words, but Nan certainly blames me for the breakup. There's no dissuading her, and I imagine she's shared some of her hurt with Josh. What did Amanda say to Josh?"

"I think she tried to calm him down, but he hung up after a minute or two. That's the only time he called her, she told me."

"Did Nan herself ever call Amanda?" I may have sounded a little frantic.

"Not that I know of, Rob. Listen, kids sometimes take sides in these situations."

"Even so, Josh's call must have troubled Amanda enough to make her come out to see you in the first place."

"I suppose so," Jane answered, looking down at the conference table. There was a brief moment of silence. Then Jane looked up at me. "Was Josh ever with you when you went to the White House?"

"Several times. What of it?"

"Did he ever have dinner in the formal dining room?"

"We had Thanksgiving with the Cutlers a year or two ago. Where are you going with this, Jane?"

Another pause. "I think you know, Rob."

I did. And I was pissed. "If you're accusing my son of something, this conversation is over. He would no more kill Amanda than he would kill me or Nan. The topic is off the table." I got up to leave.

"Rob, please hear me out. I am not accusing Josh of anything. But you yourself said that we need to give the jury options. And Josh *is* an option, isn't he? He had motive. He knew the Horse Center."

"It doesn't make any fucking sense. Even if he wanted to kill Amanda—which he didn't—what's his motive to pin it on Jack? And how could he possibly pull it off? It makes no goddamn sense."

"It makes as much sense as any other option. It's a totally plausible decoy for the jury," Jane said.

"We're not doing this, Jane. I won't have Josh used as a prop. Not to mention that this line of defense would make me a witness as well. I'd have to explain my own affair with Amanda and then accuse my son of retribution. We're done here."

"No, Rob, we're not done. You invited me to this dance. You asked for my help. And now I'm giving you some. Josh may very well be as pure and innocent as last January's snowfall, but we don't know that, do we? I certainly don't, and with all due respect, Rob, neither do you. Our job is to get Jack out of this jackpot, and Josh is most definitely an option."

"Not to me, Jane. I just won't go there."

"I understand your concerns," Jane said softly. "In the meantime, go home and take care of yourself. Tomorrow is a big day."

———

I did go home, finally, as Jane had urged. It was late, a good time to sleep, but sleep came slowly. The conversation with Jane continued to haunt me.

Josh had called Amanda at work. "You stole my dad." Was Josh speaking for himself or was he channeling Nan's suspicions? And at the hospital tonight, how could he not have recognized me?

I thought back to our last good day together, Josh and me, that lunch up at Chevy Chase Circle when he told me about his "friend who never leaves." The friend who emerges when Josh is frightened. Was Josh introducing me to his friend that day? If so, why that day?

And why was Josh so convinced that Jack was innocent?

XXXI

Can we go back to the assault on your father?

    What do you want to know?

Tell me more about why you did it.

Like I said, you can only be pushed so far.

You felt that your father pushed you too far?

Not me. Robbie. Our old man was scared of me. I was bigger than he was, and way tougher. He'd never do the shit to me he did to Liddle Robbie. My brother needed me to stick up for him. He always did. Did I tell you about the school photographer?

I don't think so.

You'll love this. There was this one day, Jack and Robbie were high school seniors. Jack was serving his second term as student government president and basically running the school. BMOC, right? And Robbie was dating Jess at the time.

Briar apparently had "study halls" in those years. As Robbie told it, couples whose free periods coincided sometimes used that forty-five-minute block to find some cozy nook for makeout sessions. Thursday, fifth period, I recall, was Robbie's time to "study" with Jess. Jack got it into his head that Robbie's romantic interlude would make a nice front-page photo for the *Briar Brigade,* their school newspaper. So he tipped off the arts editor to where she might find them. And there they were, half-naked! The paper got an exclusive. Never did get published, but the photos were pretty widely shared. Everyone at Briar got a good, long look, I'm told.

That must have been mortifying for Robbie.

No shit. Robbie told me all about it when he came. He was freaked out but wouldn't do squat about it. "How long do you plan to be Jack's butt boy?" I asked him. "What's it gonna take before you see him for the bully he is? And why are you so fucking needy?"

Robbie had no answer, but I did. Without saying a word to my brother, I staked Jack out one day after school. "This one's for the study hall photo," I told him as I doubled him over with a swift shot to his midsection. He glared at me for a moment, and I have to hand it to him, he recovered and gripped my neck. Strong hands, I remember thinking. Lacrosse player's hands. But I was no slouch. I hit Jack twice in succession, the first shot breaking his grip on my neck, the second knocking him to the ground.

Just then, one of the phys ed teachers came running over and broke things up. Too bad. I had plenty left in the tank.

What happened after that? How did Jack react?

I got out of there. But Jack yelled at Robbie about it at school the next day. Robbie told me about it.

What did Jack say to Robbie?

He actually blamed Robbie for the fight, can you believe it, that smug a-hole. Jack couldn't see that I didn't need a written invitation from Robbie to stick up for my brother.

Let's get back to the night you beat your dad. How did it happen?

It was a night like any other. He was coming home from work, took the same subway at the same time every night. The D train at Atlantic Avenue. A few blocks from the hardware store. I waited in the alley. And just when the coast was clear, along comes Nathan. Batter up.

Did he see it was you?

Fucking right he did. After the first swing, I told him what the beating was for. "One for the buckle, two for the shoe, three for cigar burns, this one's for you. Asshole."

Did you ever tell Robbie about the assault?

Of course not.

Why not?

He would have freaked, just freaked. Evie had sent him out to talk to the cops. To try to find out if there were any suspects. Robbie is always so fucking helpful. Always the good boy. All the while, it was big brother who got the job done.

You told me once before that the level of abuse went way down after the assault. Why is that?

Why? Because I killed the bastard, obviously.

XXXII

D ^ay 5
It was hair day at the Cutler trial.

We knew from discovery that the prosecution planned to call an FBI analyst to testify about the gray hairs recovered at the crime scene. Charles Ehrlich, the bureau's chief forensics officer, was expected to tell the jury that the strands matched the color and texture of hair taken under subpoena from Jack.

I'd brought my own expert to court today to listen to Ehrlich's testimony. Ordinarily, judges keep witnesses out of the courtroom while other witnesses are testifying. But experts are different, since their job is to rebut what the opposing expert is saying. So I asked Diana Beardsley, a retired FBI expert on hair and fibers, to come listen to Ehrlich.

The government began its examination as expected. Sam Parker quickly established that the gray hairs found on Amanda's body had the same shape, coloring, and texture as Jack's. The prosecutor showed some blowups of the recovered hair strands and the hairs taken from Jack. To the untrained eye, the hairs looked pretty similar. Even to me.

But Parker then approached the witness and handed him a forensics report I'd never seen before.

"Mr. Ehrlich," Parker began, "did you perform any additional tests on the hairs recovered from Ms. Harper's body?"

"Yes," said Ehrlich. "I used comparative microscopy testing to see how the recovered hairs compared to a sample of President Cutler's head hair."

I shot to my feet and asked for a sidebar with the Court. Judge Edgerton excused the jury.

"Your Honor," I began, "this is the first we're hearing of microscopy testing. There's not even a hint about it in the government's pretrial disclosures. I object to this line of testimony."

Sam Parker gave it the old college try. He explained that the FBI had only recently conducted the extra testing, and thus the government's previous disclosures to the defense were not technically inaccurate.

But Judge Edgerton wasn't buying it.

"This is completely unacceptable," His Honor growled. "I won't preclude the evidence because it does appear to be probative. But there is no excuse for this late hit, Mr. Parker, no excuse at all. So if defense counsel needs some extra time before cross-examining the witness or wants the chance to find a rebuttal expert, I will certainly agree."

Unbeknownst to the prosecutors, I was perfectly happy with where things stood. Ehrlich was the government's final witness, which meant that I could call my own expert right after Ehrlich finished and the prosecution rested. "Your Honor," I said, "I think we're ready to proceed with our cross-examination today."

The jury returned, and Parker continued.

"Mr. Ehrlich, before the break you mentioned that the FBI lab performed something you called comparative microscopy testing. Could you briefly explain to the jury what that is?"

"We use a device known as a light comparison microscope to compare the separate hair strands and observe their major physical characteristics. The lab examines a questioned sample and a known sample. The questioned sample consists of the hairs found at the crime scene. They're called *questioned* because we are trying to determine who they belong to. The known sample is taken from a known suspect, in this case President Cutler. We place both samples on the platform of a high-powered microscope, which magnifies the samples from forty times to four hundred times."

"Mr. Ehrlich, please tell us how you selected which of Mr. Cutler's hairs to use for your comparison."

"Sure," said the government's expert. "So when you're comparing head hairs, you need to randomly select at least thirty to forty separate hairs from the suspect because people actually have different kinds of hair on their head, with differing characteristics. You want to be able to control for those variations by randomly selecting a large enough sample."

"What's the next step, sir?"

"You first try to identify *differences* between the two samples. If you find sufficient differences, you can be reasonably confident that the questioned and known hairs come from different people."

"What did you learn when you took that first step in this case, Mr. Ehrlich?"

"I found that there were not sufficient differences, and therefore the questioned hairs could well have come from Mr. Cutler."

"You say 'could well have come,' sir. I take it that is different from proof beyond a reasonable doubt."

"That's true. This kind of analysis can tell you only whether the questioned and known hair samples are associated with each other."

"Did you take any further steps to compare the two sets of hair strands?"

"Well, we had only the cuticles and not the roots of the hair. The cuticle is the part of the strand that sticks out from the scalp—basically, the hair you see when you look at yourself or other people. Unfortunately, you need a hair root, a follicle, to conduct DNA testing. If we'd been able to look at DNA, I could have given you a more definitive opinion. But our lab did compare the cuticles for thickness, pigment presence, and diameter. We found the same basic features in both sets of hair strands."

"Which in layman's terms means what?" Parker asked.

"It means that there is an association between the questioned hair and the hair we took from President Cutler."

"Anything else, Mr. Ehrlich?"

"We looked at one more data point. Both the questioned hair and the hair we took from the president showed the presence of hair dye, apparently a common hair coloring used to darken graying hair."

I tried not to glance over at Jack. He couldn't have been pleased that the whole world now knew his Clairol secret.

"Don't a great many people use hair dye, Mr. Ehrlich?" Parker continued.

"They do. But we also knew another important detail. According to the records taken from the White House Cosmetology Room—that's where the president and his family got their hair cut when they were in the White House—Mr. Cutler got a haircut, a shave, and a hair dyeing around the first of every month when he was in residence."

"Please tell the members of the jury why that is important."

"Each day, normal hair grows a little. As the hair grows, the new hair growth won't yet be dyed and will therefore contain its natural color. At the same time, the *dyed* portion of the hair strand will move farther from the scalp as the hair lengthens. When you cut the strand, you can actually see what we call a line of demarcation between the natural hair color and the dyed hair."

"What, if anything, did you do with this information, sir?"

"We knew that the questioned hair was likely left on Ms. Harper's body toward the end of the month, when she was killed. At that point, there was a measurable amount of natural hair color and dyed color in the strands, separated by a line of demarcation toward the top of the hair sample. We therefore waited until the last week of the month to take a sample from President Cutler. When we compared the lines of demarcation, they fell in approximately the same place. Which meant that the hair found on Ms. Harper's body had been dyed about the same time of the month as Mr. Cutler usually got his hair dyed."

"Based on your analysis, Mr. Ehrlich, do you have a professional opinion about the hairs recovered from the victim and the samples taken from the defendant?"

"I do. There is a strong association between the president's hair and the hair found at the scene of the crime."

"And just so the jury is clear, you cannot say with absolute certainty that the hairs come from the same person?"

"No. Without DNA, we can't be completely sure. And as I said, DNA testing was impossible here because the strands were detached from their roots. All we can say is that the evidence is consistent with the rest of the government's proof in this case."

The judge called for the midmorning break. During the break, our expert assured me that she was ready to testify after I finished my cross of Ehrlich. Jack looked over at me. I shot him a glance that said *I've got this.*

I began, as always, by planting a few seeds. Ehrlich admitted that the hair similarities he observed could have been entirely coincidental.

He also could not say what percentage of the entire population had the same hair characteristics as the samples taken from Amanda's body. To set things up for my own expert's testimony, I closed the cross with this exchange:

"Mr. Ehrlich, did you perform any tests on the hair samples *other* than the microscopy comparison you've described?"

"I did not."

"Did you take hair samples from anyone other than President Cutler?"

"No."

"So is it fair to say, Mr. Ehrlich, that as you sit here today, you can't tell the jury whether anyone else—say, some drug dealer in Rock Creek or any other person—may have the same hair characteristics as the hair recovered at the crime scene?"

"I cannot, that's true."

"And the hair dye you found in the questioned samples—were you able to determine the specific type of dye?"

"Not a specific brand, no. We weren't able to extract any of the dye to perform an analysis."

"All you can say is that it was some kind of dye that darkens gray hair?"

"Correct."

"A kind of dye used by millions of Americans?"

"I suppose so."

"In fact, you can't even say whether this dye is more commonly used by men than by women."

"That's true, unfortunately."

"Do you happen to know, Mr. Ehrlich, how many Americans get their hair dyed and cut around the same time of the month as whoever it was whose hair was found at the crime scene?"

"I have no idea," Ehrlich admitted.

"You haven't even looked at that question, have you?" I almost spat out the query.

"No one asked me to," said Ehrlich defensively.

"That's all I've got, Your Honor."

As expected, the government rested its case. Judge Edgerton asked me whether the defense wished to proceed.

"We do, Your Honor," I said. "The defense calls Professor Diana Beardsley to the stand."

Parker had not expected the defense to have an expert ready to go—you could hear him barking orders to one of his paralegals to try to find something online about Diana. I smiled to myself—good luck with that, guys.

"Ms. Beardsley, would you kindly walk the jury through your background?"

"Of course. I have a BS in molecular biology from Brown University and a master's of science in forensics from George Washington University. I currently teach two classes in forensic biology at GW. I've also published numerous papers in peer-reviewed journals on forensic techniques and have written a chapter on hair and fingernail analysis for the leading textbook in the field, *Forensics in Criminal Cases*."

"Thank you, Ms. Beardsley. Moving to this particular case, were you engaged by President Cutler's defense to provide expert testimony?"

"I was asked to address the hair-related testimony of Mr. Charles Ehrlich."

"And in that connection, did you consider something called mitochondrial DNA?" Parker was furiously scribbling notes. *That's m-i-t-o-c-h-o-n-etc.,* I imagined whispering to him.

"I did. Mitochondrial DNA, usually abbreviated as mtDNA, is a form of DNA located in mitochondria, tiny cells that convert chemical energy from food into a form that cells can use. In sexual reproduction, mtDNA is normally inherited only from the mother."

I looked over at the jury in feigned confusion, which surely a few jurors were actually feeling.

"For us laymen, can you explain that a little?"

"Sure," said Beardsley. "It means that this form of DNA coding is passed down only from mothers, not fathers. The mothers pass it to their children, whether sons or daughters, but only the daughters can pass it to the next generation."

"Professor Beardsley, how is mtDNA different from the DNA that most of us have heard of?"

"Ordinary DNA is found in the nucleus of the cell, whereas mtDNA is found only in the mitochondria of the cell."

"How does any of this relate to human hair?"

As we had prepped, Diana turned to the jury and put on her teacher's cap.

"Like Mr. Ehrlich explained, a strand of human hair that is lacking a root or follicle cannot be tested for ordinary DNA. But what Mr. Ehrlich did *not* mention is that a hair strand *can* be tested for mtDNA."

"Is mtDNA from hair strands sometimes used to tell whether a person in one generation is related to a person in another generation?"

"Yes," Beardsley explained. "It's commonly used for that purpose. In one very famous case from 1995, researchers went to the family gravesite of Jesse James in Kearney, Missouri. They took hair samples and four remaining teeth from what they hypothesized to be Jesse's remains and examined their mtDNA. They also located two descendants of Jesse James's sister Susan. Since Jesse and Susan had the same parents, their mtDNA would be a match. So the researchers took mtDNA from Susan's great-grandson and great-great-grandson, both of whom would have the same mtDNA as Susan and Jesse. Based on mtDNA testing, they were able to establish that the remains taken from the gravesites did indeed belong to Jesse James."

"Now you mentioned that mtDNA is passed down only on the maternal side, correct?"

"Correct," said Beardsley.

"Did you use that information to perform any investigation in this case?"

"Yes. I performed an mtDNA analysis of the hair strands recovered from Ms. Harper's body. Once I obtained the mtDNA profile, I tried to find a match on the available databases. It turned out that President Cutler's daughter, Gretchen, had taken mtDNA tests when she was being treated for childhood leukemia. I obtained those records. They were a match for the hair found at the crime scene."

"What did that tell you, Ms. Beardsley?"

"It meant that the hair strands found on the victim's body belonged either to Gretchen Cutler or to someone maternally related to Gretchen."

"Like her mother, Jessica Cutler?"

"I am unaware of any other candidates."

"So to sum up, the hair found on Amanda Harper's body and clothing does *not* belong to President Cutler?"

"It doesn't."

"It belongs either to his daughter, Gretchen, or to his wife, Jessica, correct?"

"Correct."

"Nothing further, Your Honor."

As Diana left the stand, I glanced quickly at Jess. She did not look happy.

It was Friday night of the first week of trial, and Jack proposed getting together for drinks. But my brother, Evan, had been on my mind during the past few stressful days, and this seemed like my best chance to see him. I gave him a call, suggested that we meet at my place for dinner, and ordered some takeout.

———————

Just an hour later, we're sitting together in my living room, and I'm pouring a pair of sixteen-year-old single malts. By now I've gotten most of the bile out of my system. Evan had deserted the family—he'd deserted me—but maybe it's time to let bygones, etc. And there is still so much I haven't learned about his last thirty-plus years.

"So, Evan, insurance. Not what I would have predicted for an ex–Golden Glover."

"I sorta fell into it, Robbie. Let's face it, I was not cut out for law school. Mom was right about one thing—I barely made it through high school. Insurance mostly takes people skills. That I can do."

"Start at the beginning—where did you go when you left us?"

Evan tells the saga of his years away but begins to look uncomfortable. "I know I let you down, Rob, but I had to get the fuck out. I wanted to get as far away from Brooklyn as someone without a passport could get. So I bought a cheap car, fixed it up, drove out west. Settled in Sacramento and looked for work. Insurance was, like, my fifth or sixth try, after the first few jobs petered out."

I know from our drinks at the Mayflower that Evan had never married or had kids. "Ever come close to something permanent? Any serious relationships?"

"One or two probably count as serious," Evan says. "None of them ever really clicked. How about you and Nan? What happened there?"

"Nothing in particular. We just grew distant after a while."

"C'mon, Robert. There's always something more."

"That's the truth. Though Nan might disagree."

"What would Nan say, Robbie?"

"She blamed Amanda, and she blamed me. Said I just tuned her out."

"You do forget things, Robbie, admit it. I'm the same way. Big gaps in my memory I can't recover."

I have to concede the point. "Runs in the family, I guess. Mom, too, right?"

"For sure. So tell me more about Amanda—how did you first meet her?"

I fill my brother in on the law firm, the pain-doctor trial, how things ended. How confused I am by all of it.

"Sounds like there was something to Nan's suspicions."

"Not really, no. Nan and I were drifting toward a breakup before I ever met Amanda. I suppose the affair hastened the inevitable. But it was still inevitable."

"And Josh? You mentioned he has psychiatric issues. How serious?"

"Very. He seems to have gotten the Jacobson family curse. What Mom had, and then some."

"I wouldn't wish Mom's shit on anyone, Liddle Man. I hope he's being treated for it."

"He's got great care, though there's only so much the doctors can do. Nan and I work together well, and it's been pretty amicable. But Josh's condition is serious. And incurable." I tell Evan about the suicide attempt and report that Josh is recovering slowly from his injuries.

"I'm so sorry to hear that, Rob. Our parents' legacy, obviously."

"Yeah. I'm sure of it. But you seem to have landed on your feet. How did you manage that, Evan?"

"I've got my own battle scars. It was no picnic being the dumb older brother to a superachiever like you. Did you know that Nathan and Evie took me for testing to see if I was *slow,* as Dad used to say in those days? They thought about sending me to trade school, instead of the local public school. Did wonders for my self-esteem."

"Jeez, I never heard that, Evan. That had to suck."

"Nah, it takes more than that to sink a battleship. Fuck the both of them. And that wasn't even the worst of it. Remember Evie's disappearing act?"

I have no idea what Evan is talking about.

"Really, Rob? How did you miss it? You and I would sit with Mom, both of us trying to get her attention. And she just focused on you. The smart son. The son who was college material. And when she was really manic or just fucking nasty, she would deny I even existed. She just disappeared me. You gotta remember, Robbie. How could you have missed that priceless moment of parental affection?"

I have no memory of that but don't want to admit it. "Jesus, Evan, it does ring a bell. Maybe I blocked some of it out. I guess I figured that since I'd cornered the market on Dad's belt buckle, maybe you were doing okay. I'm sorry I didn't speak up for you."

"Forget it, Rob. Listen, you were taking the real blows for both of us. Compared to you, I got off easy. I'm not sure I could ever have survived one of Nathan's hot dogs."

I must have looked puzzled.

"Holy Christ, Robbie, have you had electric shock? Is your memory really that fucking bad? Nathan's hot dogs. That's what the old man called his nasty cigars, after he'd smoked them about halfway to the tip. When he got good and pissed at Mom, he'd call you over when the hot dog was ready, then flick the ashes on the back of your hand. You'd run upstairs screaming and run the cold water over the burn. Then you'd start biting and sucking the redness until the pain passed. How the hell can you not recall that? It must have happened at least three times until I finally clocked the bastard."

Again, I have no memory of any of that. How does Evan remember all this shit?

We sit silently for a few minutes, and I pour a couple more scotches.

Evan then asks, "So why did you sit shiva for them when they passed? Are you still religious?"

"Not really, no. I guess I did it because that's what Jews do."

"Well, not this Jew, Robert. I never looked back after the day I left."

"I know. I missed you. You took such good care of me when we were kids."

Evan looks pained. "Did I? I didn't take the belt buckles for you. I didn't take the cigar ashes. I wasn't even around most of the time. How did I really 'care' for you all those years, Robbie? I didn't do shit."

"You did what you could with what you knew. You stuck up for me with Jack, that's for sure."

"And fat lot of good that's done, Rob. Here you are, still cleaning up that bastard's mess. That's what really puzzles me. Why are you still carrying water for His Eminence?"

The big question. "The truth is, Evan, I'm doing this trial for me, not for Jack. It's the case of a lifetime, right? What lawyer could possibly turn it down?"

"I get that. But from what you said at the Mayflower, I think you're still carrying a torch for Amanda. What if the asshole is guilty? How do you really know he isn't the killer? Or maybe you even know that he is, and you're still willing to defend him."

"Evan, you know I can't get into stuff Jack has told me. But I have a hard time believing that Jack is capable of murder."

"C'mon, Rob, people are capable of all kinds of shit. Didn't Jack nearly kill his old man? Spiked him in the face at a lacrosse match and damn near knocked him through the bleachers? Remember telling me about that?"

"Yeah. But that was so many years ago. And Sherm had it coming that day."

"And then there's our little battle with el presidente in the Case of the School Photographer."

"That was nothing, Evan."

"Nothing? You came home crying your eyes out. Boo-hoo-hoo. That's why I had to go sort Jack out a little, remember?"

"That was your battle, not mine."

"Yet Jack blamed you for the fight, Robbie, correct? Not me, you. And how about the way your client has treated Jess? All those affairs, all those years. Don't tell me you've lost that lovin' feeling for Jess?"

"It's a long road from infidelity to murder, Evan. That's why the judge kept all that evidence from the jury."

"Sure, Robbie. But how about the rope burns on Amanda? Does your client beat up women? Did he beat up Jess like that, too? Inquiring minds want to know."

How could Evan know about the spousal abuse? It had to be a guess. "I can't get into any of this, Evan."

Evan is quiet for a few seconds. "I know. That's why I took care of it myself," he says, looking down as he swirls the last drops of whiskey in his glass.

"What are you talking about?"

"I'm talking about you being Jack's butt boy. Tidying up his messes. Feeding him his lines. Finding him his *women*, for chrissake. I could not bear it any longer. I feel your pain, Robbie."

Huh? "Evan, what are you talking about?"

"Jack does not deserve you. He has no fucking right to your help. But you'd never come to that conclusion on your own. So I gave the situation a little shove, that's all."

"What kind of shove?"

"I called the prosecutors and mentioned your fling with the victim."

"I'm sorry, you did *what*?"

"I called that Hannigan lady and told her about you and Amanda. Told her you had a conflict."

"Goddamn it, Evan, you are fucking kidding me! Why the hell did you do that? You nearly got my ass kicked off the case."

"That was the plan, Liddle Man."

"What plan, what fucking plan?"

"I get you kicked off the case, Jack has to find a new lawyer. Someone without your skill set. Some second-stringer who will probably get your buddy convicted. Which is exactly what His Eminence deserves."

Count to ten, Robbie. "How could you, goddamn it? I *confided* in you when we met at the Mayflower. That was a confidence between two brothers, for god's sake. You went to *the government* with that?"

"I did, and I'd fucking do it again, dipshit. I can't watch you go down on your knees for that asshole anymore. It should have worked—you've got no business defending this case. This guy probably killed Amanda, for chrissake."

"Don't 'chrissake' me, shithead. You almost cost me the case of my life."

"On behalf of a client who cost you the love of your life."

We sit in silence for a minute or two.

"Can we please change the topic, Robbie? Let's talk about your cooking skills. Or something else. What do you say?"

Just then my cell rings.

"Evan, sorry, it's Jack. I have to go see him."

"Off you go, Liddle Man. Cleanup in aisle 8."

Jack sounded pissed on the phone, and in retrospect I could see why. From a purely legal perspective, we'd had a good day in court, torching the government's hair fiber case and pointing to an alternative culprit—Jack's wife. But Jack was not in a "purely legal perspective" frame of mind. No, indeed. When I got to his townhouse, Jack was sitting at the kitchen table in an

NYU T-shirt and shorts, nursing a three-quarters-empty Grey Goose. He sat silent for a minute or so, then looked up at me with bloodshot eyes.

"Was I speaking in tongues, Robbie? Was I unclear?"

Here it comes, I thought.

"Are you proud of yourself? Feeling your oats, Counselor?"

"I thought we had a pretty good day, yes," I said. "What's on your mind, Jack?"

"I could have sworn, I could have SWORN, that I gave you a direct fucking order. I told you not to point a finger at Jess. Wasn't I sufficiently clear about that when you and Jane pitched that idea?"

I was annoyed and probably came off as defensive. "Jane and I have a job to do, Jack. We were just showing the jury that Amanda could have been killed in other ways, by other people. Options the cops never considered. We didn't accuse Jess of anything."

"The hell you didn't. This is my wife, Robert. You know, Jessica? The woman you've had a hard-on for all these years? 'Imagine my surprise,' as you like to say, Robbie boy, when I learned in court—*in court,* for chrissake—that you were gonna prove that my own wife's hair was on Amanda's body. I would *never* have authorized you to do that. I *didn't* authorize you to do that. Jess has paid a high enough price for my, my *thing* with Amanda."

"And that's exactly why it was better to beg forgiveness than to ask permission. If I'd asked you in advance, you'd have said no, just like you did before. Jack, this is a tough enough case without tying both hands behind my back."

"I don't buy it, Counselor." Jack was bellowing now. "Maybe you're just trying to win Jess back, asshole! Maybe this is more payback for some high school prank. Another shot to my midsection, Robbie?"

I needed to lower the temperature. "Jack," I said slowly, "I'm in your corner. Always have been."

Jack sat for a minute, then softened his voice. "I know, Robbie. I know." He paused for another beat. "You don't seriously think Jessica could have done this? And framed me for it? It's just not possible, Rob, is it?"

I had no idea. It had occurred to me that placing Jess's hair at the crime scene would be a good way for Jack to deflect from his own guilt. Or he could have left the hair there unwittingly, maybe during his last tryst at Amanda's place.

"Look, Jack, there are all kinds of explanations here. We're just trying to give the jury some reasonable doubt. Here's all I really know: giving the jury some alternatives is the only way to get you out of this jackpot."

"I will need to mend fences with Jess. After all I've done? I can't have her thinking that I authorized you to put her in harm's way. Shit, I haven't even confirmed the affair to her."

"Come on, Jack, she's heard about the affair a million times already. The press. The government's witnesses. This is old news."

"But she hasn't heard it *from me*. I still have to have that conversation, about the kink. About the pregnancy. And the kids, my poor kids. What have I done, Rob?"

"Jack, let's have some coffee and prepare a little for next week. Jess will get past all of this, I'm sure. And the kids will forgive you."

But what did I know? My own son hadn't forgiven *me*.

XXXIII

S aturday morning

I stopped by the hospital midmorning to check on Josh. He was sleeping when I arrived, and Nan was at his bedside reading the *Post*. The two of us went for coffee while Josh rested.

Even on our best days together, Nan can be frosty, and this was not one of our best days. My ex hadn't slept much since Thursday. Her auburn hair was a tangle, sprouting from under a gray stocking cap, and she'd wrapped a dark woolen scarf around her neck and narrow shoulders. Nan fixed me with a thousand-yard stare.

Here goes nothing, I thought.

"Have you been able to talk to Josh this morning?" I asked.

"Just for a few minutes. He's been in and out of sleep most of the morning. The doctors say that he's likely to stay this way until the meds taper off."

"What's Josh on now?"

"They've switched cocktails," Nan said, barely looking at me. "Mixed and matched some of his antidepressants. Something to help him sleep and remain stable."

"Have the doctors said anything about how long Josh will stay here?"

"Not yet. I guess they're watching and waiting at this point."

"Is he eating much?"

"Some Jell-O. A little fruit juice. Intravenous fluids, mostly."

"Has Josh said anything to you about Thursday? Like what he was thinking at the time?"

"Not really," Nan said. "I don't think he's ready to discuss any of that. He keeps apologizing. As if he did this to us, not to himself."

A few seconds of silence. Then: "Nan, did you ever see this coming? Did Josh ever talk about hurting himself?"

Nan's eyes flashed. "You mean why didn't I stop him from doing this? Don't make this about me, Robert." She was speaking in one of those hushed voices that sound like a full-on marching band. "Please don't tell me this is my fault."

"Nan, I'm not saying you should have prevented this. I'm just asking if it's as shocking to you as it is to me."

"I'm sure it's shocking to you, Robert, because you hardly ever see him. You'd probably be shocked to discover that Josh has friends. Would it shock you to learn that he's been dating a girl from the neighborhood? Have you even *talked* to Josh since the trial started? He reads every single story about the trial, he brags to everyone he meets—total strangers, for goodness' sake—about his dad, his famous lawyer dad, the president's defense counsel. Did you know any of that, Robert?"

I was beaming inside, I'll admit it, but figured a hurt look would better suit the moment. "No, I didn't. How could I? He refuses to take my calls, and you know that."

"Do you blame him? This trial has taken every moment of your time. Even before that, you always had your nose buried in your work.

Jack this, Jack that. I say Jackshit, Robbie, and I bet Josh sees it the same way."

The truth hurt. But I was in full battle mode at this point. "You know perfectly well why he's stopped talking to me."

"Do I? I suppose that's also my fault, right? It couldn't possibly just be your preoccupation with Jack's case, could it? It couldn't possibly be your fixation on your *career.*"

"I suppose it's a combination of things, Nan. But it can't help matters that you're forever blaming me for bailing on our marriage."

"That's ridiculous, Robert. You *did* bail on *us*. You just shut down. Either you were at the office or in court or with your buddy Jack or somewhere in the ether. Josh and I were just appointments you had to keep between client visits."

Down the rabbit hole again.

Nan was not finished. "You didn't hear us. You were never listening. Like that Chinese dinner. You didn't say a word to our son all night. It was his *birthday,* and yet you couldn't be bothered to say a word to Josh. Not a single word."

That same old bullshit. False and pointless.

"Nan, we've been through this countless times. Please."

"Not to mention your little office dalliance."

Amanda. I really didn't need another chorus of Amanda. "Nan, how many times are we going to have the same goddamn conversation? You and I were over long before Amanda came along. Long before. We were living apart under one roof. So blame me all you want—I probably deserve it. But Amanda doesn't—didn't. None of this was her fault."

"She didn't help matters. She didn't help at all, Rob."

"Did you know that Josh called Amanda at the White House?"

Nan paused. "He called her?"

"I figured you knew, Nan. I figured you put him up to it."

"That's ridiculous. What did Josh say to her?"

"He told Amanda she'd stolen his dad from the family."

"I don't believe it. You get that story from her?"

"No, I got it from Jane, who got it from Amanda. I'm sure it happened just that way. And what I'd like to know is where Josh came up with the notion that Amanda caused our breakup."

"Well, he didn't need to hear that from me, if that's what you're imply-ing, Robert. He could see it for himself. Firsthand."

This was not going to end well. "Nan, that isn't true. We've been over and over this. Amanda is simply not the reason you and I split up."

"Nothing is ever *the* reason, Robert. There's never just one reason. But she made it easier for you to do what you obviously wanted to do anyway."

A sudden thought came to mind, then darted quickly out of reach. Nan fiddled with her coffee cup for a moment.

"Nan, did you ever call Amanda yourself?" I asked, perhaps a bit more sharply than I had intended.

"Never. And don't use that lawyer's tone with me, Rob. It doesn't scare me anymore."

"Did you communicate with Amanda in any way?" *Keep your voice down, Robbie.* A couple of other families in the cafeteria glanced over at us, while pretending not to hear.

"Stop it, Rob. I'm not here to be cross-examined, so don't talk to me like I'm some fucking witness. I'm going back in to see our son. Do me a favor—come back this afternoon, after I've left for the day. I'll tell Josh you were here."

"I'll go tell him myself, just for a couple of minutes." I got up to leave. "You can go see him after I'm gone."

XXXIV

Day 6, morning session

"Your Honor, the defense calls Dr. Sasha Casey."

Dr. Casey was the William Joseph Bratton Professor of Forensic Science at John Jay University in New York, a chair endowed in the name of a former New York City police commissioner. She had spent twenty-plus years as a CSI analyst with the NYPD and had been teaching forensics since her retirement six years ago. She also did consulting for the Innocence Project, a dedicated group of lawyers and scientists who exonerate wrongly accused prisoners, some on death row. This was the heart of Jane's direct examination:

"Professor Casey, there is evidence that fingerprints and DNA belonging to President Cutler were found on the victim's clothing and on her body. In your professional opinion, does that mean that the president actually touched Ms. Harper at or around the time of her death?"

"Not necessarily," said Casey.

"Can you explain, please?"

"First off, fingerprints can remain on a surface for an extended length of time. I examined the fingerprints in question, and their clarity was only fair at best. That suggests that the prints may have been left quite some time earlier. In general, estimates of the age of latent prints—and by *latent*, I mean prints that you need to dust or expose to a light source to perceive—are highly unreliable."

"Does the surface on which the prints are found make a difference in determining age, Professor?"

"Absolutely," Casey answered. "Take clothing, for example. Clothing has what we call a nonporous surface. A print left on clothing may remain there for a long time, unless the clothes are washed. And even after a washing, the print may remain detectable."

"So I take it, Professor Casey, that means that Mr. Cutler's fingerprints may have been placed on Ms. Harper's body and clothing some time before the killing, is that correct?"

"That's correct."

"Is it possible to plant someone's fingerprints at a crime scene?"

"It probably doesn't happen often, but it's not hard to accomplish. I wrote up the basic technique years ago in a journal. Suppose you have a glass surface bearing someone's fingerprints. Even a child could take a paintbrush, dip it into cocoa powder, and then dust the powder on the surface of the glass. The dusting will reveal the latent print on the glass. If the child then takes a piece of cellophane tape, she can literally lift a copy of the print from the surface. By pressing the tape onto another surface, the fingerprint can be transplanted from the glass to a new surface."

"Such as a shirt collar? Or a human body?"

"All possible."

"Let's talk about DNA now, Professor. There has been testimony in this case that DNA belonging to the president was found at the crime scene. In your professional opinion, does that mean that President Cutler was in contact with Ms. Harper around the time of her death?"

"No."

"Tell us why."

"For one thing, depending on the conditions, DNA can also survive on an object for a long period of time, sometimes for years. So even if the president was in contact with Ms. Harper, it is almost impossible to say how long before her death that contact took place. Beyond that, it is possible that President Cutler didn't have contact with Ms. Harper at all, and yet his DNA could be found at the scene."

"Explain, Dr. Casey, how that could happen."

"There are several reported cases of transplanted DNA. Back in 2012, for example, a homeless man named Lukis Anderson was charged with the murder of a Silicon Valley multimillionaire. It turned out, however, that Mr. Anderson had an airtight alibi: he was completely intoxicated and under medical care at the time of the crime. The same medics who treated Anderson earlier in the day responded later that day to the crime scene at which the wealthy Silicon Valley executive had been killed, and they inadvertently transferred some of Anderson's DNA to the victim. The Innocence Project has seen cases like that before. It happens."

"Can someone deliberately transfer DNA from one person to another?"

"Absolutely. There's a well-known study in our field in which a wash-cloth that was wiped across someone's neck picked up the person's DNA and then transferred the DNA to someone else. Most of the time, DNA transfer is accidental, but there's no reason why a motivated person could not perform such a transfer on purpose."

Jane then decided to blunt the expected line of cross-examination with her next question.

"I take it, Dr. Casey, that you cannot identify anyone who may have planted President Cutler's fingerprints or DNA on Ms. Harper's clothes and body, correct?"

"That's correct. I have no knowledge about this case in particular. My opinions are limited to what I said: it's difficult to tell when DNA or fingerprints were first placed on a surface, and it is even possible that someone's prints or DNA may appear on a surface that he or she never actually touched."

"Nothing further, Your Honor."

Sam Parker stood up for the government.

"Professor Casey, let's talk about the fingerprints and DNA on Ms. Harper's clothing. Would you agree, Professor, that a good cleaning would likely cause that evidence to disappear?"

"A cleaning could, but need not, wash away prints and DNA."

"Do you have any reason to doubt that Ms. Harper washed her clothes from time to time?"

"I imagine that she did."

"So unless the washing machine was surprisingly ineffective, you wouldn't expect to see any remaining fingerprints or DNA on Ms. Harper's shirt collar, apart from her own?"

"I can't speculate about that."

"But, Ms. Casey, you would agree that *if* Ms. Harper washed her clothes thoroughly enough, then the president's fingerprints and DNA must have been placed on the victim closer to the killing?"

"If your assumptions are true, I would probably agree with that conclusion."

"Now let's talk about your 'planting' testimony. You have no basis for believing that someone in fact planted the president's prints or DNA, correct?"

"That's correct," Casey conceded.

"So all you're really telling the jury is that planting prints and DNA is theoretically possible?"

"Correct. I have no knowledge, one way or the other, as to whether someone actually planted evidence on the victim. All I can say is that it would be easy to do so."

"Well, it's not that easy, is it, Dr. Casey? The bad guy would first have to get access to the president's fingerprints and DNA, from a glass, a piece of paper, or some other object, right?"

"That's true."

"And then that mystery person would have to go to Ms. Harper's apartment or at least find her dead body in the park, then plant the prints and DNA, while making sure not to get caught."

"I suppose."

"Are you able to identify someone who did any of those things, Ms. Casey?"

"Of course not. Again, all I can tell you is that it is physically possible to do all of those things."

"Dr. Casey, how many cases have you seen in which all of this forensic evidence was present, but the owner of the DNA and fingerprints did *not* touch the victim?"

"I can't cite a case, but it is entirely possible. Plus, the suspect may have touched the victim long before the killing, and the DNA and fingerprints could still be there."

"Dr. Casey, have you come to learn that President Cutler was interviewed by the police and denied that he ever touched Ms. Harper at all?"

"I may have heard something to that effect," Casey acknowledged.

"Can you explain how someone can leave their fingerprints and DNA all over a crime scene and yet never touch the victim at all?"

"Only if the prints and DNA were planted there."

"And just to close the loop, you know of no one who did anything like that in this case."

"I do not."

Judge Edgerton called the lunch break. *Saved by the bell,* I thought to myself.

XXXV

D ay 6, afternoon session
    "Your Honor, the defense calls Humberto Mercado."

Hummer remembered to put on a suit, so that was a good start. Jane walked our PI quickly through his background in law enforcement, then turned to his assignment.

"Mr. Mercado, what were you asked to do in this case?"

"I was hired by defense counsel to investigate some of Amanda Harper's bank records."

"I show you what's been marked as defense exhibit 1. Do you recognize these documents?"

"Yeah. These are the records I looked into."

"Do these records reflect both cash and charge transactions by Ms. Harper last year?"

"Yeah, they do."

"And do they also reflect the individual items purchased at each particular vendor?"

"Yeah. They're broken out by items."

"Tell the jury what you discovered when you reviewed these banking records."

"First off, once a month, and always on a Saturday, Ms. Harper withdrew exactly a thousand dollars in cash from her ATM. Then the very next day, a Sunday, she would use her credit card to purchase a bunch of products at Overdon Pharmacy in Southeast D.C."

"Can you briefly describe the pharmacy to the ladies and gentlemen of the jury?"

"Sure," said Hummer. "It's a one-story building, glass-enclosed, green awning, which takes up the entire block between Orseck and Untereiner in Southeast. I suppose I should say 'took up the entire block,' because I betcha the cops shut the place down ten minutes after I finish my testimony."

"Did Ms. Harper live near the Overdon Pharmacy?"

"No. She lived in Northwest D.C., a short walk from Rock Creek Park, where her body was found. Overdon Pharmacy is at least a half hour drive."

"Mr. Mercado, during the six months ending January 31 of last year, how many times did Ms. Harper engage in this pattern of withdrawing a thousand in cash on a Saturday and the next day making credit card purchases at Overdon?"

"Once every month, for a total of six times."

"Did that include the month of January last year, when she was killed?"

"Yes. On Saturday, January 4, Ms. Harper withdrew a thousand dollars. Then on Sunday, January 5, she charged thirty-five dollars' worth of sundries at Overdon."

"Did you make a list of the items that Ms. Harper purchased by credit card on the six Sundays that she visited the pharmacy in the last half of last year?"

"I did," Hummer said. "Cough drops three different times, some other cold medicine on four occasions, and nasal mist spray twice."

"Ms. Harper must have been fighting one nasty cold, Mr. Mercado."

That drew the obvious objection, but Jane quickly moved on.

"Did there come a time, Mr. Mercado, when you and some of your colleagues took a closer look at Overdon Pharmacy?"

"Yeah. After we got through with the bank records, two of my investigators and I went to Overdon and poked around."

"What did you learn?"

"Well, the first thing was that the store is supposedly open only Monday through Saturday. There's a sign posted on the front door with the hours of operation, and it says the place is closed on Sundays."

"Yet Ms. Harper charged various products, and only on Sundays, did she not, Mr. Mercado?"

"Yeah, she did. So the boys and I staked the place out on one particular Sunday, starting at about seven a.m."

"And what, if anything, did you observe?"

"The store was closed all morning," Hummer began. "There's a metal grating that covers the front of the pharmacy, bolted with a padlock. But at exactly two p.m., a short unsub—sorry, unknown subject—female, shows up at the place, unlocks and raises the grating, and goes inside. The unsub left the CLOSED sign on the front door, but turned on the lights as she went in."

"Then what happened, Mr. Mercado?"

"Starting a few minutes after two p.m., a few customers show up and also go inside the premises."

"Did any of the customers appear to hesitate when they saw the CLOSED sign?"

"No, they went in like the sign read OPEN."

"What did you see next?"

"Over the next twenty minutes or so, the customers come back out, each of 'em holding a plastic bag with the pharmacy logo on it."

"Mr. Mercado, could you tell what was inside any of those bags?"

"Nope."

"Did you investigate any further?"

"Yeah. I went into the store with one of my guys and casually made my way to the back, where the pharmacy counter is located. I saw a small line of folks heading through a back door behind the counter."

"What happened next, sir?"

"After each unsub left the back room, he's now holding a plastic bag with the store logo, like I mentioned. Each customer would then buy a few additional items from the store and place those items in the same plastic bag, along with whatever was already in there."

"Were you able to see what was going on in the back room?"

"No. Had to be careful not to blow our cover."

"Did you observe anything else, Mr. Mercado?"

"Yeah. I noticed that all the cold medicine is shelved right next to the pharmacy counter."

"And what was the significance of that to you, Mr. Mercado?"

"It told me that Ms. Harper had charged only items within immediate reach of the pharmacy counter. As if she was, like, grabbing a few things at random to make her visit look legit."

That drew another obvious objection ("Speculation, Your Honor"), but Hummer had already made the point.

"Did you observe anything further at the Overdon Pharmacy?"

"At exactly five p.m., the same unsub comes back outside, lowers the grating, locks the place back up. She then left the premises and walked around the corner."

"Finally, Mr. Mercado, do you know why Ms. Harper was *charging* items at Overdon Pharmacy on Sundays, when she had taken out a thousand *in cash* just the day before?"

"Nope."

"Do you know whether she perhaps used some of that cash in the Overdon back room?"

"I'd have to be guessing."

Sam Parker handled the cross for the government.

"Let me get this straight, Mr. Mercado. Are you asking us to believe that Ms. Harper was a drug addict of some sort?"

"I'm not asking you to believe anything but what I'm saying. And I'm saying that every time Ms. Harper drew a thousand in cash, she'd go to the same pharmacy, nowhere near her apartment, the very next day, and use her charge card to buy the very same cold medicines, each within easy reach of the pharmacy counter. Each of these pharmacy visits was on a Sunday, when the store was supposed to be closed."

"And to be clear, you never actually saw Ms. Harper enter the store or buy anything there."

"Yeah, Counselor. She was already dead before I started investigating."

"Are you aware that Dr. Zaid's autopsy disclosed no trace of narcotics in Ms. Harper's blood or tissues?"

"I heard that, yeah. But based on my many years as an ATF agent, I wouldn't expect drug traces to remain after a body has been left out in the freezing cold for a while."

"So let's talk about Ms. Harper's death for a moment. Do you know who Ms. Harper's killer was?"

"Of course not, Einstein."

"Do you have any evidence suggesting that Ms. Harper was killed by a drug supplier?"

Hummer decided to have some fun.

"Apart from the fact that her body was found in a highly trafficked part of Rock Creek Park? Apart from the fact that she could never seem to be reached on weekends? Apart from my years doing undercover work for ATF, which acquainted me with the violent habits of your workaday drug dealer? You mean, apart from all *that* evidence, Counselor? The answer is no, I'm not aware of any evidence."

"If a drug dealer were somehow Ms. Harper's real killer, can you imagine how President Cutler's fingerprints and DNA got all over the crime scene?"

"Can I imagine? Yeah, I can imagine."

Sam didn't take the bait. This time. "No need to speculate, Mr. Mercado. But perhaps you can tell us how some mystery drug dealer managed to get hold of a knife from the James Monroe collection at the White House?"

Hummer was flashing a half-grin. *Please, Sam,* I said to myself, *please pick a fight with this witness.*

"Mr. Mercado, I repeat, maybe you've heard that a James Monroe knife was found stuck into Ms. Harper's briefcase at the Horse Barn. How do you suppose the killer got hold of that invaluable artifact?"

My prayer was answered.

"Who said that it was the killer that placed the knife at the scene, Counselor? The vic could have been killed by a narcotics trafficker, and yet someone else, perhaps Ms. Harper herself, wielded the knife. I wasn't there. Were you?"

"I have nothing further with this witness, Your Honor."

Jane decided to do a brief redirect.

"Very briefly, Mr. Mercado. Mr. Parker asked you if you could imagine how the president's prints and DNA got to the crime scene, if a drug dealer was the real killer."

"Yeah, I remember that question. I said I could imagine, but the prosecutor cut me off before I could say more."

"Could you please finish your answer now?"

"Sure. A drug dealer could have killed Ms. Harper, but the fingerprints and DNA could have been left on Ms. Harper's clothing and body by someone *other* than the killer. Sometime earlier. Maybe when Mr. Cutler and the vic had some cuddle time together."

Judge Edgerton overruled Parker's objection, since he had invited Hummer to guess.

"And just to wrap things up, did the police, to your knowledge, even consider any other suspects besides President Cutler?"

"Not to my knowledge."

"Until you did your own investigating, did the police know anything about Ms. Harper's trips to Overdon Pharmacy?"

"Nope."

"Or the thousand-dollar withdrawals in cash?"

"Nope."

"Or the mysterious Sunday hours at the pharmacy? Or the line to the back room? Or Ms. Harper's constant need for the same handful of cold medicines?"

"No, no, and no."

"Your Honor," Jane said, "the defense has no further questions of this witness."

It was 4:20 p.m., and the judge decided to let the jury go home a few minutes early. He then turned toward the defense table.

"What's scheduled for tomorrow, Mr. Jacobson?"

"We may call President Cutler first thing in the morning," I said. "Ms. Cashman and I will be meeting with our client this evening, and we will decide whether the president wishes to testify."

"That's fine," said the judge, "but I don't like surprises. Once Mr. Cutler has decided whether he intends to testify tomorrow, let Ms. Hannigan know right away."

"We will, Your Honor."

"All right," said the judge. "See you all in the morning."

XXXVI

D ay 6, evening
    You can't wait until the last minute to prepare a client to testify at a criminal trial. It takes hours, days really, of sustained practice. Not only do you have to cover the client's answers to your own questions, but you've also got to anticipate what the prosecutors will do on cross. The stakes could not be greater. If a defendant takes the stand, a jury will often base its verdict on how well the testimony goes.

Prepping Jack was a tough job. He said he was eager to tell his story, yet remained squeamish about the kinky aspects and even more so about the pregnancy. As I explained many times, however, there are no halfway measures about testifying—you have to let it all hang out.

"There's no more runway on this, Jack. The jury will want to hear from you. They'll expect it. They'll hold it against you if you don't take the stand, no matter how Edgerton instructs them. And testifying means telling the whole damn story."

"I understand, Rob," said Jack. "But the cross will be brutal, won't it? They'll go after me on my affairs. They'll ask about the rough stuff. I'll look like a moral leper. The embarrassment will haunt me for the rest of my life."

As Jack was talking, Jane grew increasingly exasperated. Finally came the kind of outcry I'd never heard from her before.

"For goodness' sake, Jack. Everyone already thinks you're a moral leper. Adultery is the least of your problems. How about letting us do our job, so you aren't haunted instead by communal showers with the Aryan Brotherhood?"

Whoa, I remember thinking. Jane surely got Jack's attention with that one. It suddenly occurred to me that maybe Jane should handle Jack's direct instead of me. Perhaps Jack would find it easier to admit what he had to admit if he wasn't talking to an old high school pal.

I turned to my trial partner. "Jane, would you mind giving us the room for a few minutes?"

Jane stepped outside. I let a few seconds pass in silence.

"I'm sorry for Jane's outburst, Jack, but she makes a good point. Maybe she should be doing your examination."

Jack darkened. "No. It's got to be you."

"Hear me out. You and I have known each other for forty-plus years. You may find it easier to tell the hard truth to a relative newcomer, instead of a guy who remembers you from gym class."

"I take the point, Robbie, but my mind's set. You have to do this for me."

A few more seconds passed in silence. And then I got to my main point: "Perhaps we should be discussing a plea, Jack."

"A plea. Are you shitting me, Robbie? I didn't kill Amanda, and I won't say I did."

"You didn't commit *murder.* I believe you. But maybe this was something short of murder."

"Rob, what the fuck are you talking about?"

"I had a visitor a few months ago, Jack. She called herself Caroline Morgan from the Distilled Spirits Council. Ring any bells?"

"Blond," Jack asked. "Maybe five-nine? Holds her booze pretty well?"

"I didn't drink with her, Jack, but given what she had to tell me, I'm guessing she can sit upright through closing time. I take it you know Ms. Morgan?"

"If that's what she's calling herself these days. What of it?"

"Listen, I didn't take a wedding vow with you, Jack, and I'm not your confessor. So I don't much care who you step out with. But Ms. Morgan shared a little secret about your . . . your *extracurricular* tastes. She said you enjoyed choking and smacking her around during sex."

Jack blanched. "She said that?"

"Yeah, Jack. She was quite anatomically precise about it. And when I met with Jess the last time she was at my office, she mentioned your need to be commander in chief between the sheets. Plus, I saw the black eye you gave your wife 'accidentally,'" I said, using air quotes. "So maybe you just got a little too excited with Amanda."

"It's none of your fucking business."

I was ready to pop the bastard, but reeled it in. "That's where you're wrong. My job is to spare you a life sentence. If I can. If Amanda's death was just some rough sex gone sideways, we might be able to work out some lesser charge with the prosecutors. Murder requires premeditation. If this was a sex act that got out of hand, I may be able to shave a decade or two off your prison term. You'd get to see Gretchen and Harlan before they're grandparents."

Jack stood firm. "This wasn't sex gone sideways, Robert. I simply did not kill Amanda. Period. So a guilty plea is a total nonstarter. As for my testimony in court, I can't see claiming that Amanda was into choking or some other freaky shit."

Of course, I knew better about Amanda. If Jack had put choking on the menu, she'd have ordered seconds.

"Jack, I need you to see how much is on the line here. If you can't admit the whole truth, 'warts and all,' as you once told me, then I can't put you on the stand. I can't let you testify falsely when the government asks about your . . . your tastes. Which means I'd have a hard time dealing with the pregnancy, with your prints, and with all the DNA evidence. Ticktock, Mr. President. You're tomorrow's main event."

Jack said he understood he had to testify and, on his way out the door, promised to do his best. I called the prosecutors, gave them the news, then headed down the hall to see my colleague.

"Why the outrage, Jane? Jack's just looking out for the history books. You can understand that."

"Oh, I understand just fine, Rob," said Jane. "But I have no empathy for the lecherous bastard."

"All due respect, Jane, but down here on Planet Earth, we mortals make mistakes. We sin. We give into our temptations once in a while."

"As you know better than most, Rob."

Where was all this coming from? "It must be lonely up in heaven, Jane."

Jane sat silently, sipping her tea for a minute. When she spoke again, her words were barely audible. "I have no designs on heaven, Rob. I deserve it even less than our client."

Huh?

"Give me some credit, Rob. You think I'm just some beacon of goodness? Just some shining example to all the younger lawyers at the firm? What do you think it was like to be the first Black female lawyer at L&H?"

"I imagine it was awful, Jane."

"No, Rob, you really can't imagine. You're thinking that I had to deal with racist remarks, maybe some misogyny thrown in, but no. The L&H

partners were far too genteel for any of that. Theirs was the soft racism of low expectations. The senior litigators figured I'd gotten into Harvard through the back door. So they gave me the least challenging assignments, work meant for a paralegal, then fawned over me when I accomplished them."

"Jesus, Jane, I had no idea."

"Of course you didn't. It was well before your time. The worst of the lot were dead or retired by the time you arrived. I'd moved up by the time you joined us."

"I never asked you how you pulled that off."

"I did it by being the smart, tough lawyer I always was. And by finding a mentor who refused to coddle me."

"Who was that?" I asked.

"I'm not naming names, Rob. Let's just say, he and I worked together, much the way you and I did. Until . . ."—Jane trailed off—"until I got too close to him. Until my husband, Phil, found out."

I guessed the rest. "I'm so sorry, Jane. I never knew any of this."

"I don't take out ads, Rob. But let's get back to the client for a minute. Did you raise the accidental death scenario we discussed?"

"He won't go for it. He's totally implacable."

"I'm sorry to hear that, Rob."

"Why's that?"

"Because," said Jane, "it's the single likeliest theory I've heard."

XXXVII

D^{ay 7}
 The crowd that greeted us this morning was larger and meaner than usual. Folks were expecting Jack to take the stand, and a who's who of his political enemies had turned out to wish him well. The Second Amendment enthusiasts suited up in military gear. You could spot the Liberty League in the middle of the pack. Pride of place went to Operation Cradle, which must have started queuing up last night. This fringe group, which spent most of its time blockading the few remaining abortion clinics in the South, was chanting above the din:

Cutler, Cutler, Cutlery,

Monroe's knife accuses thee.

Harper's trial seals your doom,

For killing babies in the womb.

My walk from the Metro gave me time for some last-minute noodling about Jack's direct. My job was to set the table. Jack would be the witness. He had to command the stage. Regardless of the judge's instructions, the burden would fall on Jack to convince the jury of his innocence. As usual, I would just be his facilitator.

I'd have to protect Jack from the prosecutors, of course. Katherine would hammer Jack with his lies to the cops, and I needed to defuse her cross as best I could during my own examination. But I'd also have to protect the client from himself. If Jack misstated a point, the prosecutors would cudgel him. Even an accidental slip could be fatal. Trial practice is always a razor's edge, this case especially.

Jane and I met Jack in the defense witness room. He had his game face on.

———

As Jack approached the witness stand, the lucky few who had scored courtroom seats snapped and crackled with anticipation. The first few rows were reserved for family and the press, so most of the public was consigned to the adjoining room and a live audio feed.

As I moved to the podium to begin the direct, I scanned the courtroom for Jess and the kids. For the first time since the trial began, they were not there. I thought I knew why. But sitting in the last row, near the far corner of the courtroom, were two people I had not expected to see.

Josh and Evan, sitting side by side.

Calm down, I told myself. *Stand still. All eyes on Jack.* I paused to let the jury take a long look at the former president while I waited for my pulse to slow. Jack, meanwhile, settled himself on the witness stand.

"Mr. Cutler," I began at last, "you've been present for the entire trial, and you've heard the prosecution tell the jury that you are guilty of killing Amanda Harper. Is there any truth to that charge?"

"None whatsoever." Jack took a deep breath. "I did not kill Amanda."

"You did know Ms. Harper, though, is that correct, sir?"

"Yes, of course. Amanda joined the White House Counsel's Office about a year before my administration ended."

"Did you have more than a purely professional relationship with Ms. Harper?"

Jack paused and for just a moment looked me dead in the eye. You could sense everyone in the courtroom waiting for the shoe to drop.

"Yes," Jack said finally. "Yes, I did. Sometime in the late spring of that last year, Amanda and I became intimate. I knew it was wrong at the time, and I'm deeply ashamed to admit it now. But Amanda Harper and I became romantically involved during my final year in office."

The crowd rumbled—Judge Edgerton gaveled for quiet. I looked back at Josh, who had a thin smile on his face.

"Tell the ladies and gentlemen of the jury how the affair began."

"There's not much to tell. In many ways, it was your ordinary office romance. During those final twelve months, the Senate Republicans started lobbing subpoenas at the White House. It was something new every day. They wanted documents about the Antarctica skirmish. They wanted my climate secretary to testify about our electric car mandate. They wanted senior officials from the Justice Department to discuss the merits of some of my pardons, especially that undocumented alien who thereafter murdered his family. No sooner did we respond to one subpoena than ten more would come across the transom. This was Amanda's docket at the Counsel's Office, and so the two of us found ourselves working together more and more often. One thing led to another, as they say."

"Just to be clear, Mr. Cutler, when you refer to the Senate Republicans, you aren't suggesting, are you, that they are responsible for your affair?" *A little rough, Robbie, take it easy.*

"Absolutely not. This was my mistake. No one else's."

"And you concealed this affair from your wife, Jessica?"

"I certainly tried to. And that's the most shameful part of this, the constant deceit. The lies to Jess. I admitted the whole sordid business to her only last night, when I knew I'd have to tell the complete truth in the courtroom this morning."

"So you waited several months before you shared that news with your wife, didn't you, Mr. Cutler?"

Jack shot me a look. Just a quick flash—I'm sure no one noticed.

"That's true, Mr. Jacobson. I waited much too long to tell Jess the truth."

"What was your wife's reaction when you finally told her, Mr. Cutler?"

"She was hurt, but not surprised. Jess hadn't recalled this originally, but she'd come by the White House dining room one evening when I was having dinner with Amanda. Jess noticed that we'd already drained a bottle of red wine and were working on a second. Turns out she'd had her suspicions for a while. Of course the pregnancy, and the, um, graphic details, were something else."

"Do you recall whether you were using the James Monroe silverware that evening you had dinner with Amanda?"

"We used that silverware most nights in the dining room. I don't recall the place settings that particular evening, but the Monroe setting was customary. Let me add one more thing, if I may, Mr. Jacobson. I did not kill Ms. Harper, but I have done incalculable damage to my marriage and my family."

I could feel my stomach tensing. "Maybe that's something you should have thought of before you launched into an affair with a subordinate, Mr. Cutler."

Jack glared at me again, just for an instant. "That *is* something I should have considered, you're right, Mr. Jacobson."

"And it's fair to say, sir, that Ms. Harper was alone with you in the Oval Office on one or more occasions?"

"That's true. We spent many late nights working on responses to the Hill. I took those subpoenas personally. And Amanda was my lead lawyer. It was on one of those late nights in the Oval that our relationship crossed a professional line."

"Tell the ladies and gentlemen of the jury about the last time you saw Ms. Harper."

"I continued to see Amanda after I left office. That's why I gave up my security detail right after we moved out of the White House. The last time we met was at Amanda's apartment near Rock Creek Park. I took a car over to her place, we went to bed together in the late afternoon, then ordered takeout for dinner."

"Do you recall the date of that last visit, Mr. Cutler?"

"Sometime in late January, maybe a week after I left office, about a day or two before Amanda was killed," Jack answered.

"Do you recall what Amanda was wearing?"

"Not exactly, but Amanda wasn't big on fashion. She had maybe three variations of the same basic outfit. As best I recall, she was wearing the same thing she had on when her body was found."

"Do you recall touching Ms. Harper and her clothing during your last visit to her apartment?"

"I'm sure I did. We were intimate, Mr. Jacobson. As I told you only a *minute* ago."

Jane coughed softly—our signal for a quick consultation. I went over to the defense table and bent my ear toward Jane.

"Rob, you're overdoing it," Jane whispered. "The client is getting rattled. Please dial it back."

Fair point, I thought. I went back to the podium to settle things down a little. En route, my eye caught Evan, who was smiling broadly as I resumed questioning Jack.

"After that tryst in late January, did you make plans to see each other again?"

"Yes. I was infatuated with Amanda. And I believed the feeling was mutual."

"But you did not see her again, is that correct?"

"That's correct. I tried her cell several times in the week or so that followed, but she never picked up. I assumed that she was either too busy or just needed a break, so I stopped trying to reach her. In early February of last year, when the first police reports came out, I realized why I couldn't reach her. I was shocked and deeply upset."

"Mr. Cutler, we've heard testimony that Ms. Harper was pregnant with your child at the time of her death. I take it you don't contest the paternity finding."

"No, I don't. I'm sure the child was mine."

"Did you know that Ms. Harper was pregnant prior to her autopsy?"

"I had no idea. She did not appear pregnant when I last saw her. And she didn't tell me about the pregnancy. Ever."

"Based on your knowledge of the victim, why do you think Ms. Harper concealed her pregnancy from you?"

Katherine was on her feet to object, but Judge Edgerton allowed Jack to answer.

"Amanda was, let's just say, self-reliant. She had no illusions that I'd leave Jessica and start a new family with her. I'm sure Amanda simply felt that she could raise her child alone or with some new partner."

"Mr. Cutler, the police eventually questioned you about Ms. Harper, correct?"

"That's true."

"And you were not straight with them, correct?"

"Also true."

"In fact, sir, you flat-out lied to the cops, didn't you?" I asked sharply, pointing at the witness and holding Jack's eye.

"I did," Jack answered weakly.

"And why is that, Mr. Cutler?"

"Look, I was mortified. The thought of airing my laundry in public or even in a prosecutor's office was unbearable. Particularly given some of the kink, the rope restraints, the marks on Amanda's wrists and ankles. It's all so humiliating. I lied about it, and I'm sorry for that. But I did not—I did not kill Amanda. The fact is, I loved her, or at least I thought I did."

"That kink you mention—that was consensual between you and Ms. Harper, am I right?"

"Do we really need to get into that?" Jack asked softly.

"Yes, we really do. Did you use restraints in your sex life with Ms. Harper?"

"We sometimes used some light rope restraints."

"We've all seen the photos of Amanda's wrists and ankles. Those didn't look light to me."

Jack visibly reddened. "You weren't there, Counselor, were you?"

"And when you say *there,* Mr. Cutler, where exactly do you mean? Where did you and Ms. Harper use the ropes?"

"In her apartment. In the bedroom."

"Did Amanda ever protest when you tied her up?"

"No." Jack was fuming at this point. Anyone could see that. Maybe just a question or two more.

"Did she scream? Or call out to stop? Or stop breathing at any point?"

"No, no, and no."

"Just to be clear: you're saying that Ms. Harper was never harmed by the ropes on her wrists or ankles?"

"Never. We were very careful. She was experienced, if you will, and always in control."

"In control, Mr. Cutler? *You* were the one in control, am I right? Ms. Harper was the one who *submitted,* correct?"

Jack was gritting his teeth. "Yes, correct."

"Which is what attracted you to Amanda in the first place, isn't that so?"

"That's nonsense, Mr. Jacobson. I thought Amanda was beautiful and smart and challenging. That's what I found attractive."

"Really, Mr. Cutler?" I found myself saying more sharply. "Level with us, sir: You like women who do your bidding. You love submission."

Jack paused, then mumbled, "Maybe. Maybe that's part of it."

Out of the corner of my eye, I noticed Evan and Josh. *Both* of them were smiling now, rooting for me.

"Can you explain how a knife from the James Monroe collection ended up in the crime scene?"

Knife must have been their cue. About a half dozen spectators in the last row of the courtroom jumped to their feet, removed their jackets, and revealed T-shirts with anti-abortion messaging. These Operation Cradle protesters got only as far as "Cutler, Cutler, Cutlery" when the judge gaveled for quiet and signaled the marshals to escort them from the courtroom. "If there is another such outburst," Judge Edgerton warned, "I will empty the courtroom for the balance of the trial. Is that clear?"

Jack took a moment to regroup. I poured him a cup of water, then reminded Jack of my last question: How did the James Monroe knife end up wedged into the briefcase?

"I've tried to imagine," Jack said slowly, "but I can't. I didn't give any such gift to Amanda, plus it's White House property. As I mentioned, Amanda did have dinner with me a couple of times in which the Monroe silverware was set out. But I have no reason to suspect that she pocketed a piece of cutlery and took it from the White House. I don't suspect that of *any* of my other dinner guests over the years. Like your family, for example."

Time to get back on track. "Let's talk about your whereabouts in the weeks following your last encounter with Ms. Harper. Are you able to say where you were during the two-week period surrounding your final visit to her apartment in late January?"

"I've checked my calendar. Apart from one overseas trip right after the Melvin inauguration and my last visit to Amanda's, I was at home continuously, in my study, working on a memoir of my White House years. I was reviewing some official papers and focusing on the first draft. I've promised the publisher the first few chapters by next month, so I haven't had much time away from the grindstone."

"Where was your overseas trip?"

"I was in Paris to give a talk to EU economists about the aftermath of Frexit. There are lots of photographers and reporters who can corroborate my whereabouts for those three days."

"And otherwise, Mr. Cutler, you were at home?"

"That's correct."

"No visits to Rock Creek Park or Northwest D.C. in the days following your last visit with Amanda?"

"None, Mr. Jacobson."

"You *have* been to the Horse Center before, though, correct?"

"Yes."

"In fact, you've kept a horse there for several years, am I correct?"

"That's true. *Lots* of people use the Center."

Jack sounded defensive. But I needed to blunt the questions the government would inevitably ask. Looking back, maybe I should have given Jack more of a heads-up. Sometimes you just have to trust your gut.

"So let's review the bidding, Mr. Cutler. You lied to your wife?"

"Yes," Jack said, his jaw tensing.

"And you lied to the cops?"

Jack paused, his eyes flashing at me again and his right hand gripping the witness stand. "Yeah, I did. I admitted that already."

"That's just what politicians do sometimes, right?"

Judge Edgerton looked over at the prosecution. No objections.

"I suppose so, Counselor."

"So why should this jury take your word . . ." I caught myself mid-sentence and lowered my voice. "Why should *anyone* believe you when you deny killing Amanda Harper?"

Jack paused and took a deep breath. "Because it's the truth. It is the goddamn truth." He spat the last words out.

"Anything else you want the members of the jury to know before I sit down, sir?"

Jack turned and faced the jurors, looking from one to the next.

"It pains me to appear so completely a cliché, but I really did love Amanda. She was a brilliant, beautiful, formidable lawyer and human being. She brought energy into the room. I would never, never have harmed Amanda in any way."

"Thank you, Mr. Cutler. Your Honor, I pass the witness."

Judge Edgerton called a midmorning recess. Jack joined Jane and me in the witness room.

"Jane, would you mind leaving Robbie and me alone for just a moment?" Jack asked.

After Jane left the room, Jack turned to me, his voice on a low boil. "What . . . the fuck . . . was that? What the hell were you doing in there?"

"You need to calm down, Jack. And lower your voice," I added, motioning toward the prosecution's room just across the hall. "The direct went fine. Those questions were designed to steal the prosecutors' thunder. Now, when Katherine does the very same stuff on cross, the jury will have heard it all before. It won't have any impact. She may not even touch some of that material."

By now the two of us were inches apart, on our feet, and facing each other in the small conference room.

"You don't know shit about people, Robbie. You never did. When the jurors hear my own lawyer accuse me of being a pervert and a liar, what the fuck are they supposed to think? When they hear *my own lawyer* attack me for having an 'affair with a subordinate,' they're gonna start measuring me for an orange fucking jumpsuit. For chrissake, whose side are you on, you *little shit*?"

On *little,* Jack shot his right hand out and grabbed my throat. I was stunned for just a moment and gasped for air. Jack still had a lacrosse player's grip.

With a sharp shot to the underside of his arm, I broke the hold.

"You still have that move down, huh, Robbie?"

I had no idea what he was talking about.

"And asking whether I enjoy dominating women, all that 'submission' bullshit, how does that help me with the jury, not to mention with the history books?"

"That's a total exaggeration, Jack. You need to trust me on this. Watch how the cross goes. Take your time. Like we said back in my office, don't get rattled. I've let the air out of Katherine's tires—that's what all those questions were designed to do. I'm on your side. Like always."

Katherine Hannigan tried throwing a few howitzers in the very first round.

"Let me see if I've got this, Mr. President. The victim was pregnant with your child on the day she was killed. Your fingerprints and yours alone were all over the crime scene. Your DNA and yours alone were on Ms. Harper's neck and nearby clothing. And a knife from a priceless White House collection was wedged into Ms. Harper's briefcase. Yet you didn't kill her. Is that your testimony?"

"That is my testimony, Ms. Hannigan."

"Do you consider yourself unlucky, sir?"

"Actually, I've always counted myself blessed in a great many ways. Other than this trial."

"Well, I ask, Mr. President, because it seems like a stroke of remarkably bad luck to find your fingerprints and DNA all over a crime scene, with no one else's fingerprints or DNA anywhere in sight, and yet you are *not* responsible for the crime."

I broke in. "I can't tell if that's a question, Your Honor."

"Move along, Ms. Hannigan," Judge Edgerton ordered.

"Sorry, Your Honor. Mr. Cutler, did you happen to see the photos taken of Ms. Harper's body?"

"I did."

"And you noticed that Ms. Harper had rope burns on her wrists and above her ankles?"

"I did."

"You put them there, Mr. President, didn't you?"

This attack might have landed harder, had I not already covered the same ground.

"I did. You cannot imagine how humiliating it is to say this in public, but Amanda and I sometimes engaged in light restraint play. No one ever got hurt."

"Really, sir? *Light restraint play?* Didn't the ropes burn into Ms. Harper's skin?"

"They may look that way. I can understand that. But in the privacy of our relationship, we had this strictly under control, Ms. Hannigan."

"Did your light restraint play also involve pressing down on Ms. Harper's neck sometimes?"

Jack winced a little. "Sometimes. But again, we were always very careful. Amanda had a safe word in case she became uncomfortable."

"What was the safe word, Mr. Cutler?"

"Really? You really need to know those details?"

The judge directed Jack to answer the question.

"The word was *subpoena*."

That drew a few titters from the crowd, which Judge Edgerton gaveled into silence.

"Let's talk about the knife, Mr. President. You cannot account for its disappearance from the White House?"

"I cannot."

"Any idea how Amanda or some other mystery person got the knife out of the White House undetected? People have to pass through metal detectors, don't they?"

"That's generally true."

"What do you mean, *generally*? Are you suggesting that maybe Ms. Harper eluded the metal detectors after she pocketed the James Monroe knife from your dining room?"

"I can't really speculate about that. Maybe I walked her out of the White House one evening. If so, we wouldn't have gone through the detectors. I don't recall. All I can say is that no system is foolproof, and I'm sure people have managed to take things out of the White House before."

"Let's talk about the Secret Service for a minute, sir. You were under round-the-clock protection by the Secret Service during your four years in office, correct?"

"Yes."

"And that's because presidents are in harm's way all the time, right?"

"Yes, they are."

"And that risk doesn't magically disappear after presidents leave office, does it?"

"There's still a risk, yes."

"Which is precisely why former presidents are automatically given security protection even after they leave office."

"Correct, Ms. Hannigan."

"Yet, you gave up your security detail the very day you left office, right?"

"I did."

"Only one former president in history has ever relinquished his security, am I correct?"

"I've seen that reported, yes. President Nixon did so."

"And the reason you did that, Mr. Cutler, is that you could never have gotten away with murder if you were being watched by a security detail."

I took in a slight breath. Katherine was scoring some points now, and I had not anticipated this line of cross. Damnit.

"No, Ms. Hannigan, that is entirely false. My wife and I agreed to give up the detail because we wanted some semblance of privacy again. And I wanted to be able to visit Amanda without being followed. In retrospect, I wish I'd kept my security detail. The Secret Service would have been my best alibi."

Nicely done, Jack.

Katherine changed topics again. "Mr. Cutler, you admit that you are the father of Ms. Harper's child, right?"

"I do, yes."

"And you admit that you were unwilling to leave your wife, Jessica, to start a new family with Ms. Harper."

"I admit that as well."

"I notice that your wife and children are not in court today. Am I correct?"

"You're correct."

"And that's because your wife was terribly upset when she finally heard from *you*—not from the press, not from the internet, not from trial witnesses, but from the proverbial horse's mouth—the full nature of your relationship with the victim."

"I suppose that's true, yes."

"You yourself admit that the news of the affair has done terrible damage to your marriage, am I right?"

"Yes."

"And your wife was especially upset to learn that her husband—you, Jack Cutler, former president of the United States—fathered a child with another woman."

"She was, yes. My conduct is inexcusable."

"If you could have spared your wife from learning about the affair and the pregnancy, you would happily have done so, right?"

"Perhaps, but I had no choice in the matter. The autopsy results showed my paternity."

"But *before* Ms. Harper was killed and *before* the autopsy, you were trying your best to conceal the affair and the pregnancy from your wife."

I rose to object, but the judge overruled me. "The witness may answer."

"May I hear the question again, Ms. Hannigan?"

"Of course, Mr. Cutler. At the time of your final tryst with Ms. Harper, you were still hoping that your wife would never learn about the affair."

"That's true."

"Or the pregnancy."

"I didn't know about the pregnancy myself, so the thought never entered my mind. Not even the medical examiner could tell that Amanda was pregnant before the autopsy results came in."

"But Ms. Harper may have *told* you about the pregnancy *herself*. And you would have given anything to spare your wife and kids hearing about that news, right? Even if you had to kill Amanda and her child to conceal everything, correct?"

Jack raised his voice. "Amanda *didn't* tell me. And if she had, I would never, never have done what you accuse me of."

"At the time of Ms. Harper's death, did you know that doctors can now establish the paternity of a fetus as early as five weeks?"

"I did not know that until I heard it in court."

"So at the time of Ms. Harper's death, you could well have believed that by killing Ms. Harper at that early stage of her pregnancy, no one would ever learn who the baby's father was."

I stood to object, but Jack insisted on answering.

"Ms. Hannigan, I will tell you again, and for the last time: I did not know Amanda was pregnant before she died. And I would never, never have killed her. Not to cover up paternity, not for any other reason."

"But in fairness, Mr. President, we have only your word for this, right?"

"I suppose that's true."

"There's really no way to know whether you're telling the truth, other than to take your word for it, is there?"

And that, my friends, is what Trial Practice instructors call "asking one question too many." We had prepped him for this exact possibility, but never imagined we'd get this lucky.

"Actually, Ms. Hannigan, there *is* a way to tell if my testimony is true. Would you like to hear it?"

What could Katherine do? If she didn't bite, the jury would hold it against her. And I would come back to the issue on redirect anyway.

"Okay, Mr. Cutler. How can anyone tell if your testimony is true?"

"By subjecting me to a lie detector." As we had prepped, Jack told the story of the fMRI testing and the results. This was the only way we could possibly have paraded his passing score in front of the jury. Katherine had stepped in it. And the jury seemed enthralled.

We then caught another break, this time from His Honor.

"We will break for an early lunch," Judge Edgerton declared. "And resume at two p.m." The jury would now have more than an hour to focus on the fMRI results.

Over lunch, Jane and I reminded Jack to keep his cool. Let the lawyers be the bad guys, we told him. Your job is to be respectful and respond to the questions.

"Ignore the badgering, Jack," I added. "Just concentrate on the questions she asks, pause a split second before answering, then respond. That's all you have to do. An hour or so more and you're done."

————

Jack returned to the stand ready to go.

"Mr. President, before the lunch break I asked you why the jury should trust the things you've told them. You will admit that you've been lying to your wife about the affair for many months."

"I have, that's true."

"In fact, you used a Burner app on your phone precisely so that it would be harder for your wife or for the police to connect you to Ms. Harper?"

"I was trying not to advertise my affair with Ms. Harper."

"You also lied when you were interviewed by the police?"

"Yes, Ms. Hannigan."

"And when it's been in your self-interest, Mr. Cutler, you have not hesitated to lie, whether it's to your own wife, to the cops, or to others."

"I'm afraid that is all true."

None of that hit the mark, I thought. The jury had already heard the same questions when I asked them earlier.

"And you're also willing to blame others for your own failings, are you not?" Katherine continued.

"I don't accept that accusation, no."

"Well, when you told the jury on direct that your wife, Jess, suspected your affair with Ms. Harper, weren't you hoping that the jury might blame Ms. Cutler for this murder?"

"Ms. Hannigan, that never occurred to me. I was simply answering my lawyer's questions."

"So it's your lawyer's fault?"

"Not at all what I said or meant. My point is that I was not accusing Jess of anything. I would never do that."

"The fact is, Mr. President, despite the lawyer's insinuations, you haven't the slightest reason to suspect any other person of having committed this crime?"

Oh my, I thought—Katherine had stepped in it again. Another break for us.

"Since you ask," Jack responded, suppressing a smile, "I actually do have reason to suspect someone else of this crime."

"Okay, Mr. President," Katherine said with a soupçon of resignation in her voice. "Whom do you suspect?"

"I don't have a name, but it wouldn't surprise me if Amanda were killed by her narcotics supplier. She confided her use of Ecstasy to me when we were together. And when I heard Mr. Mercado's testimony about Overdon Pharmacy, it rang true to me."

"The fact is, Mr. President, you really have no firsthand knowledge of any such drug dealer who might be responsible for this crime?"

"If you're asking, Ms. Hannigan, whether I can identify Amanda's Ecstasy source or whether I can name Amanda's actual killer, then no, I can't."

"Let's turn, finally, to your so-called alibi. Basically, your testimony is that, other than a three-day trip to Paris, you were at home, day and night, for the two weeks following your last visit to Amanda's in late January. Do I have that right?"

"That's correct."

"So no midafternoon strolls up to Woodley Park, no midnight pizza runs, just all work, all day long, in your home study, is that correct?"

"That's right."

"Do you keep any kind of journal of your daily schedule or your comings and goings?"

"No, I don't."

"So other than your say-so, what basis does the jury have for finding that you were at home during the time Ms. Harper was killed?"

"I have nothing more to offer except the truth."

"Your version of the truth," Katherine said as she sat down.

Judge Edgerton sustained my objection to the prosecutor's comment. I then advised the Court that I had no questions on redirect. I thought that Jack had handled himself well on cross and that redirect would make us look needlessly defensive. Jack resumed his seat at the defense table.

"Your Honor," I announced. "The defense rests."

The judge adjourned for the day. We spirited Jack out of the courtroom, trying to avoid the crush of reporters and photographers. But as we left, I cast a final look around the packed courtroom. Josh had apparently left already, but there was Evan, still planted in the back of the courtroom. He was staring directly at me with a broad grin on his face. "Very nice work, Robbie," he called out.

XXXVIII

So were you really in court that day?

Yeah, I was.

Why did you decide to attend that particular day?

How could I miss it? Jack and I have a history, right? When I roughed him up a bit back in the day? For messing with Liddle Robbie? I was there for moral support. Give my bro some spine, you know? Put a little more oomph in his questions. I should have passed Robbie a few notes during his examination of the bastard. You know, help him channel my thinking.

How did it feel to listen to the president's testimony?

It felt pretty good. Cutler looked so small up there, bellyaching about how much he loved Amanda. All I could think was how much I wanted to throttle the bastard.

So anger again.

Anger as always. But I was angry a few times at Robbie as well. Ask Jack about the juicy stuff, little brother! Ask how it felt to tie Amanda up. Ask about the choking. Hey, Mr. President, Your Excellency, did you put your hands around Amanda's throat and press up? Is that what she asked you to do? Did you maybe get a little overexcited one night? Get a little stiffie, Jackie? What did Amanda sound like when you pressed a little harder? Did she squeak? Did her eyes glaze?

Is that what you imagine actually happened?

I have no idea. Maybe she told Jack she was pregnant, like she told me. Maybe he believed her, like I did. Who the fuck knows?

Were there parts of the president's testimony that bothered you?

Sure, Doc. When Robbie asked His Excellency about the last time he was with Amanda. It brought back my last visit with Amanda. This is something I haven't even told Robbie yet, so let's keep it between us for now, okay?

XXXIX

D ay 7 after hours, and Day 8
At about ten-thirty that evening, Katherine Hannigan called my cell. I was still in the office, working on the closing argument I expected to give in the morning.

"Rob, sorry to be calling so late, but I thought I'd better reach you tonight. We're planning to call a rebuttal witness tomorrow."

I could feel my heart racing. Sure, the prosecution sometimes calls a witness to rebut testimony offered during the defense case. But it doesn't happen often, and I had no reason to expect rebuttal in this case.

I asked for the name of the witness.

"I'd like to tell you," said Katherine, "but I can't risk the chance that your client will try to keep our witness off the stand."

That as much as told me who the prosecutors would be calling. I phoned Jane and told her the news. "I guess I'm not surprised," she said. "Just keep your cool. They can bring in fifty bishops to swear Jack is the killer, they can bring Amanda back from the dead, they can do whatever they want—just brace yourself for cross. You can definitely handle this witness."

I tossed and turned much of the night, hoping Jane was right.

Right after the jury was seated at 9:30 a.m., Katherine approached the lectern. It was just as I had expected. "Your Honor," she announced, "the government calls Jessica Friedland Cutler."

Bedlam. The crowded courtroom buzzed, and Jack whitened at my side. I jumped to my feet and asked for a sidebar. Judge Edgerton, obviously displeased with the government's tactic, called us into chambers.

"Your Honor," I began, "I'm sure the Court can appreciate that this comes as a complete surprise to us. We received the prosecution's witness list a month before trial, and updates to the list at least two weeks ago. This is the first we're hearing that the former first lady will be testifying for the government."

Judge Edgerton turned to the prosecutors. "Why are we learning about this witness at the eleventh hour?"

Katherine spoke up. "President Cutler opened the door to this testimony just yesterday, when he claimed that he was at home working on his memoirs during the weeks surrounding Ms. Harper's death. Ms. Cutler was not in court yesterday, but after she heard about that testimony, she contacted us and offered to appear as a government witness. Until then, we had no reason to believe she'd even be willing to talk to us. As soon as we heard from her, I alerted Mr. Jacobson."

"Your Honor," I protested, "when Ms. Hannigan called me late last night, she declined to tell me the name of the witness. There was nothing I could do to prepare."

"We couldn't take chances," said Katherine. "If I revealed that the former first lady would be testifying for us, the defendant might try to persuade her otherwise. And Mr. Cutler can be very . . . persuasive . . . when he wants to be."

Jesus, what did Katherine know about that? What had Jess told her?

The judge broke in at that point. "All right, I've heard enough. I don't like surprises any more than Mr. Jacobson, but under the circumstances, I will allow the witness to take the stand. Mr. Jacobson, if you need a short recess to prepare a cross-examination, I will allow it."

"Your Honor," I protested, "that resolves only the issue of unfair surprise. It still leaves open the marital privilege. Ms. Cutler is not allowed to testify against her husband about any confidences they may have shared."

Katherine smiled broadly. "Your Honor, we have no intention of asking the witness to repeat anything she or the president said to each other. We will ask her to describe only things she saw with her own eyes. There is no privilege that prevents her from doing so."

Katherine was right, unfortunately. There are two different kinds of spousal privilege. The first privilege allows a spouse to refuse to testify against the other spouse *at all* unless she chooses to do so. But Jessica Cutler evidently wanted to testify. The second privilege forbids a spouse to testify about marital *confidences*, but Katherine Hannigan had just sworn she would not elicit any communications between Jess and Jack. The testimony would go forward.

We returned to the courtroom, and Jess took the stand. As if to rub Jack's nose in it, she was wearing the same almond-white tailored suit she'd worn on the *60 Minutes* episode that helped get her husband elected.

I remembered that outfit well. During his first run for the White House, Jack had been accused of stashing a much younger woman in an Upper West Side penthouse for his occasional fundraising trips to New York. Taking a page from an earlier playbook, he agreed to do an interview on *60 Minutes*. Jack was convincing enough, but it was Jess's star turn that saved the campaign. Looking fierce yet vulnerable in the same off-white outfit, Jess turned to the cameras and said, emphatically, that she believed Jack, that theirs was a loving marriage, and that the accusations against Jack were false and hurtful. Like Nixon's Checkers speech and some TV spectacles that followed, the White Suit Interview, as it was thereafter known, was a great success. Jack's poll numbers shot up throughout the fall.

Now, when she took the witness stand, Jess did not meet Jack's eyes or mine as Katherine led her methodically through her testimony.

"Ms. Cutler, where do you presently reside?"

Jess provided her current county of residence in Maryland. She pursed her lips as she spoke and carried herself like a reluctant witness. I was not convinced.

"Prior to that, where'd you live?"

"I lived at the White House until President Melvin was sworn in," Jess answered.

"And after the inauguration?"

"We moved into a townhouse in Georgetown."

"Did you reside at that townhouse in late January of last year?"

"Yes, with my two children and with my husband, Jack Cutler."

"That would be the defendant, sitting to my left at the defense table?"

"Correct."

"Ms. Cutler, the jury has heard testimony that Ms. Amanda Harper was killed on or about January 28, just after the Melvin inauguration. I take it that both you and your husband were living together on that date?"

"We were, yes."

"Your husband has testified that he was at home for the entire three-week period surrounding Ms. Harper's death, except for a trip to France and one evening at Ms. Harper's residence. Can you tell the ladies and gentlemen of the jury whether that testimony is true?"

"It's not."

Jack's right hand began to tremble as he sat next to me at the table. I placed my left hand over his to steady him. Judge Edgerton also had to gavel the courtroom to silence before Katherine could continue.

"How do you know that the president's testimony was untrue, Ms. Cutler?"

"When Jack—when my husband first ran for president, I began to keep a journal of our lives together. I would jot down little details, private moments in a harried life, in case I wanted to write my own memoirs someday. About three weeks ago, I was looking through my notes from around the time of Ms. Harper's death. I saw that I'd made a short notation, 'Jack out,' on each and every one of the days during the week she was killed. I make such entries only when Jack is gone on business or otherwise away from home."

"Ms. Cutler, I show you government exhibit 42. Do you recognize this document?"

"It's my journal," said Jess. "It's got my name, and the handwriting is all mine."

"Directing your attention to the pages for January 21 through 29 of last year, do you see the notations you've entered?"

"Yes. On each of those days, I've written 'Jack out.'"

"What did you mean by that notation, Ms. Cutler?"

"It meant that for some significant part of the day, my husband was somewhere other than at our home in Georgetown."

"Just so we're clear, Ms. Cutler, you're not saying that your husband was specifically with Ms. Harper when he was away on any of those days?"

"That's right. I have no idea where he was or what he was doing. I just know that he wasn't home with me."

Jess spat out that last line with some force. She obviously wanted the jury to absorb its full import.

"Thank you for coming in today, Ms. Cutler. I know this can't have been easy for you."

I decided to take Judge Edgerton up on his offer. "May we have a short recess, Your Honor, before I begin my cross?"

The judge gave us a half hour. I asked my paralegal to go back to the office and find a manila envelope in the upper righthand drawer of my desk.

Jack looked distraught. "The jury seemed to be eating from Jess's hand."

"Stay tuned, Jack."

My paralegal returned with the envelope about fifteen minutes later. I removed a small item from inside and waited for court to resume.

Jess returned to the witness stand, composed herself, then turned to face me for the first time that day.

"May I offer you some water, Ms. Cutler?" I began. Jess assured me that she had what she needed.

"Ms. Cutler, you've been in the courtroom almost every day since the trial began, am I correct?"

"Yes."

"That includes the day the jury heard testimony about the hair found at the crime scene?"

"Yes, I was here for that."

"And you were sitting here when the defense expert explained that the gray hairs found on the victim belong either to your daughter Gretchen or to you?"

"I was."

"And can we agree that Gretchen's hair isn't gray?"

"Correct."

"So that leaves you. Did you have anything to do with Ms. Harper's death?"

"Absolutely not."

"You do have your hair cut the same time of the month as your husband does, right?"

"Yes. Around the first of the month."

"And forgive me for asking, but you also use a hair dye to darken gray hairs when you get your hair cut, correct?"

"Correct."

"Just like your husband does?"

"Yes."

"You don't have any basis for disputing that the gray hairs found at the crime scene were yours?"

"I don't know one way or the other."

"Do you have any idea how your hair got on Ms. Harper's clothing and body?"

"No, except I certainly didn't put them there."

"So let's move forward in time. You were also in court for the first few days of the defense case, too, correct?"

"Correct."

"But then, on the day your husband testified, you did not come to court, right?"

"Correct."

"And that's because, the night before he testified, your husband told you the details of his affair with Amanda Harper, including the choking, rope restraints, and paternity?"

"That's true."

"I'm sorry to pry, Ms. Cutler, but I imagine you were deeply upset to hear that from your husband's own mouth."

"I was."

"But you weren't really surprised, were you?"

"What do you mean?" Jess asked.

"I mean, Ms. Cutler, that even *before* he told you about it the other night, you suspected your husband of having an affair with Amanda Harper, correct?"

Jess paused, then grudgingly agreed.

"In fact, you suspected the affair at least as early as the evening you walked in on the two of them having dinner together and polishing off two bottles of wine."

Jess agreed again. Score a big point for the defense—Jess had motive.

"And because you were so upset by your husband's graphic affair, you decided not to attend trial the next day."

"Yes. I was hurt."

"Actually, Ms. Cutler, you were more than hurt—you were humiliated, were you not?"

"I was."

"You were *infuriated* by your husband's affair with Ms. Harper."

"I was angry, yes."

"And you're feeling all those feelings right this very moment—hurt, humiliation, and anger?"

"That's true."

"It feels like a kind of darkness, a deep darkness that Jews sometimes call *choshek*, am I right?"

Jess gave me a quizzical look, then agreed.

"Do any of those dark feelings account for your decision to challenge your husband's alibi for the days surrounding Ms. Harper's death?"

"Absolutely not. Jack was out of the house big portions of each of those days."

"Ms. Cutler, may I ask you to turn again to the pages in your journal that Ms. Hannigan asked you to review?"

Jess did so. Then glared back up at me.

"Now, Ms. Cutler, you were asked by the prosecutor to examine the days January 21 through 29. What I'd like you to do now is to look at the pages in the journal that *precede* January 21. Do you have those days in front of you?"

Jess turned to the pages. "Yes."

"Do you notice any difference in the writing between the days *preceding* January 21 and the eight days you testified about?"

"No, Mr. Jacobson, I don't. All the writing is mine."

"How about the color of the ink, Ms. Cutler?"

"The pages that precede January 21 are written in blue ink. I now see that the pages Ms. Hannigan asked about are written in both blue and black ink."

"How about the pages *after* January 29?"

"Again, blue ink only."

"So it's fair to say that the only pages bearing a *combination* of colors are the pages for January 21 through 29, which contain the words *Jack out*, correct?"

"That appears to be correct."

"And in fact, Ms. Cutler, the black ink is used only to make the notation *Jack out* on each of the eight pages?"

"That appears to be correct."

"And you would agree with me that, from the face of the journal itself, we can't tell *when* the words *Jack out* were actually written in the journal. There's no way to date the ink on those pages, is there?"

"I really don't know, but it's my testimony that Jack wasn't home for chunks of each of those days."

"Ms. Cutler, didn't you add the words *Jack out* in black ink sometime well after you entered the balance of the entries on those pages in blue ink?"

"That's not true. Jack was somewhere other than at home for portions of each of those days. I'm certain of it."

That's when I picked up the contents of the manila folder.

"Ms. Cutler, I'd like to play you a recording and see if you recognize any of the voices on the tape."

And with that, I played a tape of my second office meeting with Jess, which I had made by activating a tiny recording device placed beneath the conference table:

This is also why I cannot help you with an alibi. Jack and I have led pretty separate lives since we left the White House. I cannot tell you where he is or where he goes from one day to the next. I've considered divorce, and sometimes still do. But lately . . . I've spent some quality time in therapy. And I've found some companionship of my own.

Jess looked ashen.

"Ms. Cutler, do you recognize the voice on that recording?"

"I do," Jess admitted.

"And do you recall making those statements in my office about three months ago?"

"I do."

"Do they refresh your recollection that you cannot be sure when the president was or was not at home with you?"

Jess paused—long enough to defrost a freezer, I thought. "I guess so," she said at last.

"And regardless of when you made the notation *Jack out* in black ink, am I correct, Ms. Cutler, that you really can't say with confidence that your husband was out of the house at the time of Ms. Harper's death?"

Another long pause. Ticktock. Finally: "I guess I can't say that with confidence."

Katherine Hannigan tried a redirect, but the damage was done. Jess left the stand and hurried from the courtroom, distraught.

The government rested its case. "All right," Judge Edgerton said. "We will hear closing arguments in the morning. Get a good night's sleep, everyone."

XL

Day 9, closing arguments

Those of you who watch lawyer shows on TV may have the wrong idea about closing arguments. On television, closings are short and dramatic. I don't think I've ever seen a summation on *Law & Order* that exceeded two minutes.

Real life, as you might imagine, is different. In a case like this one, there's a lot of ground to cover. I had to offer the jury an innocent explanation of as much of the evidence as I could, or at least raise doubts about the government's case. I also had to equip the jurors with arguments they could use during deliberations to dissuade fellow jurors who were inclined to convict.

Of course, the prosecutors would be trying to do the opposite.

Katherine Hannigan approached the lectern without a single note in front of her. She was that confident. She ticked off all the forensic proof, item by devastating item. She showed the jurors, more slowly this time, each of the crime scene photos—Amanda's death mask, her disfigured eyes and lips, the matching fingerprints and DNA clusters. And she hammered home her theory of motive—that Jack had killed Amanda to cover up a pregnancy that would end his marriage and sully his reputation. Katherine was pointed, emphatic, and, I have to admit, pretty compelling.

But only for the most part. Katherine had failed to address the two big weaknesses in her case. Now it was my turn, and I intended to capitalize.

I looked slowly from one juror to the next, pausing a bit longer when I got to my favorite juror, number 5, the secretary for the public defender. I thought I saw a twinkle in Shirlene Mills's eye.

"Ladies and gentlemen. On behalf of Jack Cutler, Jane Cashman and I want to thank you for your patience and for your close attention this past week. I know you've been following the case intently, and very soon Jane and I will be placing Mr. Cutler in your hands.

"You have been called to perform one of the most difficult and consequential duties of American citizenship. You will be judging a man's fate.

"Notice I did not say 'a president's fate.' I said 'a man's fate.' As Judge Edgerton will instruct you, President Cutler is not entitled to be treated any better than any other defendant. He is entitled to nothing more than a fair shake under the same rules that apply to any other defendant in an American courtroom.

"But neither should he receive anything *less*. Kings and vagabonds must get the same treatment under the law.

"And that treatment should be exactly what you would want for yourself if you ever had the misfortune of sitting where Jack is.

"So ask yourselves: What would you expect if *you* were the person accused? What protections would you insist on? What kinds of proof would you demand, and what kinds of arguments would you tolerate?

"If it were *you* in President Cutler's position, I bet you'd start by insisting that the presumption of innocence be taken seriously. I didn't hear much about the presumption of innocence when Ms. Hannigan was speaking. And I guess I can't blame her. *Presumption of innocence* is not a prosecutor's favorite phrase.

"Again, don't take my word for it. Take it from the judge, who will instruct on the law after I sit down. I expect Judge Edgerton will remind you, as he did the day you were sworn in as jurors, that Mr. Cutler stands before you presumed to be innocent. That means he starts this case with a heavy thumb on the scale in his favor.

"And that thumb stays on the scale in Mr. Cutler's favor unless and until all twelve of you are convinced, beyond a reasonable doubt, that he committed this terrible crime. If you cannot reach that awesome judgment, you must find Jack Cutler the man, not the president, not guilty.

"What else would you expect if you were in Mr. Cutler's position? One thing you'd expect is for the prosecutors to play it straight. You'd expect the government to admit when it made a mistake. You'd want the prosecutors to admit when they overreached a little or tried a little too hard or fought a little too aggressively.

"So if *you* were the one on trial, I bet you'd be mighty unhappy to hear Ms. Hannigan make no mention in her summation of the gray hair found at the crime scene. Remember her opening statement a week ago? Remember when she listed all the evidence she'd be offering? She told you—and I wrote this down—that the government would prove that gray strands matching the president's hair were found on Ms. Harper's body.

"But when the rubber met the road, the government couldn't prove that. Instead, it fell to Jane and me to clear up the origins of the gray hair.

"As Judge Edgerton told you, the defense doesn't have to prove anything. The burden is always on the prosecution. It still is.

"But we brought our own expert, Diana Beardsley, into the courtroom. She told you about something called mitochondrial DNA. She told you how mtDNA can be extracted from a hair strand, even when it lacks a follicle needed for DNA testing. And she told you that when she performed mtDNA testing on the gray hair strands found on the victim, they matched Jessica Cutler, not Jack Cutler.

"I wasn't surprised that Ms. Hannigan simply ignored what Ms. Beardsley had to say. I suppose that if I had called an expert as pathetic as Mr. Ehrlich, the government's hair and fibers guy, I might be tempted to ignore the whole subject, too.

"But facts are facts, even these days. The gray hairs at the crime scene came from Jessica Cutler. That's a fact, not an opinion.

"So let me ask you again: Did Ms. Hannigan say a single word about the gray hair? Did she offer any explanation as to how Jessica Cutler's mtDNA got onto Ms. Harper's body?

"She did not.

"If *you* were the one on trial, you'd wonder about that. You'd be worried that perhaps the government wasn't leveling with the jury. You might even be angry about the basic fairness of the process.

"But then you'd get even angrier. You'd ask yourself why Ms. Hannigan never mentioned the stunt she pulled at the end of the trial, when she called Mr. Cutler's wife to the stand as a rebuttal witness.

"Who can forget that dramatic moment? The prosecutors waltzed Jessica Cutler into the courtroom to try to torpedo her husband's alibi. But what happened? I played Ms. Cutler a tape recording of her meeting at my office, when she admitted to me that she had no idea where her husband was at the time of the murder. She recanted her trial testimony and left the courtroom in tears.

"Once again, Ms. Hannigan never mentioned that sorry little episode in her summation. Why do you suppose that is? I suggest that she omitted Ms. Cutler's rebuttal testimony for the same reason she never mentioned the hair strand evidence: because it points to the president's wife as the killer, and not the president.

"If you were the one in Mr. Cutler's shoes, you'd be angry that the government tried to sweep this evidence about Jessica Cutler under the rug. You'd be angry, but you'd also be frightened.

"You'd be frightened that a government so intent on conviction cannot be trusted to play things down the middle.

"But the law *demands* that the prosecution play things straight. And it hasn't. The government's bogus use of the gray hair strands and its willingness to sponsor Jessica Cutler's false rebuttal should make you hesitate. If you were the one on trial, you would not stand for this.

"Did Jessica Cutler actually kill Amanda Harper? She *did* know about her husband's affair with Ms. Harper back when it was still going on. She admitted that right on the witness stand. Remember how Jessica walked in on her husband and Ms. Harper when they were having dinner one evening and had already polished off a bottle of wine?

"If Ms. Cutler did not kill Amanda Harper, how did her hair strands end up at the crime scene?

"In the end, I can't tell you whether Jessica Cutler killed her romantic rival. But neither can the prosecutors. They never even investigated that possibility. They started and ended with a single suspect, Jack Cutler, and they pressed blindly ahead until he was sitting in front of you in court.

"As the judge will tell you, the defense doesn't have to prove anything. It's always the government's burden. And the prosecution never investigated Jessica Cutler. Instead, they let her come in and lie to you. And when Katherine Hannigan stood before you earlier this morning to sum up her case, she didn't even bother to explain this enormous hole in the government's case.

"That's how much they want to convict Jack Cutler.

"They want to convict Jack Cutler so badly that the prosecutors likewise didn't tell you the full story about Amanda Harper. Yes, she was a great lawyer. Yes, she had a long and wonderful life ahead of her. Her death is a terrible tragedy. I totally agree. We all do.

"But that's no reason to sugarcoat the life she led. That's no reason to ignore the part of Ms. Harper's life you learned about when Humberto Mercado testified. He told you how Amanda Harper would go to the Overdon Pharmacy, nowhere near her apartment, and always on Sundays, when the pharmacy was supposedly closed for business. He told you about the line of customers that went into the back room on Sundays. He told you how Amanda Harper withdrew a thousand dollars in cash on Saturdays, then went into the pharmacy the next day and used a credit card, not the cash, to buy a handful of items, usually the same items week after week, all of them within grabbing distance of the pharmacy counter.

"What do you suppose Ms. Harper used the cash for? The cash she'd taken out only the day before? Isn't it highly likely that she used the cash to buy whatever was for sale in that back room behind the pharmacy counter? Used cash, not the credit card, so that those backroom purchases would never show up on her bank records?

"You heard from White House Counsel Mathews how Amanda Harper would sometimes be unreachable on weekends. He told you how she would return from wherever she'd been with renewed energy and focus.

"And, ladies and gentlemen, you know from your own common sense that scoring drugs in the middle of D.C. can be a dangerous affair.

"Was Ms. Harper killed by some drug dealer? Once again, I have no idea. But that's not my burden, as the Court will instruct you. It's the government's burden. And the truth is, they have no idea, either, because they never considered that possibility. They'd never even heard of the Overdon Pharmacy until my private investigator did the work the cops should have done in the first place.

"Now I will give the devil his due. The government has offered some circumstantial evidence against Mr. Cutler. His fingerprints, his DNA, and a knife from the White House collection.

"But as our experts explained, fingerprints and DNA can remain on surfaces for a long time, even after a thorough washing. And fingerprints and DNA can be planted as well. If you were the defendant sitting next to me at trial, you'd want the jury to take that possibility seriously.

"The fact is that every piece of this circumstantial proof can be easily explained. The fingerprints on Ms. Harper? President Cutler acknowledged he had an affair with the victim. She was even carrying his child. So of course his prints might be on her clothing.

"Mr. Cutler's DNA? Same thing. I bet your DNA can be found on your loved ones right this very minute.

"The James Monroe knife? Any number of people had access to it. Amanda Harper herself. Jessica Cutler. And Jack Cutler, too, of course. But you'd be guessing, just guessing, as to how that knife ended up stuck into the opening of Ms. Harper's briefcase.

"How about the cellphone calls and the iPhone locator function? What about the data showing that Ms. Harper called President Cutler numerous times and that she was in the Oval Office some nine times in the final months of the administration?

"So what? Of course Amanda Harper called her client from time to time. Of course she stopped by the president's office to do her job as his lawyer.

"Then there are the president's misstatements to the police. As painful as it was for him to admit, Jack Cutler tried to mislead the cops when they questioned him about Ms. Harper. He denied that he'd spoken very much with Ms. Harper. He denied that he'd ever been alone with her. Those statements were not true. Mr. Cutler told you himself that he lied, and he is ashamed to have done so. It's the same shame that caused him to use a Burner app when he spoke to Ms. Harper. She was his subordinate, he was her boss, and he was married. He was not proud of his interest in kink, either, even though Amanda Harper enjoyed rough sex as much as Mr. Cutler did.

"But you are not here to judge Jack Cutler on his marriage vows or his morality. That's between Mr. Cutler and his family, between Mr. Cutler and his god.

"You're here to judge Jack Cutler as a man charged with murder. And I submit, in the strongest possible terms, that lying about an affair is not proof of murder.

"Having a child out of wedlock is not proof of murder, either.

"The prosecution wants you to convict my client for being a cad, not for being a killer.

"In fact, Ms. Hannigan even tried to turn Mr. Cutler's affair with the victim into a motive for killing her.

"You heard Ms. Hannigan offer a theory, a truly horrifying theory, about a man so fearful of having his paternity exposed that he deliberately killed both his lover and his own child.

"That is monstrous, ladies and gentlemen. It is monstrous, and it is false.

"Jack Cutler took the stand and told you, point-blank, that Amanda Harper never told him she was pregnant. Not even Dr. Zaid, the state's chief medical examiner, could tell that the victim was pregnant. Not until months after her death, when the autopsy was finally completed, did Dr. Zaid discover the pregnancy.

"Same for Arlen Mathews, the former White House counsel. He saw Ms. Harper nearly every day, but never had a hint that she was pregnant.

"Did the government offer a single shred of evidence to support its monstrous theory of motive? Did Ms. Hannigan produce a single witness, perhaps a friend of the victim, maybe an office colleague, who knew about the pregnancy?

"You can be sure that the government, with all its investigatory re-sources, turned cartwheels trying to find evidence that Jack Cutler knew about the pregnancy. But they couldn't find any, because there *isn't* any. Jack Cutler had no idea Amanda Harper was pregnant.

"So Ms. Hannigan simply *asserted* that Jack knew. She hopes that you will substitute your feelings about proper moral conduct for the govern-ment's lack of actual evidence.

"When Judge Edgerton gives you your final instructions, he will tell you that you must not take the bait. In this country, we judge people based on evidence, not emotion. Kings and vagabonds alike.

"That's how much the prosecutors want to bag this big fish. They have concocted a bogus motive as part of a matching set with the bogus hair evidence and the bogus rebuttal testimony of Jessica Cutler.

"Now, in a few minutes, the case will be in your hands. When you consider the evidence you've heard, ask yourselves whether you would hesitate if it was your neighbor or your spouse or yourself in Jack's shoes. Ask whether you would hesitate when the government cannot bring itself to explain the hair strand evidence, or the phony rebuttal testimony, or Sundays at the Overdon Pharmacy, or the fragile, easily explained, and entirely circumstantial nature of the evidence in this case.

"If one of you was sitting next to me today, you would demand more of your government.

"You should demand nothing less for Jack Cutler."

XLI

Day 9, after hours
It was after midnight when I fed the last crumpled pages of my closing argument into the office shredder. The buzzer rang at reception, and I went to see who could possibly be here so late.

It was Jess.

I'd spent the last couple of nights rehearsing, but only in my head, what I'd say if I ran into Jess again. In truth, I hadn't expected to see her, certainly not this soon. Maybe ever.

We greeted each other uncomfortably and walked to my office.

"That was a pretty good cross the other day, Robbie," she offered. "Set me up and then took me apart."

"Jess, I'm sorry, but I had a job to do."

"No, that's fine, Robbie. I understand. And that tape, you really pulled the rabbit out of the hat."

I apologized for having recorded Jess without her permission. It was a cheap lawyer's trick, although under the circumstances I felt completely justified.

"And Jesus, Jess," I protested. "You could at least have given me a heads-up that you were going to take that shot at Jack in rebuttal."

Jess laughed it off. "And spoil the fun, Robbie? Where's the joy in that?"

"Jess, trust me when I tell you that I took no joy in going after you like that on cross."

Jess laughed again, more darkly this time. "Oh, for god's sake, Robbie," she said. "You really should stop believing your own press. You think I didn't see you reach under the conference room table right when we sat down that second time? Do you really think I didn't see you activate a taping system?"

I stopped and calculated. "What are you telling me?"

"Yes, Sherlock, I *knew* you had the tape. I *knew* what was on the tape. I *knew* what you would do with the tape if I made up some bullshit about Jack being away from home on the critical days. And I knew you'd never fall for those two different-colored inks, even if Ms. Hannigan was too enthusiastic to pay attention. How'd you like my performance in court—the scorned wife seeking revenge on her wayward husband? 'A tale as old as time.' I guarantee you, the jury enjoyed seeing my performance as much as I enjoyed giving it. Marlene Dietrich herself couldn't have improved on it."

I remembered the movie, *Witness for the Prosecution,* a classic from the late fifties. "You perjured yourself for him, Jess? Jesus, really? If this ever comes out, you'll be in harm's way."

"I can take care of myself."

"For chrissake, Jess, the case is going well. We've got a shot here—Jack could've walked away from this, even without your running this kind of risk."

Jessica scowled in disbelief. "Who are these jurors? What do they know about Jack? They go home every night, eat their comfort food, have a good night's sleep, then get up in the morning and judge my husband. How much would *you* bet on their powers of discernment, Counselor? Or your own?"

We sat in silence for a few moments. Then in a hushed tone, I said, "You love him that much, Jess? Even now?"

"He's our Jack. He has his appetites, and he will be served."

Infuriating. "He's not *my* Jack, Jessie, and he's not yours, either. How many women does he have to shtup before you've had enough?"

"Robbie, let's not."

"No, let's, Jess. Let's talk about it. Has it been worth it? Are you happy with your choice? Looking back?"

"Robbie, stop. That's ancient history."

"You never stopped blaming me for Maddie."

Jess looked at me with the saddest eyes I've ever seen. "Rob, it was never about Maddie."

"Come on, Jess. The darkness—the *choshek*—that set in that day. You never looked at me the same way again."

"Rob, forgive me. The *choshek* set in long before Maddie fell through the ice."

"Meaning what?"

"Robbie, don't make me say this."

"Say what, Jess? Just tell me."

"We were kids, Rob. We were babies. And you wanted a relationship so badly, you just showed me what you thought I wanted to see. Like a witch's mirror, reflecting back to me what you imagined I'd like."

"I see. So my mistake was giving you only what you really wanted?"

"What I wanted was *you*, Rob, not some ideal. I wanted you. But what I got was a great blankness. You gave me *choshek*. *Choshek* is in you."

"Jessie, I always tried my best."

"I'm sorry, Rob, but your best wasn't good enough."

And with that, Jess left my office for the last time.

XLII

L *et's go back to your last visit with Amanda. What can you recall about it?*

We met at her apartment, I remember that. I went there to boost my brother's morale when he went over to Amanda's to plead his case. But I was a bit late, Robbie was just leaving, and I ran into him as he was heading to his car. Liddle Man filled me in on the conversation he'd just had with Amanda. Just pathetic. That simpering little fella, begging a woman to love him. Pissing into the wind, if you ask me.

What else did Robbie tell you about that conversation?

We had just a few minutes to talk—he was pretty shaken up. He kept saying, "Too many tics. Too many tics." Those three words, over and fucking over.

Any idea what he was referring to?

I had a pretty good idea, yeah. Robbie's got some nervous twitches. Had 'em since he was a kid. Mostly hand biting, right where our old man used to burn him with cigar ash.

Jesus, cigar ash. I guess I'm not surprised, given what you've told me about your family. Do you know why your brother was referring to the tics when he left Amanda's place that night?

They'd had an argument, he told me. My brother, God bless him, was still pining for that woman. Still trying to convince her that they were meant for each other. Like her feelings might respond to a well-honed jury argument. "You can't start it like a car, you can't stop it with a gun."

Bottom line: Amanda was sticking with Jack. Married or not, Jack was her man.

You say that Robbie was shaken up. Do you know where he went after he told you about the conversation with Amanda?

No clue. I sat with him for a moment in the car, but then I had my own work to do.

How were you feeling after your brother told you about his conversation with Amanda?

How would you suppose, Doctor? My poor fucking brother. Trailing behind Jack again.

So what did you do?

I decided to support my brother's case. Cyrano, right? I grabbed a few items and went up to her place. Amanda was a little startled to see me, as I recall. That's how it seemed to me. "You again?" she asked me.

What happened next?

I told her that Jack would never leave Jess for her. That she was just one more pin for Jack to knock down.

At first Amanda seemed to empathize. She understood I was doing my best by Robbie. But as I kept talking, she got more and more flustered. "What do you want from me?" she asked me. It seemed like Amanda was frightened. Of me!

I asked her what Jack did for her that Robbie didn't. I asked her if Jack gave her what she wanted in bed.

At that point, Amanda just lost it.

"Jack gives me exactly what I want," she said. She pulled down her turtleneck to show me a couple of markings on her throat.

"Does he place his hands right here?" I asked and cupped her neck with my own hands. Big hands. Big hands belonging to big brother.

"Right there," she said. "Right there," and coughed a little.

"And does he apply a hint of pressure? Just like this?" I asked.

"A little, then a little more." More coughing.

"Maybe he pushes up a little on the sides?" I asked, doing so myself.

"Yeah." Raspier now. "But his hands are firmer. Tougher. No bite marks on his hands. No purple blotches. No tics. No fucking tics." Spat it out at me.

"I can push up just as well."

"You don't do anything just as well. You don't even exist to me." A line I'd heard before. A long time ago. My mother Evie's voice.

Then she starts scratching. Thrashing around the apartment. A few heaves as she tried to get some air. I just held on for dear life. So to speak.

Just a little more pressure, and out came the red spots.

From there it gets blurry. We're in my car. At some point that evening I'm walking in Rock Creek Park, looking for a spot, not too public. I pull on some gloves. It's cold out tonight. Snow's been falling for hours. God's own weather.

XLIII

D ays 10 and 11
    Another blustery day in the nation's capital. The jury was a tum-
ble of snow boots, fleeces, and overcoats against another February freeze.

Judge Edgerton charged the jurors in about an hour, then directed
them to begin their deliberations. This is always the toughest part of the
trial, for the defendant of course, but also for the lawyers. You watch the
clock all day and wait to see if the jury sends out a note, giving you some
window into their thinking.

Just before lunch on the first day of deliberations we received the first
question from the jury. The court security officer took the note to Judge
Edgerton in chambers, and he came out to the bench to read it to us.

"Back on the record at 11:42 a.m.," he began. "We've received a note
from the jury, which I will mark as court exhibit 2. It reads as follows:
'Can we hear a readback of the gray hair testimony of Charles Ehrlich?'"

It's usually impossible to interpret jury notes. For one thing, you
never know how many jurors actually care about whatever the note

asks. A single juror may be hung up on a particular issue. Or the opposite may be true.

Still, it was hard to see the first note as anything but discouraging. Charles Ehrlich had been the government's ridiculous hair-comparison witness. Had the jury forgotten how I'd blown that idiot out of the water? Did they remember our mtDNA proof? Had the jury really understood Diana Beardsley's rebuttal?

I tried not to convey my concern to Jack, who was even more worried than I was by the first note. Plus, what could we do about it? The jury wanted a readback, and a readback it would get. Judge Edgerton summoned the jury, read the note again into the record, then directed the court reporter to sift through her notes until she found the Ehrlich testimony. The silver lining, if there was one, is that the jury would hear not only Ehrlich's direct, but also my cross.

The court reporter's singsong recitation took about an hour, and the jury returned to its deliberations. Three more hours ticked slowly by before another note emerged from the jury room. This time, Judge Edgerton was on the bench handling a motion in another case. He looked down at the small white piece of notepaper, then announced:

"On the record at 3:32 p.m. I will mark this note as court exhibit 3. The jury asks, 'Would you please reread the instruction that asks us to listen to one another with an open mind?'"

Now it was the government's turn to fret. Obviously, one or more jurors were refusing to go along with the others. While the defense always hopes for a unanimous acquittal, a hung jury, especially if it was divided in our favor, was good enough, as Jane had explained to Jack. At the very least, we'd live to fight another day. For prosecutors, it's unanimity or nothing.

Judge Edgerton summoned the jury again and reread his instructions regarding deliberations. Our eyes were trained on the jurors, trying to pick up a cue into their thinking. One or two jurors, I thought, shot a quick glance at juror 9, a buttoned-up guy with a security clearance. The jury was clearly divided—but how deeply, and in whose favor, was anyone's guess.

At 5:30 p.m., with no further notes that day, the judge sent the jury home, reminding them not to look at news reports or go online, and directing them to return tomorrow morning to resume deliberations.

A little before noon the next day, we received yet another note from the jury. Judge Edgerton remained in chambers for about a half hour, as the rest of us wondered and worried. As he entered the courtroom, you could sense the judge's fatigue. Or maybe I was projecting.

"Back on the record at 12:28 p.m. The jury has sent in a note that I will mark as court exhibit 4. It reads: 'Your Honor, we have tried our best to reach a verdict but are unable to do so. The vote is ten to two. What should we do?'

"Ordinarily," the judge said to the lawyers, "I don't want to know the vote count until there is unanimity. But I thought it best to read you exactly what the jury wrote, so that all of you would know what I know. Let me hear first from the government. What do you want me to do?"

Katherine approached the podium. "Your Honor, the jury has been deliberating for only a day and a half. It's too early to declare an impasse. The government asks the Court to give its standard instruction on listening to one another and trying as hard as possible to reach unanimity."

"Thank you, Ms. Hannigan. Mr. Jacobson?"

"Your Honor," I began, "we now know that the jury is divided ten to two. What's more, the jury *knows* that we know that. So if you give the instruction that the government is asking for, the two dissenting jurors will think that you're aiming your instructions at them. They'll figure that you are basically asking them to capitulate. Under these circumstances, the instruction would be too coercive to the holdouts. We think you should declare a mistrial now."

Judge Edgerton considered my point but disagreed. "I think I can formulate an instruction that doesn't put any of the jurors on the spot." He read us his proposed instruction and took our suggested tweaks to the language. The judge then summoned the jury and read the instruction, taking care to assure the jurors that they need not abandon their strongly held beliefs simply to get along with everyone else.

Three hours later, the jury sent out its final note. They were still deadlocked, now eleven to one. The note expressed regret and resignation. Unanimity was impossible.

Judge Edgerton thanked and dismissed the jury, advising them, now that their service had concluded, that they were free to talk to whomever they wanted. But if they chose to speak to any of the lawyers, he wanted them to do so right now and in chambers. This was standard procedure.

As it turned out, three of the jurors wanted to talk to us. The forewoman, juror 4, did most of the talking.

"We were divided eleven to one in favor of acquittal. A single juror voted for conviction on the very first ballot and never wavered. She thought the president was guilty and could not be persuaded otherwise. She even found the government's hair evidence compelling," juror 4 said, casting a slightly embarrassed look at Katherine. "Sorry, Ms. Hannigan, but the rest of us did not buy your gray hair theory."

Both sets of lawyers shot questions at the three jurors, asking mostly about which arguments and witnesses had been persuasive and which not so much. After ninety minutes or so, I had only one remaining question for the forewoman.

"Is there anything more I could have done to persuade the last holdout?"

The forewoman thought for a moment. "I don't know. She was pretty adamant. Maybe Shirlene's just seen too much violence in her day. Maybe she's learned to be skeptical of criminal defendants. It's probably eye-opening to work in the D.C. public defender's office."

So much for the science of jury selection.

———————

As we headed to the elevator, Katherine Hannigan grabbed my elbow. "I guess I should tell you that, regardless of the jury's lean, the government plans to retry the case. I will call you tomorrow to discuss possible dates for retrial."

The following week, I met with Jack and Jane to plan strategy.

XLIV

S o am I crazy, Doc?

The question right now, as I've said, is whether you're competent to stand trial. The tests we gave you raised some serious issues, so I have a few follow-up questions. Shall we get started?

First tell me what's going on in my case. I haven't seen my fucking lawyer in weeks, and I'm going out of my goddamn mind.

I know only the basics. Despite Robbie's and Jane's best efforts, President Cutler was convicted in his second trial. But he was let out of jail shortly before your arrest. His wife, Jessica, and their private eye, someone named Mercado, found the cellophane you used to lift the president's prints. The PI also found another print on the tape. He turned the cellophane over to the cops, and they found a match for the unidentified fingerprint.

Yeah, they must have matched it to the partial on the baseball bat, right? The one I used on Nathan back in the day?

That's it, yes.

Well, at least Jack did a few years after he got nailed at the retrial. No way Liddle Robbie was ever gonna win the second time around. With all that evidence against Jack? With the government now wise to the mtDNA evidence? And Jessica unable to do her Marlene Dietrich routine a second time? I told Robbie the retrial was fucking hopeless. I told him to just plead the bastard guilty and get on to the next case. But you know my brother—Robbie, the Great Avenger, off to the rescue.

Let's talk about that, Evan. How did it make you feel to watch Jack get convicted at the second trial?

It felt great. Like this finally settled something I should've finished all those years ago in Brooklyn. Something Robbie would have done for himself if he'd had the stones. So as usual, it's a job for his big brother.

Why do you say that, Evan? Why was killing Ms. Harper and pinning it on the president something you had to do for Robbie?

Why? Where do I begin? First, pretty boy Jack scoops up Robbie's ex-squeeze and marries her. Then he takes Amanda, too. And Jack l-o-o-o-ved Amanda. Did you hear him whimper about that at trial? He loved Amanda just like he loved Jess. And that Nazi TV trollop. And the bimbo from the liquor lobby. And the honey he kept on the Upper West Side. And God knows how many others. So Jack had to do a few years in jail—boo-the-fuck-hoo! He did a couple of months for each girl he swiped from my brother. A couple more for the school photographer Jack sicced on him. A year or two for the PA announcement of Robbie's untimely demise. More time for making Robbie wait in the cold in Albany while he went out drinking, a couple more months for cribbing Robbie's ideas to run for office, and some bonus months for sending Robbie to solicit ladies at some motherfucking fundraiser. Then add a year or so for every black eye he left on Jess, and another for every buckle scar Nathan put across the small of Robbie's back, or every shoe our old man threw across the room, or every scar Papa dear left on Robbie's knuckles from his fucking cigar, and another year or two for every time Evie reminded Robbie what a fucking loser he was. That adds up pretty quickly, don't you think, Doctor?

That's quite a list of grievances, Evan.

And I'm just getting started. How about a few more years for every time our mother, rest her nasty little soul, told Robbie that I was just a figment of his imagination? That she had no son named Evan. That I didn't even exist.

Do you exist, Evan?

Of course I fucking exist. I'm the guy who mops up Robbie's messes. I'm the guy Robbie calls when he needs a balls transplant.

Does it ever work the other way? Can you summon Robbie when you need to feel, let's say, more grounded in reality?

I can get in touch with him, sure.

I think I should discuss all of this with Robbie. Can you contact him for me, Evan? I need to see him. There are some things I can learn only from him directly.

I haven't spoken to him for a long time. I'm not sure he'd want to hear from me right now.

And why is that, Evan?

Well, he was pretty unhappy when I finally told him what I'd done for him.

What did you do for Robbie?

It was all so fucking easy. I did it just like the defense experts said. Just like they'd said in the research papers I'd read. I lifted the prints and the DNA from the silver service the last time His Highness had dinner with Robbie at the White House. It was a simple matter of transferring the prints and DNA to poor Amanda's lifeless body. When Robbie heard Cutler utter the magic words *seeds and leads* at that last White House dinner, I knew where Jack had been planting his flag. How else did commander in chief come by that phrase? It didn't come from Robbie. It couldn't have come from Jane Cashman, since she'd never met him.

So you decided to kill Amanda? Simply because she'd been sleeping with your friend Jack?

Fuck no. First of all, Jack's Robbie's friend, not mine. Plus, Amanda had plenty to answer for in her own right. She was pregnant—she'd told me that back at Christmas when I stopped by her office. And she was delighted, just pleased as fucking punch, to have old Jack's kid, but she didn't want my brother. "Too many fucking tics," she said. And she treated me like some ghost. "Who are you?" she asked me, like I was no one. Like I didn't exist. She sounded just like Evie. I couldn't let that pass, even though Robbie did.

What did Robbie say when you finally told him what you'd done?

He was furious. Furious, can you believe it? "I did it for you, just like I sorted people out for you at Briar. Be grateful, for chrissake. If you can't fight your own fucking battles, at least let me take care of it without listening to your whining."

It was bad enough when Jack took Jess from Robbie during that first campaign, that rich entitled prick. Then Amanda, too. And naturally, that two-timing slut picked His Highness. Why stay with a rump roast like Robbie if you can have filet? It was so easy to finally wrap my hands around her neck, just as she had once asked Robbie to. This time, the pleasure was all mine. Squeeze just a little—"that's what I like from Jack, yes"—squeeze a little more—"yes, Jack does it like that, but better"—push up along the windpipe—"too many tics"—push up higher—"you don't exist to me," just like Evie—then pop!

Dragging the sack out to the park was an errand, of course. That was the only heavy lifting. C'mon, Doc, it's a good fucking joke, lighten up. I couldn't just leave the body at the apartment, could I? People might have seen me there in the past, right? Plus, the park is crawling with potential perps. It was the perfect venue. Covered in snow, even.

And it was easy to pin it on Jack! Tra-la! Of course, if I could do it all over again, I would do a slightly better job of it. I'd still pocket the silverware from that last dinner with Robbie. I'd still make sure that I took the particular cutlery Jack used and drop it in my suit pocket as he walked Robbie around the metal detectors to the front lawn. I'd still remove Cutler's prints and DNA from the knife. Totally seamless.

And I'd still leave Amanda's body in one of the horse stalls, where Jack kept his horse. I'd still take Amanda's briefcase from the apartment and dump it near her body, along with the knife. Such excellent distractions, all fingering Jack!

But I would definitely be more careful when I scooped up the stray hairs in the Cosmetology Room. Next time, I'd want to make sure the hair belonged to Jack, not to his wife. All that gray curly hair—who can keep it all straight?

But I made up for that hiccup, didn't I? Or at least I tried to. While Robbie was busy preparing his clever little crosses and his fancy PhD experts, I was hard at work, too—sending the government's motion about Jack's other affairs over to that douchebag at Smith TV. Damage the defense! I was so careful, so fucking careful, even Jack would have to admit that. I used one of those Burner apps. Those babies let you call people and even text out nasty pieces of evidence and never get your fingerprints on anything! What a wonderful new world we're living in! If only idiot juror 3 had kept his fucking mouth shut about seeing MacGregor's show. He coulda stayed on the jury and poisoned the whole lot of them. Gotten them to convict the bastard the first time around. That fucking juror has a top secret clearance but can't keep a fucking secret.

Evan, I really think I need to talk to Robbie for a minute. I'm asking you again to please help me get in touch with him.

That guy's gone. Forever. I'm in charge now. Robbie is gonna need me to handle the shit that's about to take center stage. But I sure as hell don't need him. And what an ungrateful punk Robbie has become. Has he ever thanked me, even once, for the sacrifices I've made for him?

I mean, Robbie knew, he knew, that Amanda was banging His Eminence, and that she would never give him up. But Robbie's such a fucking lapdog, he let it all pass. That knob polisher would never do a damn thing about it. But I would. Evan Hillel Jacobson. The older brother no one's ever seen.

Evan, I'm not leaving here until Robbie shows up. I'd like to hear his side of the story.

Well, keep waiting, Doctor, keep waiting. He's in here somewhere. I'll send him your love.

Acknowledgments

I f you wait seventy-two years to write your first book, you may be lucky enough to have accumulated a wealth of family and friends to help you get it written. I'm very lucky indeed.

Countless friends and family put up with my impromptu readings of different chapters at various stages of development. I'm grateful for their encouragement and forbearance. You know who you are.

A more select few have had genuinely profound effects on the final version. Charlie Stein, a friend of some sixty years, read two early drafts and reminded me that the trial of a president should look like the trial *of a president*, and not some penny-ante dispute. Susan Danoff, my sister-in-law, read two early drafts and helped me reformulate the voice of the second narrator. My former law partner Gary Orseck gave me a long list of ways to improve the draft, and I adopted almost every one of them. My former law partner Alan Untereiner offered crucial suggestions about Rock Creek Park that I shamelessly cribbed. Alan also introduced me to The Ninas Book Club, which served as a fantastic focus group for a near-final draft, and to my wonderful literary agents, Lane Zachary and Max Moorhead of Massie & McQuilkin, who took a chance on a first-time novelist, and whose every editing suggestion made the book better. Lane, in turn, introduced me to Peter Borland, my intrepid editor at Atria Books/Simon & Schuster, who took the same risk on a novice writer and whose edits have enriched the novel from start to finish.

I save the most important for last. My three sons, Jeremy, Ethan, and Noah, read and reread drafts and pushed me to do better, even when I was unduly resistant. The very structure of the novel and an array of plot points owe whatever merit they have to my boys' input.

Finally, there is my wife, Leslie Danoff. She, too, read and reread the book and provided plot ideas, structural suggestions, and painstaking line edits. More fundamentally, she told me, in the midst of the COVID year, that I would never know whether I could write a novel unless I tried. Like every other risk I've taken during our forty-three-year marriage, Leslie's the one who thought it could be overcome.

And as always, she was right.